To Nowhere

A Novel by C.E. Wilson

D1649070

Text copyright © 2015 by C.E. Wilson

All Rights Reserved

This is a work of fiction. Any resemblance of characters to actual persons, living or dead is coincidental. The author holds exclusive rights to this work.

For information:

http://cewilson5.deviantart.com/

Cover Image by Maggie Munyon

To Nowhere

ISBN: 978-0-9883055-9-5

To my incredible daughter, Quinn.

Thanks for all the naps.

One

"You just moved next door to the old Shaw place, didn't you?"

As I turned around I suddenly realized I was being treated to a very attractive guy standing in line for coffee behind me. This whole new town my parents had moved into had that 'Pleasantville' vibe going on and not a single green and tan label was in sight at the coffee shop. I glanced around for a moment like a total dork and tried to play it off when in reality I was making sure the owner of the husky voice was actually talking to me.

"I'm sorry, do you have hearing problems or something?" he asked next with a frown. His chin lowered and gave a look which could only be described as pity and my face reddened at the thought that I was being neither smooth nor charming.

"No, I'm fine!" I blurted. I tucked a piece of thick red hair behind my ears. Hopefully he could see I had about ten piercings in my right ear... if he was into that kind of thing. Or if it wasn't... I still loved having the chance to show them off. "I wasn't sure if you were talking to me."

He arched an eyebrow. "So did you?"

"Did I what?"

He rolled his eyes. They were a particularly lovely shade of green. "Did you or did you not move next door to the old Shaw place?"

My face brightened. I could finally answer one of his questions and not look like a total spazz. "Oh! Yeah, we did, actually. It's vacant, right?"

"Yeah. No one's lived there for years. They say the place is haunted." He stepped up to place his order at the counter and shot a smile down in my direction. I was so distracted that I almost missed the fact he had butted in front of me. Whatever, I got a pleasant view of his jeans and the body which filled them. "What can I get you?" he asked.

"You don't have to get me—"

"What can I get you?" he asked for a second time.

I flushed wildly and willed my face to stop smiling like an idiot in front of this delicious (and possibly older) piece of man candy. My god he was good looking. Some girls didn't always go for the dangerous look with thick rimmed glasses... *oh who the hell am I kidding*, of course they do!

"Do you function on a two minute delay or something?"

Right! Right! "Sorry! I'll have a white chocolate mocha. Iced, please."

The woman at the counter shot me a look which was more reserved for a disgruntled surgeon working the late night shift and delivering triplets rather than a woman who took coffee orders. She rolled her eyes and snapped her gum. "We don't make that here. Wrong place, hunny."

"Give me a medium black," the stranger said to the woman. She nodded with approval and started to grab him a cup.

"No white chocolate mochas?" I arched my brow at the beautiful stranger.

"They don't call them that here," he explained.

"What the hell do they call them?"

He smirked. "White *creme* mochas."

"What the hell? Are you serious?"

"Dead serious," he said with a chuckle.

8

"That sounds dirty as hell."

"Or hot as," the stranger said. His eyes trailed up and down without shame. "Depends on the person, I suppose. So how about it? You want to try some white creme in your mocha?"

I tried not to flush at his banter. "I'm willing to try anything once." I glanced up at him through my mascara. "My name's Lyris, by the way."

His face changed slightly and I wondered if he was taken aback by the strangeness of my name. It was probably best not to tell him my full name was actually Lyris Christmas. Might be a bit of overload for the guy, or any guy. Luckily, the look was fleeting and left as soon as it appeared.

"I don't like to know names," he said with a smirk.

Weirdo.

Once we had our drinks the stranger invited me to sit with him outside.

"I work until ten," he said offhandedly, taking a sip of his coffee. "That's why I need this."

I wondered what it would be like to kiss a guy who drinks his coffee black. Most of the guys from my old home wouldn't be caught dead at a coffeehouse let alone drinking an actual cup of coffee. Most couldn't stand the taste. I have to say I'm one of those people.

"You enjoying the creme?" he asked. The corner of his mouth tilted upward in a teasing way.

I took a tentative sip and glanced at him over the rim of my coffee cup. *Damn he was fine.* Much too good looking for me normally, but I did have that whole 'fresh meat' thing going on. It was probably best to strike while the iron was hot and this guy... was scorching.

"Again with the two minute delay." He rolled his eyes and I worried he was starting to get bored. "Seriously, do you have some sort of learning disability? Because if so, I'd like to know now. I don't like damaged goods."

What the hell? "Damaged goods?"

"Yeah," he said, growing surprisingly serious. "I need to know if something's wrong with you."

I shook my head, too damn excited to win this guy over. "No, I'm good. No problems on my end."

He seemed to relax in his chair as he took another pull from his cup. Watching his Adam's apple throb with each swallow was, dare I say, hypnotic? He had a strong jaw and to say there was a hinting of a beard would be a laugh. The guy was shaggy like one of those guys you see on the cover of a romance novel – the new ones. I actually wondered if he shaved his chest. His stark green eyes were dangerous and his shaggy near-black hair rested right over his eyebrows.

"So what's your name?"

His eyes narrowed slightly with annoyance. "I thought I said I didn't do names."

"I thought that only meant for me."

Another smirk. "Well played. I guess if you must know, my name's Wy-um...Wyatt." A slight grimace crossed his face as he stuttered.

"That's cool." I tried to play it off like having a conversation with a beautiful man was something I did on a normal basis.

"Coming from a girl named Lyris, I'll take that as a compliment."

10

I finally worked up the courage to smirk back at him. "I thought you said you didn't do names."

"You *are* a clever one," Wyatt said with a pleasant mixture of sarcasm and approval. "That will definitely work in your favor."

"Will it? Are the odds in my favor?" I asked, hoping to tease him.

"Oh, hell yeah," he said. He winked as he took another sip from his cup. I couldn't tell if he got the joke or not. "Humor goes a long way. It can make difficult situations a little more fun, a little more tolerable, if you will." He waggled his brows and I swear I was on cloud nine. This was almost too good to be true.

"So what's this you said?" I asked, still trying to keep conversation going with him.

His jade eyes turned back to mine. "About what?"

"You asked me if I moved in next door to the Shaw place?" He nodded. "So, what's the big deal about that?"

"Did I say it was a big deal?"

"Is it?" I asked.

He shrugged. "Just that it's haunted."

I frowned. "Haunted?" I wanted to laugh, but Wyatt seemed to be quite serious. "You don't actually believe in that stuff, do you?"

"Believe in what stuff?"

"Haunted houses." I tried to laugh which was met with a blank expression. "I mean next thing you'll be saying that you believe in the Easter bunny."

"Don't you believe in the paranormal?" he challenged,

11

ignoring my comment.

"I think I'm a little old for haunted houses," I said, trying to play it cool. I figured this guy had to be at least three or four years older than me which would put him a little out of my league.

"And you think I'm not? Just how old do you think I am, Lyris?"

Oh God. Just hearing him say my name, watching it flow from his mouth. No one from my old school would ever believe this was happening. Guys like Wyatt just didn't flirt with girls like Lyris Christmas. And yet it was happening. In real life.

"I dunno," I said as I glanced across the street. We weren't that far from a college campus. "What are you, a freshman?"

"Is freshman an age?"

"Smart ass," I grumbled. "Seriously, nineteen? Twenty?"

"Right the first time," Wyatt said. "I'll be twenty this fall. Looking forward to it, but not as much as I am for the big ole' two-one. Oh man, that's going to be wild." He leaned back in his chair, and looked up at the sky. "I plan on taking my boys to Vegas and partying it up for an entire weekend."

"So what? You're a trust fund baby?" I teased.

His expression darkened, but just like before it passed before I could focus on it. "Not exactly, Lyris."

He lifted his head and looked in my eyes and I quickly tried to focus on a couple walking down the sidewalk. They looked compatible enough. The guy was a bit too tall, but other than that they looked like a decent pair.

"So then tell me," Wyatt spoke up suddenly. "How old are you?"

"A little too young for you."

"Nothing's too young for me."

"You might not want to say that in a courtroom," I teased.

"Answer me."

I flushed as he barked his command and wondered if this wasn't the only place he liked to be bossy. "I'm seventeen."

"Seventeen's a perfect age," Wyatt said. "Probably one of the best. I know I'd do anything to be seventeen again."

"Why? You can't drink, you can barely drive, you can't vote—
"

"Vote?"

"You know what I mean. You can't do much."

"That's true. You can't. But you're also young... and beautiful." His eyes flickered to mine. "Seventeen is one of my favorite ages."

"Alright now you really sound like a creeper." I tried to giggle off Wyatt's strange way of talking, but it was getting pretty damn difficult, especially with those sharp green eyes completely focused on me even when a very slim and bouncy blond jogged past. I tried to tell myself that even if he was a little weird, what was so wrong with that? He was gorgeous, older, and probably in college... so what if he spoke like he was sizing me up to sell?

Wyatt chuckled, disrupting my train of thought.

"Sorry, I don't mean to weird you out. When I heard a new family was moving in the house next to the Shaw place, I had to find out if it was true. And you're better than anything I expected."

"Are you being serious?" I asked. I hoped I didn't seem

desperate for his kind words and attention.

"Am I?"

"You're too charming and odd for your own good."

"So charming and odd that you'll go out with me after work tonight?"

This surprised me. I choked *oh so elegantly* on my drink and quickly attempted to regain my composure. "Yeah, uh huh. Right. You. Me. The stars." I tried to play off his suggestion as a joke so it wouldn't burn so much when he joined in my laughter, but it didn't come.

"I'm serious. I work till ten, but I'm sure I can get off at nine."

"Why?" The words slipped out before I had a chance to censor myself and he looked amused.

"Why not? You're a girl. I'm a guy. I think you're interesting."

"Aren't I a bit young for you?" *Why was I saying this?* Was I trying to blow my chance at going on a date with the hottest guy who'd ever approached me in my entire seventeen years of life?

"I told you, Lyris. Seventeen is the perfect age."

When he spoke and his voice came out like a purr I knew in that moment I would go anywhere with him. It was frightening how much I was drawn to him already. I tried to hide my goofy smile until I was back in the comfort of my home.

Two

When I said I was willing to go anywhere or anyplace with Wyatt I was a little surprised by his actual suggestion. I didn't know if it was because I watched one too many of my older sister's 80s teen flicks, but I imagined us going to a club, watching people smoke cigarettes, or chilling under a dock near the sea. Hell, I imagined a trip to the ice cream shoppe or bowling alley.

What I had not imagined was his suggestion to meet up at the Shaw place to prove it was haunted.

At first I thought the whole concept was pretty lame, but when I thought about those emerald green eyes on mine and how Wyatt said seventeen was the perfect age, I found myself unable to resist. How lame could it possibly be? We would be together, in a dark abandoned house. It could lead to some serious making out.

I hoped he wasn't expecting too much. It was still only the first date.

I smirked at my reflection in the mirror. Did I really just call this a date? It couldn't be. Wyatt couldn't actually be interested in anything more than a casual fling with someone like me. Maybe he took all his dates to abandoned houses because his apartment was a wreck, or he didn't have a lot of money.

No. That didn't make sense. He said he wanted to fly all his friends to Vegas for his 21st birthday. He wouldn't have said something like that unless he had some major cash.

Puzzled, but not deterred, I glanced out my large bedroom window to see my parents pulling out for the night. Some stupid initiation party, I assumed. Both of them had been hired at the local university. My mother was a Sociology professor and my father was a Psychology professor. My upbringing was not an easy one. There was nothing but over-thinking. Since I turned thirteen I was pretty sure they had given up and written off everything as a phase. I assumed they'd get back to me after I turned twenty-five and was more mature.

Who knows? I was just happy they were gone for the evening. No reason for them to know about my date with a guy three years older than me and a possible trust fund baby. Not at least until things got more serious. *Heh...* if they got serious at all.

About an hour later I was ready to head out. My wavy red hair flowed down my shoulders and a few stray strands brushed over my eyes. My hair color often brought a lot of attention, but it was something I'd gotten used to. I stood out with red hair, but other than my hair I was a pretty average looking girl. Hazel eyes, light skin (not that cool, super pale skin like porcelain), just light. I had a decent build and was pretty tall, but also pretty skinny. I had one of those Jennifer Aniston type bodies which really worked for some guys, but turned off a bunch of others.

Whichever.

I stood outside the Shaw place and waited for Wyatt to show up. When he was five minutes late, I started to worry that maybe I was being stood up.

When ten minutes passed, I checked my watch – an expensive 'I'm sorry we're moving to the East coast' gift.

At fifteen minutes late, I looked towards my house and wondered if it would be best to save myself the embarrassment of being stood up. Maybe his friends were hiding nearby and watching as some poor, innocent girl actually tricked herself into thinking she had a date with a guy like Wyatt. Just the idea of being watched made my cheeks hot and I started to spin on my heel.

"What are you doing out here?" a voice shouted from behind.

I jerked around to find Wyatt. He stood there, looking as delicious as before with his long hands tucked in his jeans pockets. He was at the front door of the Shaw place and the door was swung wide open like he owned the damn place. I tried not to look as self-conscious as I felt.

16

"I thought you said we would meet at nine thirty," I shouted.

"Shh!" he hushed and waved me closer to him. Like an obedient dog, I followed and quickly jogged to the front door. "Not so loud. Isn't this like a prestigious neighborhood where all the richies hang out?"

"I don't know. I just moved here. I thought you said—"

"I've been waiting for you since nine twenty," he grumbled. "I thought I made it clear. Meet at the Shaw place at nine-thirty."

"I was outside waiting."

"So why didn't you knock?"

"Because no one lives here?" I said, sounding a bit annoyed.

Without warning, Wyatt pulled me through the front door and closed it quietly behind him. I was ready start some sexy argument about not understanding his vague directions, but before I could catch my breath he slammed my back against the door and pinned both my arms above my head. We were almost the same height so I could tell immediately that he was a smoker when his breath hit my nostrils. I didn't know what it was, but it actually smelled better than how I imagined it would be.

"How long were you waiting outside?" he asked softly.

"I don't know," I stuttered, surprised to find myself in such a vulnerable position. "Five minutes?"

"Liar. Tell me." His eyes locked on mine and they smoldered with what I wanted to say was passion, but it was more like urgency. Since it was summer it wasn't completely dark yet and I could hear him take in a ragged breath. "Did anyone see you?"

"You're scaring me a bit, Wyatt," I admitted at last. His grip on my wrists loosened and I exhaled loudly in his face.

"Better?"

I nodded, but my heart still pounded loudly behind my thin tank top. Actually there's one more thing I should mention. Despite having what I described as a Jennifer Aniston-like body, there was one thing that was very un-Jennifer Aniston like. In fact, I dare say it was a bit more Angelina Jolie-like.

"Two minute delay," Wyatt huffed angrily. "Are you still scared? Do you want to leave?"

I tried to hold his gaze. "Should I want to?"

"Now's not the time for games. Answer me."

His eyes warned that he wasn't playing around. If this was the type of interaction he enjoyed, I guess this was his way of giving me a way out, but I was hooked. Despite being almost the same height as him, I felt owned. I liked the feeling - that if I tried to move my wrists there was no way I could escape.

I wouldn't want to.

"I'm good," I said. "And no. No one saw me." He released my wrists completely and took a step back. My face was still warm from his breath and my chest was beginning to sweat.

"For a minute there, you really had me going," I said, trying to laugh.

"Did I?" He started to chuckle. "I never saw myself as a scary guy."

"You're not scary. I'd say you're more intense."

He turned back to face me, his face piqued with interest. "Really?" he asked, taking a step forward. "And it doesn't scare you?"

"No." My breath hitched as he came closer and practically

touched my nose with his. "Alright, maybe I'm a little scared now," I said as my eyes crossed to try and focus on him. "You're not a vampire, are you?"

"A vampire?" he croaked. I could tell he was holding in a frown. "You don't believe in haunted houses but you think I'm a vampire?"

"Are you?"

"I wish," he grumbled. He licked his lips and his eyes fell to mine. "You're an interesting girl. I'm surprised that you showed up."

"Maybe I think you're interesting too," I countered.

"That's a bad idea."

"I don't see it that way."

"You should." He looked away for a moment and his eyes darted towards the stairs behind him, to the side, past my shoulders and then back to my eyes.

"You know, if you really want to show me this house is haunted—"

"Shut up," he said, growing irritated. A hand flew up to my mouth and covered it. "Just shut up for a moment." He looked around himself and then brought his attention back to me. "Are you playing around?"

I started to speak, but my words were muffled by his hand. He slowly pulled it away. "Playing with you? You're the one who brought me here on some weird excursion to find out if a house was haunted and then you pinned me up against a door *Psycho*-style. How could *I* be playing with *you*?"

"Humor me with an answer, Lyris."

I flushed when he said my name. God, I didn't think I'd ever

19

get sick of hearing this man say my name. "I don't exactly know what you mean, but I'm not playing with you."

His eyes searched mine, but I had no idea what for. What was he trying to find? Maybe I had misjudged him. Maybe he was actually interested and worried that I wasn't interested in him. That happens, right? A super-hot guy finds a somewhat attractive girl with large boobs and then he wants her? That's like, the definition of a lot of new adult books. It made sense.

I lowered my voice to a whisper. "I'm not playing with you."

He started to lean forward, and I was struck with cigarette smoke. I wondered if he had any on him right then. I'd never smoked before, but I wondered what it would be like. Our noses touched and I swear in that moment I thought he was going to kiss me. I closed my eyes and leaned forward and the tips of our lips touched. Even with that slight graze I could tell they were rough from use. My mouth parted slightly and he swallowed hard.

He jerked away with a grunt. "We should check out the house."

My body lunged forward a few inches and I steadied myself. *Really? That was it?* Where the hell was my new-adult style kiss? Maybe this wasn't enough foreplay for him, but I was good to go. I fixed my hair and pulled myself away from the door so I could follow him.

"So you really believe this place is haunted?" I asked disbelievingly. "How?"

"There's a haunted room," he said, walking towards the stairs.

"Haunted room?"

"Want to check it out?"

"Are you sure this isn't a ploy to get me upstairs?" I teased, following him just the same.

20

"Would it change your answer if it was or wasn't?" he teased right back.

I was relieved when he settled back into innocent flirting mode. I was much more on my game when he was like this, rather than being pinned up against a wall and asked if I was messing with him. But damn. It would have been sweet to kiss him.

"I suppose not," I said at last with a shrug. "So then tell me, what's so haunted about this particular room? Is it because women mysteriously lose their virginity there?"

He smirked. "You certainly talk a big game for a girl so small. Should make things interesting, for sure."

"I'm almost the same height as you, big shot," I said with a frown. "Anyway, I'm only asking questions. What's so haunted about this room?"

"There's a wall closet," he said. He fell quiet for a few moments as we finally made it to the top of the stairs. I followed behind him to a particular room on the second floor with a shut door and he rested his hand on the knob before opening it.

"Lots of rooms have closets, Wyatt," I teased.

"Not like this one. You know, in a house like this closets usually lead to somewhere. A bathroom, another bedroom, an attic, even an outside balcony. The point is, they take you somewhere."

I waggled my fingers. "Ohhh... and tell me... where will this particular closet take me? Narnia?"

I expected Wyatt to say something sharp in response, but to my surprise the corner of his mouth crooked upward almost like a smile.

"Heh, that would be interesting, wouldn't it?" As he removed his hand from the knob, he turned to face me. "You're being weird.

Don't tell me you like me?"

I flushed. "What makes you say that?" I lowered my head.

"You *do* like me," he teased. "That's cute."

I fought off the embarrassment rising in my throat like bile. Images of his friends lurking around the abandoned house and laughing made me self-conscious. "You don't have to make fun of me for it."

"I'm not," he said quickly. "I'm really not. I'm just surprised. You're not what I expected you to be."

I flinched. "What the hell does that mean? You don't even know me."

"When I heard a family was moving next door to this place and found out that the parents were both professors, I had an image of how I pictured you."

"How was that?"

"Snooty."

"Thanks."

"Stuck up."

I rolled my eyes. "You're really turning me on now."

"Immature and spoiled," he finished off.

"Damn, please stop—"

"But you're not," he said, almost sounding angry about it. "You're gorgeous and witty. You have an insecurity about you that you cover up very well with dry humor and dirty jokes."

"You can tell all of that just after a few hours?"

"I've become very good at assessing people over the years. I know what I want and I know how to find it. But you..." something flickered in his eyes, "... dammit. You're not what I expected. This changes things."

"What needs to change?" I dared to take a step forward. "We could just... you know... hang out or something. We don't have to chill in this dank, crap home. Let's go somewhere. Do something fun?"

He shook his head. "I can't."

"Why not?"

"Because you've been targeted."

"Targeted? What the hell does that mean?" For a moment I worried that maybe I crossed the line with this guy. Maybe I had been so blinded by his beauty and charm, his wit and banter that I missed some red flags. He spoke in a funny way and there was always some sort of conflict in his eyes – even in the very short time I had spoken to him.

To my relief though, his shoulders relaxed and he started to smile.

"I'm kidding," he said in a dry tone. "You're right. We don't have to do this." He took a few steps back towards the stairs and offered his hand. "I know a place that makes kick ass hot dogs this time of night and they have an outdoor garden. Come on..." He held out his hand towards me.

"Sure, but—"

"But what?"

"What did you mean when you said I was targeted?"

His smile was warm. "Don't worry about that, Lyris. That's

23

just what I say when I think I've got a crush on someone."

"Crush?" I squeaked, too excited for my own good.

"Like I said, you really surprise me. Why? Did I freak you out?"

I took his hand. "Yes, but that's okay."

As we made our way downstairs, Wyatt led us to the front door. "Why don't you head out first, okay? I'll lock up."

"Lock up?" I let out a giggle. "No one lives here."

"Let me do my thing and I'll let you do yours. You should go back to your house and get a coat since we'll be walking."

I shrugged and nodded as I turned to leave. "Meet me out in front of my house in five?"

"How about the corner?" he asked, waggling his brows. "Not afraid of the dark, are you? Not in this gated community."

"Shut up. The corner is fine." I opened the door and started to head out when Wyatt reached out and grabbed my upper arm and slung me back. "Something else?" I asked, growing a bit breathless from his mood swings. "You really should work on your people skills."

"Promise me something, okay?"

"Sure." Our eyes met and his darted back and forth with an unfamiliar urgency.

"I'm serious, Lyris. Promise me."

I arched a brow. And he was back to being weird. "Okay, I'll bite. What?"

"That room? That room I took you to?"

"The one we didn't go in?"

"Yes, that room," Wyatt continued. "Promise me you won't ever go in that room without me, let alone open any of the closet doors."

"Damn, that place really has you spooked, doesn't it? Unless you have a red room in there."

"I don't even know what the hell that means," Wyatt grumbled, locking those green eyes on mine. "Promise me, Lyris. Don't ever go in that room unless I'm with you."

"Okay, I promise. Seriously, Wyatt. What the hell is the big deal with that damn room?"

He only released my arm. "Just go. Get out here before I change my mind."

"Change your mind?"

"Go."

I couldn't understand Wyatt's stupid mood swings, but like a child wanting the finest toy at the day care, I found myself listening to his every word. As I walked back to my house, I turned around to look at the Shaw place and noticed that a single light was on upstairs, flickering once... twice... and then going out completely. Wyatt was pretty weird, but nothing was weirder than the way he acted about that stupid room. What twenty year old guy really believes a room is haunted?

There had to be more to it than that.

Wyatt was hiding something and I was damn sure I would find out what.

Three

After a long evening with Wyatt I was so sure I was going to hear back from him the following day. And then it occurred to me. I didn't have his number. And he certainly didn't have mine. I had no idea where he lived, but he knew where I lived. I didn't have the slightest clue how to track him down other than to go back to the coffee shop and wait.

But that seemed so pathetic that I had a hard time bringing myself to do it.

I was already in a pretty bad mood because my parents didn't even come home until right when I woke up for breakfast. They spared me nothing more than a tired glance. Ugh, what kind of world did I live in where my parents were the ones to go out and party all night while I shook my head in disappointment at their actions?

"I thought you guys had an initiation ceremony," I said with disapproval written all over my features.

"We did, Lyre," my dad said tiredly. He reached for a coffee pod. "Ugh, don't we have any more dark roast?"

"It's in the pantry," my mom said. "Brew up a hazelnut, please."

"What's the point of having coffee if you're just going back to bed?" I grumbled. I shook my head and reached for a box of cereal as my dad staggered over to the pantry. I swear, the pantry in our kitchen was larger than my closet back at my old home. There were only the three of us. Why had my parents insisted on moving to a bigger house after my older brother and sister had since moved out? "And where the hell are the Mallow Bits?"

"That disgusting cereal with all the candy? I threw it out."

"Mom..." I groaned. "It's not candy. They're marshmallows. Geezus, and I was still eating it."

"There's plenty of Crunch Berries," my dad said as he pulled out a large yellow box from the pantry along with his single coffee pod. His dark eyes scrutinized the box and his thin lips down turned. "This looks overly sugared and disgusting."

"I don't want corn balls flavored with food coloring," I said with a pout.

"I'll agree with that," my dad continued. "How can you legally be allowed to call something Crunch Berries when there's not a single trace of fruit juice?" He tucked the box back into the pantry and popped in the pods for himself and my mom.

Immediately the smell of bitter coffee hit my nostrils and I scrunched up my nose.

"I'm heading over to the university later today, Lyre. I can stop at the market and get more of that junk if you want."

"Get more creamer," my mom called over. She was safely tucked away in her recliner. She was wearing her pencil skirt from the night before that was entirely too tight for my liking and had just kicked off her expensive black heels. I turned away and tried not to focus on the fact that my mother – despite being hungover – was more attractive and put together than I ever was.

"Actually, dad, I can run out myself. I don't want to be cooped up in the house all day."

"Get more creamer."

"Yes, dammit," my dad grumbled. "Dear, you'll get more creamer. It will end up here eventually." He turned back to me as I located some strawberry pastries in the back of the pantry and emerged with a smile. "I guess it's good you want to head out and explore this place. I bet you never expected to live in a neighborhood so nice, eh Lyre?"

"It'd be *nice* if we could hire a person who could keep the fridge stocked," my mother muttered sleepily.

My father finally smiled. "She's going to be knocked out before she even gets to finish this old creamer." I dared to laugh. "But seriously, are you liking this place? Are you going to go check out your school?"

"You mean that pretentious private school that you and mom are sending me to because God forbid the daughter of two professors attends a public school her senior year?"

"It'll be good for you."

"Mara and Mike didn't have to go to private school."

"Mara and Mike didn't have your grades, or the opportunities you have now," my dad said with a smile. "It won't be so bad. You should give it a chance. I'll bet you'll fit right in there. In fact, I'm pretty sure there are some kids who live in this neighborhood who go there."

"I would be more shocked if kids lived in this neighborhood who *didn't* go there," I shot back. The toaster buzzed and alerted me that my breakfast was done so I grabbed the two pastries and took a seat at the counter. "But seriously though, dad. I do have a question about this area."

"Oh?"

My dad couldn't hide his surprise that I was looking to have a conversation with him. I guess he wasn't in the mood to analyze because suddenly his hangover evaporated and he practically skipped over to me with his cup of coffee. His dark eyes blazed with curiosity. My mom was already snoring in the next room.

"Yeah," I said. "That house... the one next door..."

"The empty one?" he asked, arching a brow. "Or those horrible hipsters—"

"The empty one."

28

"Good." My dad looked relieved for some reason. "What about it?"

"What's up with that place?"

"What's... up?"

"Ugh, dad. Why is it abandoned?"

"Well, it's just an old, deserted house, Lyre. Every neighborhood – even ones like this – have that old abandoned house. I think it gives the street charm."

I resisted rolling my eyes. I could care less about the damn aesthetics of the street. People knew how much it cost to move into a neighborhood practically on a college campus. Hell, even I knew that my parents were making good money if we lived here.

"That's not what I mean. I ran into someone at the coffee shop yesterday while you guys were out and he called the house the old Shaw place?"

One of my father's bushy brows arched upward. "Uh-huh."

"Do you know anything about that?" I asked. I tried to remain patient.

"How about we start by you telling me what you already know."

"And how it makes me feel?" I asked, smiling at his attempt to suppress the analyst inside of him.

"Seriously, Lyre. What did you learn about the Shaw house?"

I shrugged. "They say it's haunted." My eyes trailed over to my father who sipped from his mug slowly. Honestly it reminded a lot of how Wyatt drank. "But that's stupid, right? A haunted house?"

29

"Well..." my dad said, elongating his response as he always did, "... I suppose you could say it's true to an extent."

"See, I thought it was stupid—*what*? Don't tell me you believe in that garbage."

"Haunted is just one way of wording it," my dad continued. Another large sigh escaped him. "Actually, I was hoping you wouldn't find out anything about that house until school started." He ran a dry and tired hand through his thinning gray hair. "Lyre, there are some things in life that are so fantastic you can't help but believe them to an extent. Do you understand what I'm saying?"

I shook my head. "Why don't you enlighten me? How is a house haunted?"

"It's not so much the house. It's—"

"A room," I finished off. "The guy I met at the coffee shop told me."

"Guy?" My father's brow furrowed and I thought about warning him that he was going to get more wrinkles if he didn't stop doing that.

"Yes, a guy. The opposite of a girl," I grumbled.

"Did you go over to the house?" I looked away. "I hope you weren't trespassing."

"I have better things to do than explore some grimy old mansion. But I'm curious! Tell me about the house, dad. What's up with the room? Wyatt said—"

"Wyatt?"

"Dad. Focus, please?" My mother groaned for a moment in the background, but we both ignored her. If she wanted her damn coffee so bad she was going to have to push her 117 pound frame up off the recliner and saunter over in her pantyhose. "He said there's a room to nowhere."

My dad chuckled which irritated me.

"What?" I groaned. I took a hearty bite from my pastry in the way some alcoholics must gulp their liquor. "What's so funny?"

"A room to nowhere. That's a funny way to word it."

"So it's true?"

"I can't tell you for sure," my dad said. "All I know is that back in the eighties there was a family there. Not much different than our own! Two professors and they had three sons. But unlike your mother and I, the father was supposedly an astronomy professor and the mother was a... well, I'm not really sure what."

"So how does this lead up to having a room that leads to nowhere?"

"Apparently this couple was obsessed with science-fiction," my dad continued with a shrug. "They grew up watching and reading things such as *2001: A Space Odyssey, The Day the Earth Stood Still, The Twilight Zone*, the whole thing. Honestly, everyone was into science-fiction for a while, but one of the professors told me that the mother took her interest to a different level."

"Meaning?"

"She was obsessed with finding black holes and portals to other dimensions."

My face fell. That. Was. It? "Black holes? Other dimensions?" Inwardly and outwardly I groaned. "I was at least hoping for a murder mystery or something, dad. Not some—"

"Not a murder so much," my dad continued. His voice remained as calm and stoic as ever. He rarely raised his voice and he rarely grew irritated. It infuriated me to no end. "But a disappearance."

31

I was instantly hooked anew. "And?"

"And what happened was—"

"Stuart, give me my damn coffee," my mother groaned, suddenly coming to life. She shifted her frail corpse up into a sitting position and started to stand. "I asked you to do one thing and you couldn't even do it."

"I was spending time with Lyre."

"Lyre doesn't want to spend time with us. You read the books. She's seventeen years old. She needs to be free and if you don't want her to hate us in her thirties and visiting our colleagues for counseling, you'll leave her be." She staggered into the kitchen and reached for her mug. "It's not even warm."

"You've been on the chair," I countered, standing up for my dad. "Seriously though, what about the disappearance?"

"At first it was the youngest son—"

"Stuart. Enough," my mom huffed. "Come to bed. I want to lie down."

"So go."

"Yeah, mom," I grumbled, growing impatient with her. She really was like a child sometimes. How this women was a college professor was beyond me. "Go to bed. Dad and I are talking."

"Dad has something a little bit more important to take care of than talking," she huffed, leaning over my dad's back.

Like me, my mom was a stick except for one very important feature. While my gift was natural, my mom's was bought and paid for as a Christmas gift from my dad when I was thirteen. She pressed those rock hard orbs into his back and whispered something in his ear.

32

"Eww, mom, seriously? Gross. Lower your voice."

My dad turned red and abruptly stood up from the table. "Eh, sorry, Lyre. I'm going to have to take a rain check on this. Another time, okay? You don't mind, do you?"

"Would it matter if I did?"

My mom tugged my father by the sleeve of his button down and with an irritated growl, I polished off the last of my breakfast. Still, I couldn't complain too much. I had another piece of the story.

A room leading to nowhere.

A rich, kooky professor couple obsessed with lame books and movies.

A disappearance.

At least it was something.

As I figured that it wouldn't be harmful to go downtown and pick up some actual cereal, I pushed my empty plate away and made sure to grab my cell phone. Hell, I didn't know if I was going to run into Wyatt or not, but I wanted to be prepared.

***

After a quick trip down to the local market, I came back home to an empty house. My parents had left a note on the refrigerator, a reminder to tell our maid Jessa to pick up more coffee creamer if I forgot. *Dammit.* I threw my mother's stupid creamer into the back of the fridge and threw the note in the garbage before Jessa would see it and panic that she wasn't doing her job. It wasn't Jessa's fault that my mother was scatterbrained.

After collapsing on the couch in the family room, I went to flick on the television when something caught the corner of my eye. From the window I could see the Shaw place hidden behind some trees. I had been so obsessed with finding Wyatt on my walk that I had forgotten everything my dad said. Ugh, maybe if his voice had a little personality I wouldn't be so quick to forget. I sat up straight in my chair and looked at the side of the house. Each window and each balcony clearly led to somewhere. I didn't know why, but I was expecting some random door with nothing beneath it except open air. That would have made sense.

I stood up and walked to the window, and pressed my nose against the warm glass to get a better look. I couldn't see everything, but I didn't see any damn door that led to nowhere. *Stupid mom.* Dad was just about to say what was going on with that place when she had to distract him with her sloppy, disgusting offer of parental sex. That was the last thing I wanted to think about.

So why not a distraction?

I smiled and ignored the TV to put a baseball cap over my head so I could head outside. The weather was still warm, but the mature trees on our street provided shade that was much needed in the early summer. As I started to go for a walk, I stopped in front of the Shaw house and looked around. The light I had seen flickering yesterday was off, and the place looked as dead as I remembered it except for yesterday when Wyatt had given me a tour.

If the house was abandoned, I wondered if the front door was locked. Wyatt certainly didn't seem to have any problems getting inside.

"Still curious, eh?" a voice said next to me.

I jumped and jerked my head in the direction of the voice and found the very boy in question. "Wyatt," I gasped, "you scared the shit out of me."

"That language is far too mature for a girl your age," he said. He grinned widely and stepped up beside me.

"I thought you said you liked my age."

"I said seventeen was the perfect age. There's a difference."

I rolled my hazel eyes and took the opportunity to check him out. Even though it was downright balmy, Wyatt was dressed for an autumn night football game with dark jeans and a v-neck sweater. I could see the sprinkling of dark chest hair poking out from the top. I wondered if he ever broke out into a sweat. I was dying just looking at him. "Whatever. What are you doing here, anyway? Don't tell me you squat in this house?"

"Trust me, Lyris. I don't squat anywhere."

"So where do you live?"

"That's my business," he said shortly, turning his attention back to the house. Dark hair fell over his even darker eyes. "I had a feeling you'd be more curious about this place today so I decided to stop by and low and behold, here you are, staring away." He turned his head. "You do remember what I told you?"

I frowned. "Which part?"

"Don't go in there without me."

"What's the difference?"

His frown deepened and he shoved his long hands into his jeans pockets. "If you're half as smart as I think you are, you'll just listen to me, okay?"

"Whatever," I said.

"Whatever," he mocked back. "So seriously, what are you doing today?"

"I don't know. Depends."

"Depends on what?"

"Depends on what you're doing," I said, waggling my brows

35

as he smirked. I couldn't deny it, I loved it when I made him smile. He was usually so serious so whenever he let down his guard, I was excited. "Let's forget the house for now and get some lunch."

"Oh? Are you cooking?"

"I hadn't thought about that." For the first time he had truly caught *me* off-guard. I had planned on going someplace for lunch, but Wyatt looked past my head.

"Don't you keep food in your house?" he asked.

"Yes, but—"

"And I don't see any cars in the driveway."

"That's not the point."

"What is, then?"

"I don't really know you, dude," I said, standing my ground. "Let's just go somewhere and I'll pay." My voice faltered and I wondered if I was coming across as a prude so I snuck a look over at Wyatt. "Please?" I said in a softer voice.

To my relief, he chuckled. "You really aren't playing around," he said with a laugh. "Come 'ere..." He trailed off as he started to reach for my arm and I jerked away like his hands were on fire. "What?" he asked. "What do you think I'm going to do?"

"What *are* you going to do?"

"Come 'ere and find out," he said, holding out his hand. Slowly and tentatively I slipped my hand into his, surprised at how close they were to the same size. He pulled me close and locked eyes on mine. I swear the tip of my nose started to sweat. "Hold still," he said, softly but in a way that wasn't up for argument. "I want to kiss you now."

"So do it," I said.

He didn't hesitate as his lips came closer. I was shocked that he wasn't in the mood to banter and let out a grunt of surprise when his lips crashed against mine. They were warm and dry and they smelled like smoke, but I didn't mind. The owner of those lips was well worth it. Despite kissing him, I focused on what I remembered before I closed my eyes. The way his jeans clung to his slim hips, the way his cologne smelled like mint and blueberries. The way I could tell he used to have his eyebrow pierced, but had let it close up at some point. I could picture his simple v-neck sweater.

"Screw it," I grunted between kisses.

"Huh?"

I smiled. "Come inside. I'll make you lunch."

Four

The next few days were sort of a blur filled with grilled cheese sandwiches, blueberry and mint cologne and cigarettes on my parent's deck. I never took more than a few puffs at a time, but I swear I was beginning to understand why people in the movies liked to smoke after sex. After a heavy make-out session with Wyatt it was hard to calm down my nerves otherwise. It was getting more and more difficult to stop him when he started to pull up my shirt or unbutton my jeans.

After a blissful week when I suddenly realized I hadn't given much thought about the house next door. It was strange because every time before Wyatt left he would always remind me about the damn place.

Don't go there.

Don't go there alone.

Don't go there without me.

He would never say why and honestly until that point I didn't really care. However, my curiosity was starting to bite at me and as I was about to send Wyatt through my window on the eighth night of heavy making out, he noticed my attention flicker to the house next door.

"Don't do that," he warned.

"Do what?" I kissed the tip of his nose.

"Don't start thinking about that place again."

"Why not? You were all about taking me there before. In fact, for a while I swear that was the only reason you were even talking to me. You wanted to take me back to the creeper house where women go to lose their virginity." I started to laugh, but it fell on hollow ears.

"I was set on taking you there," Wyatt admitted. "I swear, when I have a target I can't think about anything else."

"And by target you mean having a crush?" My lips parted nervously.

"Yes," he said, though his voice grew a bit rushed.

Wyatt was lying about something. I wasn't so smitten with kisses that I didn't notice it. And the weirder he got about the house, the more pressure I felt to go there. Just once. That way Wyatt and I could laugh about it on my one thousand thread count sheets.

"You're not my target, though," he continued. "Not like that." He shook his head. "Lyre, I know you're seventeen, but I have to say, I legit like you."

I smiled. "Well, I legit like you, too."

"And that's why I'm saying. Don't go to that house. Don't look at that house. Don't even think about that house."

"So stop talking about it so much! How can I stop thinking about it if that's all you want to talk about?"

"I'm trying to drum it into your thick head," he said. His hand reached up and long fingers laced into my messy red waves, sending feelings of warmth and tingles all the way down to my pink and yellow striped socks. "Your thick, lovely, delicious head," he said in a softer voice. His forehead pressed against mine and we both closed our eyes. "I won't bring it up again if that's what it takes for you to stop thinking about it. I wish I never brought it up with you until I got to know you. That was my stupid mistake."

"It was stupid," I said in a teasing tone.

He choked out a laugh. "It was. Alright, then, it's done. No more talk of the house." He pulled his forehead away from mine and smiled. It was a weird smile because it looked genuine. His words about liking me started to seem too real and I looked away.

"I'm taking you out tomorrow," he said suddenly. "For a real date. A real dinner."

"Yeah right."

"I'm serious, Lyre," he said, grabbing my hands. Both of us looked shocked. "Will you go out with me tomorrow night?" His smile was hopeful and slightly wavering which almost caused me to fall out the window in shock. *Was this my life? Was this really happening?*

"S-Sure," I stuttered. "I'd be happy to."

His smile turned confident as he leaned forward and kissed me deeply on the lips. To show my gratitude for being taken out on a real date, I slipped some extra tongue inside and gently tugged the hair on the back of his head. He pulled back with surprise.

"God, you are nothing like I expected," he mumbled. "I'll call you tomorrow with the details. Wear something cute."

"Actually, I wanted to dress like a bum."

"Smartass," he said, winking as he started to climb down the trellis.

My parents watched the TV loudly downstairs, and there was no way they would see Wyatt. After only seven days he was a pro.

"Remember," he said suddenly. I looked down at him. He pointed at the Shaw place and then shook his head. He didn't say another word, but the seed was planted.

Dammit.

I was going to that house before things with Wyatt got too serious.

I had to know what the big deal was and why he went from

practically dragging me into the house to not wanting me to have anything to do with it at all.

When he was out of sight, I quickly climbed down the trellis to the ground floor just like I had seen him do.

***

The great thing about summer was that it was always warm. Even on the east coast around midnight the air was warm and sticky. Some people hated that feeling, but as a slimmer person I have to say I loved it. I was always so miserable in the damn winter that I could hardly stand it. In the summer, I could run around my parent's backyard in socks, night shorts and a tank top and practically break into a sweat. *Sweet.*

The trip from my parent's house to the Shaw place was a surprisingly easy one because apparently in rich neighborhoods the whole place shuts down after eleven. Not a single person was to be seen and not a single light was on. I double checked the second floor of the Shaw place. *Nope.* Not even that place was alive like the night Wyatt took me there.

As I crossed over to the next house, I noticed the grass was still immaculate. Someone must have been embarrassed enough about an unkempt lawn in their neighborhood that they must have cut it themselves, or at least hired someone else to do it on their dime. Abandoned houses didn't usually look like the Shaw place. The gutters were still clean and the paneling was smooth and white. The brick parts also seemed to have a cleanliness to them. Damn, the old place was in better shape than my old home when my family and I still lived there!

The back porch was actually very similar to the one at our house so tiptoeing up to it, I wondered if it was actually unlocked like the one at home. My parents seemed to think that 'gated community' meant that doors didn't need to be locked anymore so maybe the Shaw place was the same. I closed my eyes as my hand fell around the bronze handle and gave it a quick turn, half-hoping it was locked, half-hoping it was open.

41

The door let out a pleasant THUNK as it opened inward and I was punched in the face with the smell of old-people house and wood.

"Seriously?" I was surprised that the door was actually unlocked. I guess I secretly hoped that it wasn't so that way I could at least say I tried and could run back home and tuck myself back into my expensive sheets. But that wasn't the case and because of that I started to get a little nervous.

Without Wyatt, the house seemed cold and unwelcome and the lack of furniture made the house seem even bigger than it was. It was like a doll's house and as my socked feet crept over the hardwood floor towards the foyer and staircase, I wondered if I should have turned back. I could have turned around. I could have listened to Wyatt and remembered the fact that he legit liked me and we were going on a date the next day.

Why spook myself out?

After going on a real date with Wyatt, I would probably never feel comfortable betraying him again. As I stood at the bottom of the stairs, I looked upward and tried to will my body to go through with this. I pictured the first time I was in here and how easily I had followed Wyatt up those same stairs like a willing dog, but without him my knees shook.

It was wrong.

Oh so terribly wrong and I couldn't figure out why.

Oh wait. Breaking and entering. Trespassing.

I shook my head and let out an uncomfortable laugh and started to walk up the stairs. Maybe I wouldn't even remember what room it was. I could say I gave it the 'old college try' and then decided to call it a night.

Dammit.

All doors were open on the second floor but one.

As I approached that particular door, I chanted in my head.

Just a house.

Just a room.

Just a rumor.

Just a disappearance.

Dammit, the last part of my chant took me off-guard and as I stood in front of the closed door, my hand faltered to reach for the knob. Maybe if I had just asked Wyatt, then we could have gone together. He just said to never to go to that room without him. Maybe Wyatt was playing some sort of trust game to make sure he wasn't getting together with a liar. Maybe there was nothing behind the door but proof that I wouldn't make a good girlfriend.

And all of that would have made sense if not for what my dad had started to tell me.

Dammit again! Why didn't I ask him to finish that story?

My mind raced.

Ask him, then.

Ask him tomorrow.

Ask him and then decide what you're going to do.

Ask him and then talk to Wyatt.

"No," I grumbled, already infuriated with myself. "It's just a damn room! There's no such thing as haunted houses, haunted rooms, or closets that lead to nowhere. This isn't fracking Narnia." Before I could stop myself I reached forward, grabbed the knob and yanked the door open.

Five

"What the hell?" My voice must have come across like a groan because that is certainly what I did after I opened the door. I didn't know what I was expecting, but if there was one thing I hoped for, it was a little excitement to meet my expectations. Instead, it was like waiting in line for three hours for a roller coaster that is rumored to be bad ass and then ends up being lame ass. The room looked like nothing more than a standard nerd hang out complete with overly filled bookshelves and overly organized paperwork in one part of the room and a complete mess of chaos in another.

Wyatt was intent on keeping me away from here? He was drilling into my head to ignore an office? I had to wonder if Wyatt had some sort of mental problem hidden behind those scrumptious dark green eyes of his. No matter. At least I could have a good laugh with him tomorrow on our date and let him know I visited his little room and was bored to death.

As I started to turn away with a smirk, I decided I could at least do a little exploring. There was plenty of light in the room so I didn't have to worry... *wait*.

I hadn't turned any lights on.

So why was there...

As I slowly turned back around to face the room, I noticed that a single closet door had a bright light spilling out from beneath. I tilted my head and tried to make sense as to why someone would have such a bright light in a closet, but the moment I stepped forward it flicked off, cloaking the crack below the door in darkness. I frowned and realized my curiosity was piqued again. Not enough to open the door quite yet, but enough to at least flip on the main light in the room and take a quick look around. At the flick of the switch only a single lamp turned on and I glanced at the ceiling for some recessed lighting. *Huh.* Wasn't that a big thing to have in offices and kitchens? Ugh, I was beginning to sound like a wasp.

I shook my head at the fact that I was indeed probably a little spoiled and ventured over to the nearest bookshelves. Maybe Wyatt stored some of his personal favorites in this room and what better way to learn more about him than by learning what he liked to read.

Several titles caught my attention right off the bat and not simply because I was curious. I remembered some of the titles my dad mentioned to me. Several others of the same genre also caught jumped out at me.

2001: A Space Odyssey

The Great Works of Richard Matheson

Foundation

Dune

Brave New World

Huh. My dad had mentioned a few of those, but I hadn't really expected to come across some of the titles so quickly. In fact, there were several copies of Richard Matheson books and over ten copies of *2001*. Some of them looked downright ragged. With a tentative hand, I reached up and took one of the copies from the shelf and opened it. My eyes widened as I glanced down at the pages. They were filled to the brim with notes. Notes everywhere. Notes in the margin, notes between paragraphs and notes written vertically in the spine.

So many notes.

I closed the book and quickly shoved it back into the shelf, getting a little freaked out for reasons I couldn't even comprehend. Maybe Wyatt was right and I shouldn't have come here alone. The room smelled funny and I didn't think it had anything to do with the old books. Something was wrong. I turned away and saw an old-style secretary desk with a surprisingly new-looking office chair behind it. If the house really was abandoned in the 1980s there was no way that chair had come from the same era. It looked like a cheap chair from a Staples back-to-school sale. I touched the chair and

46

wasn't surprised that it felt as new and cheap as it looked.

Wyatt really did hang out here.

I titled my head, and noticed that the top of the desk was pretty clear of papers with only a few scattered folders over the top and a single pen.

Trust. I was breaking trust with Wyatt.

He was weird, but I had promised him that I wouldn't go to that room without him and yet there I was, scrounging through his things. The whole 'don't go into that room' was starting to seem more and more like a test. Still, I couldn't shake my father's words away. He had specifically said that this place was mysterious and I couldn't ignore that crucial piece of information. Wyatt's word was one thing, but adding my father's to the mix was quite another.

My fingertips brushed over the folder, but I couldn't bring myself to open it. It was so wrong. I had to get out of there.

Until a light flashed under the closet door again.

The room to nowhere.

First it was the youngest son who disappeared.

My father's and Wyatt's words hung heavily in my mind as the light flashed once, twice and then a third time under the closet door. *Wyatt couldn't have been there.* I saw him walk down the street so unless he decided to come back...

"I know what you're doing," I said in a sing-song voice. "I knew it! You're testing me, aren't you? You wanted to see if I would go into your room and go through all your things in this stupid little hide-out, didn't you? Well, I'm sorry, but the jig is up. Come on out, Wyatt. I'm sorry." I narrowed my eyes at the door, expecting him to burst through, half angry and half turned-on with my desire to go against my word and his, but no one came.

"Wyatt?" I took another tentative step towards the door. The light under the crack of the door flickered, once. Twice. "Wyatt, come on. This isn't really funny anymore. Are you really there?"

Another flickering. On the light came. Out the light went.

"This isn't funny," I said, stopping in front of the closed door and brushing my socked foot close to the opening. The light switched on and off and my socks flickered at the signal. My face grew hot. "Wyatt? Can you please stop now? I'm not laughing."

Light on. Light off.

"I hate you," I grumbled and turned away, prepared to stalk off.

The lights switched on and off at a rapid pace and I stopped and turned around.

"Seriously? You're sick," I muttered. "You think this is funny? You think it's cool to try and scare me?"

Darkness.

I didn't know what was actually more frightening, the flickering or the darkness, but I was pretty damn freaked out either way. I approached the door for a second time and braced myself for Wyatt's stupid face, but nothing happened. Not even a flicker.

"I'm going to open the door now," I said. "And I swear if you're behind it, I'll never speak to you again. You're an ass and I don't think this is funny. Alright? Are you happy? I legit admit it. I'm freaked out. You're freaking me out, Wyatt." I touched the doorknob and gripped it slowly. The coolness of the metal knob was surprising at first, but I think at that point anything would have been freaky. I gripped it tighter and the light slowly came on.

"I'm coming to get you, ass," I said, swallowing my fear and yanking the closet door open.

A bright light nearly blinded me and I held up my hand to block it. "Geezus, Wyatt..." I groaned. "You want to turn down the light—"

"Oberti," a voice came from above.

The light was so bright I couldn't see the owner of the voice, only feel where it was coming from. Above and high above at that. Was Wyatt standing on a stairway? Were there stairways in a closet? Was he talking from the damn ceiling or something?

"What?" I asked, squinting my eyes. "Wyatt, stop playing around and turn off that spotlight."

"Dea insigni," the booming voice rumbled overhead. "Oberti! Oberti!"

"Seriously Wyatt, what the hell are you talking about?" I trailed off as my eyes became more used to the light. But my eyes must have been playing tricks because what I saw in front of me couldn't be real. It wasn't possible.

My eyes were trying to inform me that a boy with a wide grin was crouched on one knee above me and only then did I understand why the voice sounded so far away. The man... the boy – whatever he was – towered above me as he knelt in a room the size of an Olympic stadium. His hand alone looked almost as tall as I was! I went to shield my eyes and blinked several times, but the horrible image wouldn't go away.

"What the hell..." I started to back away, but the huge being reacted wildly and a hand lunged out and stopped me from moving back any further. I screamed as my back collided with his skin and stumbled forward.

"Brohere," he said in a softer voice than before, "Brohere, insigni." His grin of delight softened into a careful smile and he said some other words he probably assumed were soothing. Still, all I could focus on was his hand touching my back and how I was being brought closer to him. More words came, but the only one I caught

49

was 'insigni'. It was like that was my name.

Well, I wasn't about to have any of that. It was time for the dream to end.

"Let me go!" I screamed. "Wyatt! Wyatt, if you're playing some sort of sick game this isn't funny!" I batted away the boy's fingers and he seemed to show a mixture of surprise and amusement at my flailing.

"Killi, killi, insigni," he said with a nervous laugh. Another long flow of words poured out from his mouth, but I couldn't understand a single one. His hand started to move closer and with horror I realized those humungous fingers of his were starting to wrap around my body.

"What are you doing? NO!" I screeched as the pressure increased around my body. The being didn't stop and only continued to mutter something about insigni. He appeared to ask a question several times about something called a 'mard' and checked around his person a few times. After he finished his inspection, he looked at me and smiled again.

"Dea insigni." He added something else and before I could react, my stomach fell to my knees.

The boy was standing up.

"Wait! No!" I screamed and realized that not only could he not understand me, but he was taking me away from my only chance to get back home. "Put me down! Put me down this instant!" I screamed.

When the moving stopped, the being looked down with curious, almost concerned eyes and it dawned on me how strangely they were colored. One was light brown with flecks of blue, but the other was a bright teal. I'd never seen an eye so bright before. It wasn't like a blue eye back home, but more like the color of water in the Caribbean. I was shocked into silence for a moment as the being shook his head, moving some blond strands away from his face and revealing even more of those incredible colored eyes. He looked confused by my outburst.

"Please," I begged him. "Put me down. I want to go home."

He gave another soft smile, but I wanted to retch.

"Killi, killi," he said softly. More words flowed, but they were too fast to try and figure out.

What I did understand was him lifting his free hand and outstretching his pointer finger towards me. I flinched as it came my way, half-expecting him to pinch or poke, but all that happened was the finger landed sloppily on the top of my head and stroked from there to the middle of my back.

And then he repeated the action.

"Killi, killi," he said. My body rocked forward from the rough impact and he pulled his finger away as quickly as it came. The being's cheeks even seemed to grow pink and he looked away. "Ahhh," he said, as though realizing something. He brought his finger back and started to stroke my head and back again. "Gaspen. Disellus, insigni."

Was he actually petting me?

Fury and embarrassment flooded my features to the point where I couldn't even fathom anything else happening. I just wanted everything to stop.

A giant.

Trapped in a giant hand.

Being pet.

Trapped.

After a few slightly gentler strokes the giant muttered

51

something else and cupped me close to his chest. I let out a puff of air as my body collided with his and he started to walk.

As the lights went off, all I could hear was the giant's footsteps below and a horrible pounding in my ears. I didn't know where it was coming from at first, but with a horrible realization I came to the conclusion that the pounding was coming from his chest. Fear dominated all feelings at that point. It was then that I started to scream and wail uncontrollably.

Six

The giant started to grow worried as he went to leave the room and darkness guided us through wherever he was walking. He repeated a few words, but I continued to scream.

"Domodo, insigni," he whispered. "Domodo... brohere."

Tears started to flow at an uncontrollable pace as the reality of the situation continued to dawn on me. This was why Wyatt didn't want me to go into that room. *This. Was. It.* I couldn't believe what was happening. It still seemed like it could be a joke, but I started to lose hope that I was going to wake from his horrible nightmare. Painful sobs racked my body and I found I was no longer able to speak coherent words. My wails seemed to fill the air despite how tiny I was.

The giant was still insistent that petting my head would be the best option.

"Killi, killi." He kept his voice soft. Being so close to his chest, his voice pounded against my ears like a thunderstorm and I tried to get away from him.

"Don't!" I screamed. I was so out of breath at that point that I doubt my voice even reached his ears. He stopped and for a brief moment, I was able to stop crying and look around. I couldn't see anything and with a moment of dread, I decided to look up at the giant to see what he was doing. All I could see was the underside of his chin as he continued to stare straight ahead, muttering something to himself, which of course, I couldn't understand.

And then his chin dipped and he was looking right at me. His lips moved and said something which I assumed was a question by the way his rumbling voice rose slightly at the end.

"I can't understand you," I said between sobs. "Please. Just let me go. You don't look like a monster. Can't you just let me go?"

His face softened slightly in the dark and a finger came up to

53

pet my head. I angrily started to bat it away.

"No! Stop! Stop petting me! I'm not a damn dog!"

The finger stopped moving and I looked up at him. I was so helpless in that large hand.

"N-no?" He repeated my word and tilted his head slightly. His voice sounded like a man's who had a heavy accent and despite the simplicity of the word, it sounded foreign and strange on his larger tongue. His finger rose and came closer.

"No!" I screamed, waving my arms around.

His hand completely froze in the air, and didn't attempt to pet me again. His eyes took on a curious nature which I couldn't decide was a good or bad sign.

"No?" he repeated. "No?"

My lip trembled under his gentle attention. He was suddenly being so patient. I had to wonder if I was being given a chance to get through to him. We obviously didn't speak the same language so just the fact that he was starting to understand a single word had to mean something. I shook my head hard.

"No."

Another smile. "Ahh... no en cacen non."

Blankly, I stared up at him and had no idea if I was getting through to him or if he was merely entertaining himself. I didn't have too much time to think about it as he nodded and lifted his chin, looking at whatever was in front of him. As his hand finally moved away from me, I watched curiously as he started to reach for something in front of him and a loud sound filled my ears. A loud creaking came next and a soft blue light filtered through the darkness.

A new room.

The giant walked in slowly at first, looking around and I followed his lead, trying to figure out where we were going next. My stomach caught in my throat as I realized where the blue light was coming from.

Cages. Lights in cages.

I sucked in another scream as I saw at least three cages sitting on shelves at the giant's level. Inside the cages was something I never could have imagined.

People. People like me.

"Oh my God," I hushed in a voice low enough that the giant couldn't possibly hear. I jerked my head up and noticed he was searching the room for something and muttering under his breath. I couldn't understand a single word, but the message was clear. People in his world were kept in cages. Cages like animals. It explained the petting from earlier.

And soon I was going to be put in one of those horrible places.

As the giant started to move around the room, I wasn't sure whether to scream and make a scene, or take in the whole thing in silence. Most of the people in the cages were either asleep or curled up in a corner facing away from the giant. My heart hiccupped and I started to tremble horribly in the giant's hand as I realized that this was to be my fate. Of course the same thing would happen in my world if we suddenly discovered a race only a few inches tall. We'd call them the scientific discovery of the century and test them, pet them and do only God knows what else.

"Killi, killi, insigni," the giant whispered. A long stream of words flowed from his mouth after that, but I couldn't figure them out. It was obvious already that 'insigni' referred to me, but I had no idea what it meant. Killi sounded like some sort of calming word, but I wasn't in the mood to be calm.

One of the men in a cage stood up and looked ahead as the giant started to fumble around in drawers. When he realized the giant had spotted him, he froze in his spot for a moment before backing away as the giant drew close to the cage.

My captor muttered something to the person and tapped on the cage a few times, but I couldn't see his facial expression. All I saw was the person give a sad nod and turn away from him, and then make his way back to the corner to take a seat. The giant seemed pleased and went back to searching the room. Like the office back at the Shaw place, the blue-light room also had a large desk in it and the giant flopped down into the chair in front of it, rocking me in his hand.

"Disellus," he muttered. "Uhh..." His voice trailed off as he started to look around the desk and then back at me.

His face seemed to be determining something, fighting with himself in his own mind. A loud string of words flowed out in a questioning tone, but it fell on my deaf ears. I couldn't understand a damn word he was saying so I just stared up at him blankly.

"Ugh." He seemed annoyed for a moment and I flinched, prepared for some sort of reprimand for not understanding him, but he repeated several increasingly familiar words. "Disellus, disellus, insigni."

More soothing words, I could only assume.

As the giant kept me locked in his fist, he started to rummage through the large desk, obviously still looking for something. I wondered what it was. Why wasn't I in one of those cages yet? Did I need an ID and tag like a dog at the shelter? I started to squirm in his hand out of instinct. Sitting there like a damn Pomeranian made no sense.

"Cacen non," he muttered to himself, turning in my direction.

He still managed to search the desk drawers with one hand, but I was so frightened of what he would pull out that I continued to

56

struggle. His grip tightened around my body and my leg was starting to hurt. I started to grow more worried. My left leg was caught between his third and fourth finger and when he squeezed me, it bent in an unnatural direction. It was dangerous, but it had to be better than whatever he was searching for in the drawers and my fate awaiting in a cage. I at least had to try and escape.

I struggled harder and a rougher squeeze came. I tried to wiggle my way out through his fingers while he was distracted with his search.

"Cacen non," he said, his voice firmer than before. "Domodo, insigni. Cacen non."

"Let me go!" I screamed suddenly, growing more frightened as his search continued. I heard a sound through the doorway from another room and my panic overwhelmed me. "Let me go! Let me go! Let me go!"

"Cacen non, insigni," he said. "Cacen..."

My struggles grew harder and his grip tightened. Another light flickered on behind us and the giant jerked his head around towards the open doorway. Someone else was here and whoever or whatever it was, was coming towards the room. The giant grumbled something under his breath and shoved the drawer shut, obviously upset he hadn't found what he was looking for.

"Brindt?" a loud and low feminine voice called from behind us. It sounded like 'Brint-a' and the giant tensed up, pressing me further into his hand. My leg screamed in agony. Another question from the female voice filled my ears and I started to tremble. One giant was enough, but two? I started to fill my lungs with air so I could scream, but the giant shook his hand gently.

"No."

His word shook me to the core. It sounded so different than the words he spoke earlier, but it was obvious he understood the meaning.

57

"Insigni, no."

"Brindt?"

The giant didn't answer, but started to fumble around and quickly gathered what he could in one hand and shoved it into his pockets. I watched in horror as he looked at me, no doubt thinking the same thing and before I could scream, I was shoved into a dark place, his hand tightly wound against my frame. My leg exploded into pain and suddenly I couldn't take any more. I had pushed my luck too far and I had actually hurt myself.

"Shit!" I groaned. The pain pulsed in my left leg as the giant's grip tightened. The darkness was filled with tiny nick-knacks and I couldn't identify a single thing... maybe a tiny cup.

Oh God.

A tiny cup.

Only one of us could drink from a cup that small.

A door slammed overhead and footsteps pounded below as the giant moved to another place. More footsteps. Another door slam. The female voice disappeared. The male giant spoke to himself sounding out of breath and worried. I couldn't help but wonder who the female giant was and why the younger giant had run from her.

It wasn't like I could ask him.

The fingers around my body loosened suddenly and without the support, my leg cramped and I winced loudly in the darkness, reaching to cradle the injury. I knew the injury wasn't serious, but it certainly was going to rule out a full-strength sprint for a little while. Fearfully, I wondered if the giant actually knew what he was doing when he held me in such a way. Maybe he had done it so I wouldn't be able to run. By temporarily hurting my leg. Maybe that's why he ran from the female voice. Maybe I was damaged goods.

Fear washed over me as a latch was turned nearby. A few moments later, light suddenly blinded me and I jerked up to see four large fingers coming down towards me.

"N-no," I gasped, not wanting to be held. I scrambled around in the darkness despite my hurt leg, but found that I couldn't find purchase. It was like running in a large sleeping bag.

"Please, don't touch me. I'm hurt! Don't touch me!" The fingers didn't listen, but continued their search until they were able to wrap completely around my body along with a few other smaller items. I cried and reached for fabric to hold onto, but there was nothing for it. If the giant wanted me, I was helpless to stop him.

My world rocked as I was pulled out from the darkness and into the light. Everything around blurred as the giant shifted his hand and brought me up towards his face. My crying was both for my pain and fear as those incredible bi-colored eyes settled on me. They were both curious and soft as they danced over my figure and I tried desperately not to give in to panic. That teal eye almost looked comical and I tried to focus on that instead of my overwhelming fear. I was weak enough in his presence physically – there was no need to come across as an emotional wreck.

But I was still so scared.

My eyes felt itchy and I could only imagine how red and puffy they must have looked in the giant's eyes as he searched me over. He was silent and offered no more soothing words which I suddenly missed. In the silence I could only focus on him focusing on me, and that was just too much to take in. He looked so much like I did. One brown eye, one teal eye, a soft, young face, sandy blond hair that fell across his eyes and long enough that only a bit of his pointy ears poked through.

I sucked in a sob.

Pointy ears? I narrowed my eyes through my tears and tried to take a better look as he continued to scrutinize me and there was no mistaking it. The giant had pointy ears just like a little Christmas

59

elf. You know, a Christmas elf who's about sixty feet tall. I swallowed and tried not to focus on the differences. I had to focus on the similarities otherwise it would seem as though all hope was lost. We really weren't that different other than size. He looked human enough. Younger than me, but still not a child.

He tilted his head, still looking until his eyes fell around my legs. I was only wearing shorts and it dawned on me just how cold it was suddenly and I shivered not only under his attention, but because I was chilled to the core. The giant bit his lower lip and muttered something before bringing me even closer to his face. I shrunk back and tried not to look at him as his large eyes filled even more of my sight.

"Banum?" he asked softly.

My face contorted. "Huh?"

His free hand lifted, and I flinched back and pinched my eyes shut. I was so sure he was going to strike me that my eyes watered as I braced myself. But instead of a pain, something brushed against my left leg and I gasped out in surprise. It felt like I was being branded because his skin was so hot and mine was like ice.

"Banum, insigni?" he repeated.

I cracked open one eye to see him pointing towards my hurt leg. "I... uh..." I couldn't seem to find my voice as the giant poked the same sore spot, forcing a pained cry to escape my lips. He winced.

"Banum," he muttered. More words came, but at such a speed I couldn't follow. "Disellus."

He finally stopped staring long enough so I could catch my breath. I had to wonder if he was talking about my leg. And there was that word again, 'disellus'. Like 'killi' it had a soothing quality to it, almost apologetic. I had to wonder if the giant understood that he was the reason for my pain and screaming... well... for different reasons, anyway.

60

I remained locked in his grasp as he moved away from the door and went towards a large blur which I assumed was his bed. He sat on the edge of it and opened a drawer in a nightstand sitting next to it. I looked up and tried to get a read on his face but he was so impassive in his search. *What was he always looking for?* I sniffed loudly and he spared a glance with an almost piteous look as he said something else and continued his search.

"Ahh," he said finally, pulling something out from the drawer and holding it out in front of him.

My heart stopped as my eyes dried up long enough to see what had him so relieved.

A cage. A tiny cage that seemed to be like a small clear purse in his hands.

***

Bile started to rise in my throat as I watched the giant 'prepare' his cage with helpless eyes. Several tissues were stuffed into the small compartment and he shot down a smile, saying soft words as though they were encouraging. He couldn't honestly think I was going to just let him shove me in a cage, did he? I started to wriggle, crying out each time my cold, injured leg brushed against the searing hot temperature of his hand, but the giant was easily able to ignore me completely and focus only on his task.

"Killi!" he said in a happy tone as he set the cage on the top of his nightstand. He shoved some books aside and they crashed to the floor with a horrible bang and I grabbed my ears. The giant hissed in annoyance and then turned with a soft expression. "Disellus," he rumbled before adding a few more words.

I wasn't in the mood to be soothed. As the giant started to move his hand towards the cage, I cried out loudly.

"No!" I wailed. "No, dammit! I'm not a pet! You can't put me in a cage!"

61

Without hesitation he lowered me inside and I collapsed against the pile of tissues he created. Were the tissues supposed to be a damn bed of some sort? A collection of damn tissues? I hiccupped loudly as his hand pulled out from the cage and a horrible sound filled my ears as he closed the lid and snapped it in place. I crashed to the floor and buried my face in my hands.

Trapped.

Trapped in a cage like a mouse at the pet store.

"Insigni?" A voice rumbled and I lifted my head for a moment to see that the giant had lowered his face down to my level. His bi-colored eyes searched me over and it looked like he didn't quite understand something. Words came as a question and I shook my head.

"I told you, monster. I can't understand you. Speak English, why don't you?"

I buried my face in my knees, and allowed myself a heavy and much needed cry. If the giant wanted to watch, so let him. If he couldn't understand why I was crying then I really was in a world filled with monsters.

Why? Why did Wyatt want to take me here? My lip trembled as the cage shook. I lifted my head to see the giant tapping on the glass just like he had done with the man back in that horrible blue light room.

"What?" I felt helpless as he looked at me. The whole situation was so strange. I was in a cage being looked at like I was some helpless and stupid animal. "What do you want? What could you possibly want to do to me now? Feed me pellets?"

"En...en – gilish?" he said, trying out the word.

I stopped crying for a moment and sniffed loudly. "Yes," I groaned. "Yes, you moron. I was saying 'why can't you speak

62

English?' I can't understand you. You can't understand me. I want to go home. I'm a person, dammit." I pinched my eyes shut. "You can't keep people in cages just because they're smaller than you!"

"Insigni..."

"And don't call me that!" I shouted, growing angry. I didn't know why I was more confident screaming at him from inside the cage, but my sadness was starting to dissolve into being outright pissed. "I don't know what the hell 'insigni' means, but that's not my name! It's Lyris, you monster! Lyris!" The giant tilted his head from the behind the glass. "You got that? L-Y-R-I-S." I sounded out the name for him several times watching as his curiosity grew. His eyes danced back and forth, and occasionally settled on my mouth as I formed the words. I must have seemed so fun and interesting to him. So entertaining.

Well, I was getting damn tired of performing for him like a circus freak.

I rolled my eyes. "Whatever." I hid my face in my hands again. "Just leave me alone, why don't you? Leave me alo—"

"Lye...ly-riz?"

My breath hitched in my throat as the giant tried out my name. I lowered my hands slightly and peered up at him.

"Lye... ly-riz?" he tried for a second time.

In his tongue, my name sounded like lye-reeze. It wasn't wrong exactly. In fact with the way he rolled his 'r' and how deep his voice sounded, I dare say it was almost pleasant. I curled my fingers under my nose so I could look at him over my knuckles, but still made sure that at least some of my face was hidden from his curious stare.

"Lyris," I said. He leaned closer to the cage, and practically pressed his nose up against the frame and I backed away. Him being so close – barrier or not – was still entirely too difficult to handle. He

63

must have noticed my discomfort because he pulled away.

"Lye-riss," he said, trying out a different pronunciation. It sounded closer to how it actually was pronounced. "Lye-ris. Lyris."

I nodded. "Yeah. Sure. Lyris." I shrugged him off, not sure how pronouncing my name was going to get me home. Not only was I his pet, but I was becoming his performing pet. I was never so humiliated.

"Brindt," the voice came repeated. It sounded like 'Brint-ah' and I looked up at him to see he was touching his chest. "Brindt." He pointed at me. "Lye-reeze. Eh! Ah! Lye-ris." He seemed to still be struggling with my name. Again with the chest patting. "Brindt," he said before pointing at me. "Lyris." Several times he went back and forth with his name and mine and looked at me expectantly, hoping I would repeat his.

I wasn't about to give him the satisfaction. I was tired of performing.

"Brindt?" he tried, touching his face. "Brindt."

I rolled my eyes and his expression darkened slightly. I was playing with fire, but I just wanted to lay down. My leg still hurt and despite my initial anger about the tissues, it was freezing cold and I needed to bundle up. I turned away from his stupid name lesson, grabbed a corner of a tissue, wove it tightly around my body, and struggled to get warm.

"Elgis?" the giant – Brindt– tried next.

I didn't answer him, and instead turned away completely and rested my face against the floor. Maybe I could sleep away the horrible dream. Maybe I would wake up tomorrow and laugh about this crazy nightmare on my date with Wyatt.

"Lye-ris?"

I groaned. *Wyatt.* Wyatt was the whole reason I was in this

64

mess. He wanted to bring me here. But why? Why would he want to show me a world where people were kept in cages like pets? What was his motivation?

"Elgis, insigni? Lye-ris?"

I ignored the giant as he asked questions several more times before he gave up. He huffed audibly and the floor creaked as he must have shifted away from the cage. I didn't dare give him the gratification of turning around to watch him. Within moments a heavy weight crashed close by and metal springs cried out. He must have been getting in bed. I guess I wasn't the only one who was sick of playing the stupid word game. He muttered one more thing to himself before darkness cloaked over the room and the giant's voice didn't come again.

"Why would you take me here?" I whispered to myself once the giant began to snore. I wondered why Wyatt would think going here would be fun. I wondered how a place filled with giants could even exist before something dawned on me.

Wyatt had referred to me as a target.

When I first asked him about it, I remembered he said it was his weird way of saying he had a crush, but when I thought about it from behind a glass wall, it suddenly made sense. It wasn't a crush at all. Wyatt had been looking for me.

He wanted to bring me to here.

He must have known of this world and its inhabitants.

But that would mean... *no.* I shook my head, and shivered hard under the tissues. It didn't make sense. Wyatt was a person like me. If he brought me here, he would have met the same fate. He couldn't have betrayed me.

Nothing made sense anymore.

Actually, that wasn't fair. Something did make perfect sense.

I was far from home... on a nightstand... in a cage... with a giant.

And I was stuck.

I couldn't speak the language and I obviously wasn't seen as an equal.

I rolled over on my side so I could see the giant. It was almost impossible in the dark, but I was able to make out enough. He looked like a person. He had pointy ears and was young, but he was still obviously a person. And though we didn't speak the same language, we were both obviously intelligent enough to figure out each other's words early on. My eyes watered as I continued to look at my captor, looking so quiet and so... human.

We were alike.

We had to be.

But the question still remained... why would Wyatt want to bring me here? My mind churned with unanswered questions until sleep finally overtook me.

Seven

The following morning I woke up shivering. At first I couldn't remember why and I grumbled loudly for my mom to turn down the damn air-conditioner. I swear... my parents were nuts. They liked the house in the 50s during the summer and in the 80s during the winter. I pulled up my comforter around my face to shield myself from the icy air. Ugh, my comforter could have used a wash so with another loud grumble, I pulled it away and sat up in bed, seriously annoyed.

"Dammit, mom! Turn down the damn—" I froze when I saw that it wasn't my mother, but a pair of large eyes. One teal. One brown. Lips parted.

"Insigni—"

"Oh God," I moaned before the voice could finish and buried myself under the comforter. I wasn't in my bed. I wasn't under my comforter. And the voice that spoke wasn't my mom, dad, or even Wyatt. It was that damn monster. Brian or whatever. He had a funny name and I couldn't remember it that morning because my mind was in such a haze. I shuddered and tried not to think about what was on the other side of the tissue.

However it looked like I wasn't going to be given much of a choice that morning. As I remained under the blankets, the giant started to say something. I could tell because of that damn word he liked to use when addressing me. Insigni. I couldn't understand anything he was saying at first, but I was already starting to pick up on some repetitive words.

And then he said my name again.

"Lye-ris," he said softly. More words.

I finally pulled the cover away from my face and sat up to look at him. As I shifted, a pain shot through my leg and I winced openly to suck in a gasp. The eyes looked shocked and then hurt as he sat up straighter and loomed closer to the cage. His eyes narrowed down and focused on my exposed legs.

"Lye-ris? Elgis?" he tried next.

"Huh?"

The word came out before I remembered who and what I was dealing with. A giant. A giant who shoved me in a cage, but had the gall to look like he was so concerned. I should have pretended to stay asleep until he left. As it was, I had no idea what time it was, what year it was, what time of year it was or even where I was. The whole thing was a little disconcerting. I stared back at him as he seemed to be just as surprised that I answered him so easily. He quickly started to talk and I waved him off, silencing him for a moment.

"I told you," I said wearily, "I can't understand you."

I wrapped the tissue more closely around my shoulders and started to shudder, my teeth chattering loudly. "How about instead of standing there, you get me something warmer than a tissue, huh?" I grumbled, not expecting him to understand. "What is it, the winter here?"

"Win... tere?" the giant asked, tilting his head.

"Yes, winter," I grumbled, still shivering. "I'm so cold. It's freezing." The giant blinked and continued to study my movements and it was then that I realized I was going to have to work to get my point across. Otherwise I was going to freeze in the cold little box. "Cold," I repeated, exaggerating my shivering. "So cold."

"Cuh...ld," he said. "Ahh... elgis." He nodded and started to turn away, leaving me stranded to only watch his face soar out of sight.

"No!" I called. "Cold! Brr... shivering? Freezing?" I frowned helplessly as he continued to move away from me, probably bored like I was last night with our little word game. His massive body carried itself into a tiny (for him) room and he disappeared. I supposed he was going into a closet to get ready for the day.

68

"Damn giant." I covered my face with the tissues so I could try to keep warm. Since it was already daytime, light shone through the tissue and I realized with a startle that a large bruise had formed on my thigh right above my knee. *Damn.* I guess that was my fault for baiting the giant. I hated that my skin bruised so easily.

A loud metallic sound cracked overhead and I pulled the tissue away from my face so I could look up. My ceiling was gone which meant the giant had opened the cage. As his huge hand started to fill the opening, I began to panic and slid into the corner. I hoped he only wanted to take the tissue away, and not the person inside.

Such hopes were for fools.

With a surprising amount of care, his hand slid in and gently grasped my body. He could so easily snatch me up with one hand that I grew frightened all over again and began to shake. His fingers curled around and his thumb secured itself over my stomach. I noticed that he didn't touch my leg as he slowly pulled me out from the cage and brought me closer to his face and as much as I wanted to squirm, his warm skin was a pleasant shock.

"Bic, Lye-ris," he said once his hand stopped moving.

I hadn't noticed until then, but as soon as his hand grasped me, I had closed my eyes. I didn't want to see the world fly past at such a crazy speed. I slowly opened my eye, and wondered why he had said my name again. I couldn't even remember his, why did he still know mine?

In his other hand, he was holding a large scrap of red fabric. It looked torn, like it was once part of a sweatshirt and he offered it between a finger and thumb. I stared up at him curiously, not sure what his angle was.

"Lye-ris elgis," he said, along with a few other words. "Bic." He thrust the red fabric into my hands and waited patiently for me to take it.

69

I wanted to fight with him. I wanted to argue and be difficult, but I was just too cold. Reluctantly, I took the red fabric from his fingers and brought it up to my nose. It smelled like the giant's hands, like sweat and cologne with a hint of spicy citrus. It was similar to how a guy like Wyatt would smell, but there was just so much more of it. Deciding I couldn't fight at the time, I wrapped the sweatshirt around my shoulders and draped it over the giant's hand as I did so.

"There," I huffed. "Happy?"

He smiled.

"Ugh, you're so confusing," I grumbled as I kept the fabric close to my skin. I had to admit it was an improvement to no longer be freezing. Not only was the sweatshirt helpful, but the giant's skin was so fracking warm. It was almost pleasant.

"So... uh..." I trailed off as the giant's eyes widened with my words and he brought me closer to his face. I winced and shrunk back in his hand, but he seemed intent on keeping me practically up against his nose so I bore with it. "I uh... I kind of forgot your name." Like he had done yesterday, I touched my chest and looked right into his eyes. "Lyris," I said clearly.

He nodded. "Perum." He pointed at me with his free hand. "Lye-ris. Lyris."

I nodded before I slowly started to point at him. "And you?"

He smiled, and though I didn't want to think about it, the giant looked surprised and happy by my action.

"Brindt," he said in a voice that was practically a whisper. He touched his chest, pronouncing his name as 'Brinta' like before with a very cool roll of the 'r'. I had to admit his accent and his name sounded cute. Far too cute to belong to a giant who kept people in cages. I shook off my one positive thought about him.

"Brindt," he said before pointing at me. "Lyris."

"Brrr...inta," I said, trying to roll the 'r' like he had done. I never took Spanish in college so of course I had no idea what I was doing or even if I was saying it right. My cheeks grew hot for some reason as I struggled with the pronunciation and he dared to smile.

"Est pomun," he said, still grinning. "Brindt."

"Brindt." I spoke more quickly as he grew more excited. He pointed at me. "Lyris."

He nodded and did the same thing. "Brindt," he said, pointing to his chest. "Lyris," he said, pointing at me.

"Yes," I said, relieved. "Can I go home now?"

His smile faded. "Eh?"

I tried not to groan. Wasn't there any way for us to communicate in a less stressful manner? I shifted in his hand and his eyes dropped down to my legs.

"Ugh," I growled. "Even giant guys are perverts, I guess," I said with a frown. "Do you mind? My eyes are up here." Though his entire face filled my vision, the damn guy seemed to be fixated on my legs. "Hey!" I shouted, wanting his attention. "Hey... uh... Brindt!"

His bi-colored eyes flickered up to me, surprised for a moment and then quickly calmed down. As I opened my mouth to speak, words poured out of his mouth at an alarming rate and there was no way I could keep up. I waved my arms around and he stopped talking.

"No." I remembered that he sort of understood this word. He arched a brow. "I can't understand what you're saying. Slow down."

His head tilted.

"Do you understand me?" I asked. "Slow. Down. I don't

71

speak your language, dude."

"Lyris," he said, lowering his eyes to my legs again. "Banum."

"Ba... banum?"

He nodded. "Banum."

His free hand made a pointing motion and started to come close. I flinched back from the oncoming digit and tried to wiggle away. I wasn't sure what I was expecting, but I kept my eyes open and watched with surprise as his fingertip stopped just an inch or so away from my leg where the bruise was showing.

"Banum," he said with concern in his eyes and voice. His finger dared to creep closer and brushed against the sensitive skin and I hissed out in pain. His hand quickly jerked away as though he had touched a flame and his large eyes grew sad. "Lyris?" He pointed at himself. "Brindt?" He spoke a few more extra sentences, but his intention was becoming clear.

He noticed I was hurt and he wondered if it was his fault.

I didn't know whether to be touched or annoyed by his gentle concern, but my body acted on instinct and I pulled my legs further away from his massive fingers. His face started to crumble as it must have dawned on him that the bruises and swelling were his fault. He started to say something, but as he remembered there was no way I would understand him, he cleared his throat and uttered out a single word.

"Disellus."

It wasn't the first time he had said 'disellus' and it was becoming more and more obvious as to what it meant. He would say that word often after he had done something he probably thought was wrong or painful or hurtful towards me so I could only assume 'disellus' was an apology of some sort.

A giant was apologizing to me.

"It's alright." I didn't like seeing his face look so sad. Despite the fact that he had put me in a cage, he really wasn't so terrible. Maybe he just didn't know any better. I couldn't stand his expression, though. It was like sadness magnified and despite my predicament, something tugged at my heart to see him so disheartened. "It's okay," I said. "I'm sure they'll fade in a few days."

The giant looked back with a confused expression. My words had obviously fallen on deaf ears. Communication, or the lack thereof, had become a major problem.

"Isn't there any way for us to talk properly?" I grumbled.

"Tah-lc?" Brindt repeated.

"Yes." I couldn't hide my surprise that he had actually picked up on the most important word. I opened and closed my mouth several times for effect and made nonsensical sounds. "Talk," I said clearly. "Blah, blah, blah. Me and you? Brindt?"

His face changed as I said his name. "Tah-lc," he said. "Brindt. Lyris."

"Yes." I was growing exasperated. "This whole thing would be a lot easier if I could talk to you."

"Talk," Brindt said again. He looked over his shoulder and then back at me. He seemed to be thinking something over. He glanced behind him, back at me, back at my leg and then back at my eyes. "Talk," he repeated.

"Ugh, you're like humungous puppy," I muttered under my breath.

Words spilled at an alarming rate suddenly as the giant seemed to finally come to a decision. "Lyris... demano?" His voice sounded hesitant as though he was asking to do something, but he didn't really seem confident to do so. It was odd to see him act so

73

hesitantly.

"Huh?" I tilted my head. He seemed to respond well to the head tilt and started to lower his hand back towards the kennel which evinced a loud screech from me. "What? No! No, Brindt!" I screamed his name, remembering how much it affected him and to my surprise, once again he listened and his hand faltered in the air, hovering over the cage opening.

"Lyris?" he asked tilting his hand so he could look at me. "No?"

I shook my head hard. "No, please. Don't put me in there. It's too scary." The idea of being put back in that cage took my breath away. Despite being his captive, I would rather be in his hands then in some kennel. It made the reality of my situation all too real. How helpless I was in his room and that someone had deliberately wanted to bring me here. I couldn't think about it.

All that I could lose.

All that could already be lost.

If I could just get him to put me down, then I had a chance of getting out there. I had to play my cards right. The giant seemed to listen sometimes and definitely liked to hear me say his name.

"Brindt." My voice shook as he leaned closer. "No." I pointed down at the cage and shook my head hard. "No, Brindt. Don't put me there. Please?"

He seemed to be thinking this over. "... Lyris," he said softly. "Lyris, banum. Lyris tah-lc." He turned his head and nodded out towards the door. I had no idea where he was going with that, so I shook my head and tried to make my voice as firm as I dared with this creature who could hold my entire body in their hand.

"Brindt. No." I shook my head. "No cage. No box. No kennel. No!"

74

His eyes flickered down to the cage. "Lyris—"

"No!" I screamed, eyes watering. I shouldn't have yelled at a giant, but I was growing desperate. Each time he humored me it felt like more of an opening to escape. If I could just get him to put me down. To trust me. I could run. I could hide. I could escape. Maybe I could even get back home. "Brindt, please. No cage."

His hand started to pull away and lowered to the desk without words. He still seemed unsure as to what he was doing, but despite that I found myself hovering over the surface. A pencil below was thicker than one of my limbs, but I tried not to think about it. I was so close. The tips of my socked feet were almost there. Chilly air bit my exposed skin, but I tried not to let it show otherwise Brindt would probably start muttering more confusing words.

"Lyris..." he started, fingers loosening. "Lyris, demano?"

I had no idea what 'demano' meant so I nodded my head in hopes that I could humor him. I could play his game. If the giant wanted to talk with simple commands I could play it his way.

"Yes," I said, nodding hard. "Lyris demano."

"Demano?" He arched his brow and a long stream of words followed, but none of them were familiar. I was so focused on getting my feet on free land that I couldn't focus. I trembled with anticipation.

"Demano," I said, knowing it would please him. "Lyris demano."

With a face that still looked unsure, Brindt's massive fingers loosened around my body and I slipped onto the desk. I stumbled as I tried to balance on my good leg, backed away and tried to gauge what the giant was going to do next. He seemed to be watching also as he pulled his hand away and leaned back in his chair. My heart pounded in my chest and I tried to keep my breathing steady as we judged each other from a distance, trying to figure the other one out. Brindt's eyes flickered to the cage for a moment and then quickly came back to me.

"Pomun," he breathed softly. He seemed to exhale.

I wasn't sure what he was expecting, but at that point I seemed to be doing exactly what he wanted.

"Est pomun, Lyris." He smiled and lifted up his free hand and I backed away, stumbling over his pencil and landing not so gracefully on my ass. "Lyris!" he hushed as I fell. That hurtful expression came and went as his hand continued to come my way.

"Wait!" I screamed, holding up my hands in defense. "Uh... no!"

The hand didn't stop, but instead of grabbing, his hand cupped behind and nudged me back up to my feet. Once I was standing, he pulled his hand away and out of sight under the desk and into his lap. His face was red.

"Disellus," he said quickly. More words. No meaning.

Honestly, my face was a little pink too after that strange interaction. Maybe I needed to stop thinking that every time he tried to grab me that something bad was going to happen. His face looked so hurt and I couldn't help but wonder what the situation must have been like for him. I tried to imagine how I would feel if a little person showed up in my house and freaked out every time I tried to touch or talk to them.

I'd probably feel like a monster.

Maybe he felt the same way.

Ugh, no! That was stupid thinking. There was a room in his house filled with people trapped in cages and I was going to be one of them soon enough. He obviously knew what he was doing. I had to get the hell out of there before I ended up in that scary blue light room. But looking at Brindt, I couldn't figure out what he was doing or what he wanted from me. I searched my memory for that word he kept saying before he set me down on the desktop.

"Um... Lyris demano?" I said in a questioning voice. I hoped this was the word he wanted to hear.

He nodded and pointed out towards the door. "Lyris..."

The first thing I really caught was my name as he seemed to explain something. I stared up at him with a blank expression as he spoke quickly in his own language, marveling at how fluent he sounded when he wasn't trying to speak mine. He stopped suddenly and looked at me carefully.

"Lyris... Brindt... tah-lc," he said.

"What did you say?" I tilted my head so he got my meaning.

"Lyris, Brindt. Tah-lc."

"Yes, I said. Talk. We're talking."

He glanced over his shoulder one last time and turned back with a sigh. "Lyris demano," he said one more time.

"Yes," I said, nodding. "Demano."

"Micuit," he said as he started to pull away from the desk.

My eyes widened as I realized what was happening. He was leaving... he was going somewhere else. Maybe even out of the room! I should be so lucky. I watched with anticipation as he slid away in his chair, started to stand up and his body unfolded into unimaginable heights. Even from the desk, I only reached his waist and realized that despite it being early, he was already dressed for the day and wearing a black belt with a silver buckle. It was so much like something I would see back home.

The similarities only made my situation all the more horrific.

I arched my neck back as he stood in front of me, somehow

looking just as uncomfortable as I felt. You think he'd be used to little people looking up at him all the time. I didn't understand what the big deal was. I was terrified, but I stood my ground on the chance that if I moved, he wouldn't trust me and would put me back in that cage. He took a slow step backward with eyes still locked on mine, but I didn't dare move.

Just stay. Stay where you are. Hold your ground.

Another step backward.

"Lyris," he said, holding up his hand. "Demano."

It was then that I realized what 'demano' had to mean. *'Stay'.* The giant asked me to stay in the same manner I used to tell my dog not to move. *Well damn.* I gave him an encouraging smile despite the fact that I was livid. I really was like a pet in his world. I didn't dare move an inch as the giant finally turned around and walked to the door.

Oh.

My.

God.

He was actually leaving the room.

He was actually trusting me to stay!

I couldn't believe my luck. I just had to behave for a little while longer before my nightmare could come to an end. I flexed my fingers several times and glanced around the desktop, trying to plot my escape as my eyes fell to a desk lamp and a cord leading to the carpet. That was it. I flickered my eyes back up to Brindt. His hand was on the door knob and he was staring right at me. I smiled and his face faltered.

"Domodo, Lyris?" he asked. Another sentence came out. "Domodo demano."

A bead of sweat formed on my hairline. Something stay.

Please. Please stay.

I couldn't think of what else he could have meant. And though I knew that the moment he left the room I would flee, I nodded my head. If I was caught then everything would be different. The fragile trust between us would be broken and he would have no reason to see me as anything other than a disobedient animal. Everything could change if I was caught after trying to escape. He trusted me after only a few hours, but I couldn't stay.

He couldn't actually think I was going to stay here with him and play his little game of 'good dog-bad dog.' I had to get away.

"Lyris?" he asked one last time, opening the door. "Demano?"

I smiled and nodded though my heart wasn't nearly as much into it. "Demano."

I expected him to smile back, but to my surprise his face only grew sadder. He nodded once, opened the door, and started to leave. "Micuit," he said in a soft voice before closing the door behind him.

I was sure he didn't believe me.

Eight

Though I had been released by Brindt's hand earlier, it was only after the door closed that another puff of chilled air sent a powerful shiver through my spine. I was only wearing a pair of thin shorts and a t-shirt with a pair of socks. Not quite the best runaway attire for a tiny girl in a giant's world, but I didn't exactly have a choice. I couldn't waste another moment. I gingerly moved towards the lamp on the edge of the desk, and tried to gauge the distance.

Damn. It was quite a drop.

I faltered for a few moments as I remembered Brindt's face right before he left the room. He didn't believe me. If 'demano' really meant 'stay' then I'm sure he couldn't have possibly believed that I was going to listen to him. Maybe he wanted me to disobey his word so he could finally treat me like an animal. The thought sent a chill down my back so without thinking too much about Brindt's hurt expression, I tugged on the lamp cord and made sure that it could hold my weight as I made my descent.

Of course it could.

Sliding down the cord proved to be easier than I expected. It was kind of like sliding down a forty foot fire pole. Actually, climbing off of the cord and landing on the carpet proved to be the more difficult task. As I jumped down to the floor, I realized all too late that my leg was still hurt from before and I let out a piercing cry as I landed on both feet.

"Dammit!" I was unable to hold up my weight and immediately crashed on my butt. It was next to impossible to be graceful in a world so big. I grabbed at my bruised leg and felt it beginning to swell under my hands. I had to at least find a place to hide until I could move better.

Borrowers did that stuff, didn't they? Hid in the walls and didn't allow themselves to be seen by humans? I could do that for a few days, couldn't I? Hide from giants?

I sucked in a heavy gulp of air and stood up gingerly to look around.

Damn. The world was a lot different from ground level. Barely any light was visible down there in the shadows, and the carpet, while clean, stirred up a lot of dust as I tried to wade through it. There had to be a way I could get to the door or at least find some hole in the wall I could burrow into for a day or two. My panicked eyes skimmed the room. I was probably already running out of time. There was just simply no way that Brindt was going to leave me alone for much longer.

I know I wouldn't have.

Ugh, why hadn't I thought this through? I had been so obsessed with jumping at the chance to make my dramatic escape that I had foolishly forgotten about my injured leg and the fact that I was still freezing, and the world through the portal was fracking gigantic. Frustrated tears filled my eyes as I limped over into the corner under the desk and hoped to keep myself as far away as possible from giant hands. Maybe Brindt wouldn't be able to reach me there. I slid to the floor, rubbed my injured knee and looked around his massive room. It really wasn't that much different than a normal boys' room, except everything was huge. Massive piles of clothes covered the floor and pencils and dried up paintbrushes were strewn everywhere. I could smell that familiar scent of spicy citrus again, mixed in with paint, lead, and teenage guy.

"Dammit, dammit, dammit," I growled into my hands.

Rumblings.

The ground trembled beneath me and I willed my tears to stop falling as I lifted my head. There was no mistaking that Brindt was coming back. It was so weird to think that those horrible rumbling patterns were nothing more than his feet bringing him back into the room. I couldn't bear to think of him this close to the ground and I pinched my eyes shut as the rumbles grew louder and closer until the door swung open, and the horrible creaking sound made me flinch.

81

"Lyris!" Brindt exclaimed in an excited voice. "Lyris... tah-lc. Lyris..."

His shoes stopped short in front of the desk as though he only just realized I was gone. I pulled my knees closer to my chest as something thudded loudly over my head as he must have placed something down on the desktop. Being so small I couldn't even tell if he had slammed it down in anger or had simply placed it down softly.

Shoes shifted.

"Lyris?" he asked, following up quickly with another question. Things shifted loudly on the desk above me, and a pencil fell to the floor and bounced off his shoe. *Ugh... oh God.* That could be me. I was shorter than the pencil which crunched under his sneaker as he moved, standing on his tiptoes to continue his search.

"Lyris, domodo. Domodo, Lyris." He grew more desperate in his movements as he continued to search.

I still couldn't tell if he was getting pissed off or worried... all I knew was that he was moving more frantically. More papers shifted around on the desk and a few coins fell to the floor.

"Lyris!" he shouted before lowering his voice to a whisper. "Lyris... domodo." Another question.

For a moment I thought about calling to him. What good was I doing hiding there? I could barely move and I was freezing to death under the desk. At least Brindt was a source of warmth. At least he had been somewhat kind so far. No matter if it was the same type of kindness reserved for a stray dog. At least he wasn't cruel, but I had still betrayed his trust.

"Lyris!" Brindt hissed loudly. Concern had left his voice. "Lyris..."

I pinched my eyes shut as he continued to speak at a fast pace and shoes finally moved away from the desk. He was still looking for me. He must have checked the entire desk. Drawers flew open and slammed shut at an alarming speed and I held my ears as he continued to call my name and search. He was mad. He was getting madder. He knew I was going to try to get away, but he probably assumed he could have found me easily.

As it dawned on me that I might be found while he was still angry, I realized I didn't have a choice. I had to get away. I had to at least hide somewhere safe until he calmed down. Maybe until he forgot about me. With so many people in that blue-lit room, I could easily be replaced. I slid on my butt and went to hide behind a magazine just a little bit away from the security of the desk as Brindt slammed another drawer shut.

"Bu domisti!" he shouted suddenly. "Bu domisti, Lyris." His movements became less violent and the chair suddenly slid as a heavy weight crashed into it and sent a puff of dust through the carpet and right up my nose.

Quickly, I went to pinch my nostrils so I could continue to slide, but there was nothing for it. A small sneeze escaped and I caught my breath.

Sneakers stopped shifting and the room fell deathly silent for a moment. I held my breath and continued to slide slowly towards the magazine.

"Lyris?" Brindt asked. He hadn't moved out from the chair yet.

I met his call with silence and more sliding. *Almost there.*

The chair started to slide backwards slowly and my heart filled with dread as the giant's bones cracked as he fell to the floor. Knees struck the carpet and more dust filled the air, but I didn't dare sneeze a second time. I would die before I would let out another sneeze. With wide eyes, I watched as the giant continued to lower himself to the ground until large hands flattened on the floor and a face started to fill the space under the desk. Desperate and huge eyes searched the ground.

"Lyris?" he asked again. His eyes somehow swept past and started over in their search. "Domodo, Lyris." He said something else when finally my body grazed against a magazine page. *Thank goodness*. I didn't hesitate to find temporary shelter hidden in the pages of what looked to be a sports magazine. I sucked in a trembling breath.

"Manno," Brindt said.

I didn't dare look out from under the magazine, but he shifted again. I could only pray that he was giving up and hopefully finding something else to occupy his time. Didn't giants go to school? Or did they have summer break like we did? And if it was summer, why the hell was it so damn cold? I shuddered and blew warm air into my hands as an unsettling silence fell over the room.

He was giving up. He was giving up.

All I had to do was...

Light poured over without warning. My shelter. Gone. My possible chance to escape. Gone. Brindt stared down from a standing position as he held the magazine rolled up in his hand. He was going to kill me. He held the magazine like he was prepared to kill a spider in the bathroom.

'Disellus' wasn't going to cut it.

I had betrayed his trust.

I had disobeyed a giant and he had found me.

"Lyris?" He sounded surprised. "Lam..." His voice trailed off as he tossed the magazine away from him. It landed on the ground with a pang and I winced violently and looked up at him. His eyes flickered down towards the desk and then back at me. Still standing, he reached over, touched the lamp cord and thumbed it carefully before looking down with a peculiar expression. It was so horrible to look up at him from the floor. All similarities I had thought we had flew from my mind as I sat level with his sneakers.

We weren't alike.

He was a giant... and I was...

"Lyris." His voice changed from surprise to concern. He started to lower himself into a crouch and I pressed myself up against the wall, quaking under his shadow. He was angry. He had to be. How could he not be?

"I'm sorry!" I shouted desperately as I saw him start to reach towards me. "I'm so fracking sorry. But I can't stay! I have to leave. I'm so sorry!" Tears came again as he merely tilted his head and continued to bring his hand close. "Puh...p-please! I'm sorry! Brindt! I'm sorry!"

"Eunt bu banum?" he asked, lowering his voice. His hand stopped close to my body, but he didn't grab me. When I didn't answer him, and only shivered more, his hand drew closer, fingers outstretched. "Lyris. Eunt bu banum?"

I thought he was yelling so I only started to sob harder, and pressed my back up against the wall. It was cold just like everything else.

"Please," I tried. "Don't do anything. Don't hurt me. I'm sorry—"

"Lyris." His voice was the firmest I had heard it. It was loud enough that it completely drowned out mine and I winced, and stared up at him with wide, watering eyes. "Eunt bu banum?"

"What? Brindt, I can't understand you..."

"Noc?" He grabbed the lamp cord and held it in one hand. "Bu?"

Was he actually trying to figure out how I ended up on the ground?

"Lyris?" he tried, holding the lamp cord and shaking it. "Bu?"

Through my fears, I nodded slowly. "Yes?"

He held the lamp cord in front of his face and then looked at me. He started to speak in a rushed voice, but I couldn't understand the words so he slowed himself down. "Bues banum?" he tried next.

Not sure what he was asking, I nodded again, but he didn't seem pleased with my answer. In fact, it seemed to anger him even more.

"I'm sorry," I said again.

"No."

I stopped crying and looked up at him. "No?"

"No," he said as he released the cord. "No sore-ee." He shook his head. "Lyris, sore-ee. No. Lyris banum."

I tried to piece together his broken English mixed in with his own words, but couldn't quite place the meaning. In my ears he only sounded aggravated.

"Brindt, I—"

"No." He lifted his hand and started to come towards me, no longer caring if I flinched or cried out. I tried to pull my injured leg closer to my body, but the swelling had gotten so bad that I could barely move. A single fingertip brushed the bruised area, eliciting a pained cry from my throat.

"Banum," he muttered. "Banum." He shook his head and mumbled something to himself. I thought I caught my name and the word 'insigni' again, but other than that, I didn't understand. He turned his eyes back to me.

"Lyris, domodo," he said, his eyes seemingly pleading with

mine. He asked another question with the same hurt expression. I shrugged because I couldn't understand what he meant and he only looked more pained. How could he be the one so sad about this? The same hand that touched my bruise started to uncurl and all four fingers and a thumb headed my way. I whimpered softly but the giant's eyes softened.

"Cen micuit, Lyris," he said as he curled fingers around my back. "Cen micuit."

I was too tired to fight with him anymore, and realized that my fate had been sealed. Despite his soothing words, I could tell he was upset because I betrayed him. I wasn't being a good pet so surely I was about to pay the price. My body fell limp in his palm as another hand appeared, hovered over for a second and then started to pet my hair. His touch was gentler than before, but he was still petting me so I tried to push his fingers away. His touch remained, no longer bothered by my shoving.

"Killi, killi, Lyris," he said as he stood up. My stomach soared down to my toes as the giant rose into the air, but his fingers never wavered and continued to stroke through my hair and down my back. "Cen micuit."

I sniffled into his touch, embarrassed because his actions were somehow comforting. *Why was this comforting?* I was in the hand of a giant who was probably still very angry, several years younger than me, viewed me as a pet and patted me like one too. Yet I calmed down as his large, but careful, fingertips sloppily wove their way through my hair. Warmth flooded my bare skin and more soothing words continued to wash overhead.

"Cen micuit," he said along with another few sentences. "Ito tabeo bu."

The world shifted as the giant found himself back in his chair. He still cradled me against him, and continued to pet my hair and back. He whispered something softly, but like most words I couldn't understand and merely nodded in agreement. His body shook and I wondered what was happening at first until I looked up at him and realized he was only laughing. He was laughing at me, but it didn't appear to be cruel. It seemed fond. Maybe I was going to be okay.

"Lyris." His voice immediately pulled me out from my pet-like state. I looked up at him. The petting stopped and his finger brushed up against my bare leg. "Bues banum." It wasn't a question and I wondered if this was his way of showing an understanding that I was hurt. Another nod came and his lower lip puckered out and he gnawed on it for a moment before turning serious.

"Brindt?" I asked, looking up at him with worried eyes. He couldn't actually be mad... not after being so kind. My body was lowered to the desktop and I gently slid out from his hand. I landed carefully on my good leg, but he kept one hand close as though he was afraid I would try to run again. "Uh... Lyris demano?" I tried, hoping to please him.

He shook his head, but didn't bother to answer, confirming my greatest fear of being caught. All chances of building trust were lost. His one hand remained close as he reached over for something else with his other. I watched until the hand appeared again holding two tiny pieces of wood, smaller and shorter than Popsicle sticks, but just as flat. He lifted his other hand away and held one piece of wood in each hand as he turned down to look at me.

"Demano," he said. His voice remained firm.

I nodded, too frightened to do otherwise at that point. If I was told to jump off the desk I would have probably listened, his eyes were so focused and scary. I held my breath as each hand descended and a flat piece of wood was pressed on either side of my knee. I poked an eye open and Brindt instructed me to do something. I tilted my head.

"Danar," he commanded. "Danar, Lyris." He pinched my leg lightly on either side and I quickly grabbed the wood to secure both sticks. He nodded with a pleased expression and reached for something else. "Danar." He held up a piece of string. His fingers were large, but surprisingly dexterous as they wrapped around my leg and the two pieces of wood several times until my leg was held securely in place.

It looked like a make-shift splint and I looked up at the giant with wide and surprised eyes. He only looked back blankly and focused on the task until everything was secure. His finger dipped under my leg, touched the back of my knee, and lifted it slowly a few times, as though testing his work. He pulled away and then he was silent.

I studied his work and occasionally glanced back up at Brindt, who also seemed to be watching closely. My leg was straight and the wood panels actually gave some extra warmth to my exposed skin. I felt around my knee, and though it still hurt a lot, the splint seemed to be helping already. Some ice would have probably helped with the swelling, but I had no idea how to get that across to the giant. Besides, he had done enough. Despite my fear of him, he had helped me.

"Uhh, thanks," I said, still looking at my knee.

He didn't answer, but I could hear him breathing steadily above me.

"Demano." He pulled open a drawer at his desk and started to search for something.

I couldn't bring myself to look at him even as the drawer closed shut, but a clanking of glass and metal caught my attention and I was forced to jerk my head upward. Brindt looked through something which could have only been a magnifying glass. My breath hitched as he glanced around the splint from all directions, resting his free hand dangerously close as he seemed to steady himself. He remained silent.

I clenched my hands into fists as I tried to gather some courage to fill the silence.

He could have hurt me, but he didn't.

He could have put me back in the cage, but he hadn't.

He could have yelled at me, but he didn't.

His teal eye continued to observe from above when I finally found the courage to speak.

I shot my head up and met his gigantic eye through the lens.

"Thank you, Brindt," I said in a loud and clear voice. I touched the splint to show what I was talking about. "Thank you."

The eye widened behind the lens. Surprise wasn't able to be hidden at such a magnitude. He licked his lips and suddenly the magnifying glass was gone, set aside and Brindt's face filled my vision instead of just his eye. He tilted his head and I touched the splint for effect.

"Thank you, Brindt."

The one corner of his mouth dared to creep upward as though he couldn't control it, but he shook his head and the start of a smile away. He looked shy as he turned away and rubbed the back of his neck. He said a few things in a low voice to himself and then turned back.

"T-tank...u?" he said, trying out the new words.

I nodded and tried to hide my shock. "Yes. Thank you." I tapped my brace again. "For this. Thank you."

With a shaky hand, he pointed at the splint and then at himself.

"Yes, thank you, Brindt." I nodded.

This time he actually smiled. His eyes crinkled in the corners and his cheeks turned a different color, which made me blush. It was hard not to get caught up in the moment of such a weird situation as I realized that Brindt probably wasn't going to hurt me.

He just wanted a pet.

"Lyris," he started, sounding unsure and careful with his words.

"Yes?" I looked up and met his eyes. It was a strange moment, but Brindt pushed forward and tried to make a point of his own.

"Lyris... demano?"

I bit my lip. Could I actually promise to stay? It was so wrong to lie to him, but it wasn't like I could go anywhere at the moment. With my leg still injured, it probably made the most sense to stay with him until I could talk more. We were already starting to be able to communicate so I imagined I could get him to understand my need to leave his world in a few days. My parents would be going crazy with concern because of my disappearance, but maybe I still stood a chance to go back.

"Yes," I said finally. I would do what Brindt wanted for the time being.

"Lyris?" He tilted his head.

"Demano," I said which brought a smile to his face. "Lyris, demano."

"Pomun," he said with a nod. "Dea insigni. Dea Lyris." He started to reach behind me and just as I started to smile back at him, I realized that something new was pinched between his finger and thumb.

A collar.

Nine

At the appearance of that collar, all trust I was beginning to feel for the giant melted away as he held it up with a smile on his face.

How dare he smile after helping me out and then pulling this?

Since my leg was tightly bandaged I found it difficult to get away from him as he started to lower it towards me. My mind raced as I tried to figure out the expression on his face. Why did he look so excited? Didn't he think we were making progress? He even understood some of my words.

Words...

Words!

"Brindt, no!" I screamed loudly. I was surprised by the shrillness of my voice and I realized then just how frightened I was of a little piece of fabric shaped like a circle that would snap around my neck. The things it would mean if I allowed Brindt to strap that around me. Luckily, despite everything, Brindt still responded well to the word 'no' and his own name so the horrible collar stopped coming as he pulled it back.

"Lyris?" He arched a brow with a confused expression.

"Yes, Lyris." I touched my chest. "That's me. I have a name. I told you my name. I have a language. I'm obviously intelligent and you obviously understand that! So why are you trying to put a collar on me?" I didn't dare allow my eyes to water, I was so enraged. "I thought you might still see me as a pet, but a collar?" I pointed to the horrible object and shook my head wildly. "Brindt, no!"

He flinched back, no doubt surprised by my words and let the collar fall from between his pinched fingers into his open palm. He rolled it back and forth a few times with a thoughtful frown. "No?" he asked, holding the collar towards me.

I shook my head. "How can you even ask me that?" I shouted. "Would *you* want to wear a collar?" I mimicked the action and hoped he would catch on, but to my horror, he only smirked.

"Insigni, Lyris." The damn fool was still smiling a bit. "Dea insigni. Dea Lyris." He held up the collar again. "Tah-lc," he said. "Lyris. Brindt. Tah-lc."

"I'm not talking you if you put that horrible thing on me... you... you... monster!" The word spilled out again and Brindt tilted his head.

"Moan... star?" he tried. "Brindt?"

"Yes! Brindt is a monster!" I shouted. I didn't know how else to get through to him so I threw up my hands and growled loudly, and barked like an idiot to make my point. "Do you understand that, Brindt? Monster! You! You're a monster!" I growled a second time. "If you put that on me, you're a monster!"

Brindt pointed at his chest with his free hand. "Moan-star?"

"MONSTER!" I roared. "You! All giants! Whatever you are. If you think you can just collar us up like pets then that makes you a monster!" My chest heaved from all the shouting and my cheeks were bright red. Brindt looked down with an expression I couldn't quite understand.

Confusion?

Anger?

Sadness?

"Well?" I asked, challenging him as he seemed to have fallen silent for the time being. I couldn't stand to see him with that collar in his hands, but when I looked at his face it was hard to actually see him as a monster. I even wondered how old he was. In my opinion, he looked old enough to know better. Old enough to understand that if something looks like you, can talk like you (sorta), and can

93

understand you (sorta), then you certainly don't have the right to collar them up and treat them like an animal. And after I thought we had made so much progress, despite my running away, I thought maybe I was getting through to him that I was a sentient and intelligent being just like him.

"Mon-star," he said softly. "Brindt." He snuck a look with the collar still in his palm. "Brindt, tomidulous." He bowed his head as though something occurred to him. "Mon-star."

"Monster," I said. I didn't care that I was baiting him. He was trying to figure something out and I wondered if the word 'tomidulous' had anything to do with the horrible shrieking I made a few seconds ago. I hoped it sunk in. "Brindt. Monster."

Something flickered across his eyes and he glanced down at the collar in his hand, curling his fingers around it. For a moment, I thought he was going to snap it on anyway, but instead he threw it at the wall behind me. I screamed loudly when his fist rose above my head and he moved with such strength and speed that I realized that if he had wanted to hurt me, there was nothing I could do about it. The tiny collar hit the wall behind the desk with a surprisingly loud snap and just as I turned back around, I saw Brindt had removed something from his ear and slammed it down next to me.

"Brindt... no... no monster!" he shouted. "Tah-lc. Brindt... Lyris! Tah-lc!"

I shook my head. "I don't want to talk while wearing that stupid thing! Monster!" I screamed. "Monster, monster, monster—" I nearly lost my breath as a huge hand wrapped around my entire body and I was hoisted into the air. I coughed and sputtered to catch my breath and locked eyes on the horrible being who thought it was fine to keep people as pets.

Words streamed out from his mouth in an angry panic, but I couldn't bring myself to even look at him at that point. I squirmed and struggled in his warm, sweaty fist as he continued to talk, but most words were lost on me. I caught his name. He kept talking about 'tah-lc' and he was set on saying the word 'no' and 'tomidulous'.

94

"Lyris?" he tried after a few minutes of pointless explaining. His voice had fallen back to a reasonable decibel, but it was just so hard to look at him. "Domodo, Lyris." More words, "... no... Brindt no tomidulous."

"Whatever." My answer was clear and he huffed audibly at my response.

"Ectu," he grumbled under his breath, probably thoroughly annoyed at that point. His hand closed more tightly and he shoved his body away from the desk.

I should have panicked. Because in that moment if Brindt truly was annoyed and no longer deemed me worthy of being his pet, I could have been taken to the blue light room. But I was so set in letting him stew in the fact that I thought he was a monster, I stiffened in his grasp as I was merely deposited back into the cage back on his nightstand. I tumbled back onto the tissue pile, but Brindt's touch was surprisingly light as though he was still worried about my leg. I didn't give him the satisfaction of letting him know I was appreciative and quickly turned my body away so I didn't have to face him.

I would find a way out of this sooner or later.

I didn't need Brindt's help. Not if I was going to be treated like an animal.

The cage lifted into the air suddenly so I was forced to tumble around a bit inside. I used the awkward time to try and figure out what Brindt was doing. He was holding the cage at waist level, practically letting it dangle against his hip as he moved around the room. I sucked in a scream, ready to make myself known if he tried to take me to that blue room but instead he went to a place I had seen him go in before.

His closet.

Unable to even stand and pound on the glass to get his

attention, I decided that the best course of action would be the silent treatment. I crossed my arms over my chest and looked straight ahead as the scenery changed from walls filled with pictures and books to dirty shirts and blankets. I frowned as Brindt cleared a shelf at his face-level and carefully slid the cage there and his eyes landed on mine.

"Lyris," he said, adding more to the sentence. "Micuit?"

Silence. His frown deepened.

"Lyris, domodo." His voice cracked slightly. He started to say something else, but as I just continued to stare at him blankly, I swear something snapped. His eyes darkened and he turned his head away muttering something about 'tah-lc'.

Whatever.

Without another word hc turned away, left the closet and shut the door behind him to leave me trapped in the darkness. I wouldn't have even minded so much if my stomach hadn't let out a very unattractive growl at that exact moment. *Dammit, I was hungry.* The giant could have at least remembered to feed me before he tried to put a collar on me.

Great.

***

By the time light filtered into the closet, I was so starving that I was weak and laying on my side. Like an animal, I had figured out a way to use the bathroom in the cage and a small pile of tissue lay tucked in a corner. I felt humiliated and humbled by the time Brindt came back and to my relief I noticed he had a small plate in his hands with brightly colored objects that I could only interpret as food.

I shifted in the cage so I could turn to look at him and gave him an encouraging smile in hopes that all had been forgotten about the collar, but his look was still cold. *Ouch.* I guess all was not

96

forgotten in regards to calling him a monster.

"Brindt," I said, trying to get him to pay attention as his hand reached for the top of the cage and lifted it. For once, I hoped that he would reach inside to get me, but instead he took a seat on the floor of the closet, set the plate of food next to him on the floor and the cage in his lap. My body rocked with all the movement, but I didn't want to complain since I was still worried about his cool demeanor. "Brindt?"

Silence filled the air as he opened the lid of the cage and peered inside. He bit his lower lip and started to reach for something and I held my breath, prepared for his fingers, but none came. Instead, the tiny collection of tissues in the corner of the cage was plucked out and set somewhere out of sight. My cheeks grew hot at the idea of him taking care of my bathroom routine, but I didn't bring it up. It was already awkward enough being in his lap in a cage. His plaid shirt and his head hung over me, but his lips remained closed.

"Brindt, please," I said. I wanted him to talk to me. Yell at me. Say he was hurt. Say something in his language – in my language! I didn't care at that point, but the silence was worse than anything!

He didn't reply, but instead reached next to him to pick up something from the plate. His hand soared overhead, entered the cage and held out the strange food in front of my face.

"Codo," he said stiffly.

I searched his eyes through the opening of the cage. "What is it?" I asked softly, pointing at the piece of food pinched between his fingers. To my relief it didn't look like pet food, but something in closer resemblance to fruit. I had never seen a fruit so bright blue before, but the texture was like a watermelon. I tilted my head up at him in hopes that I would spark a reaction, but he merely said the word again.

"Codo."

I frowned. I really was like a pet. I leaned forward in my sitting position to take the object from his fingers and was relieved that he released it immediately and pulled his hand out. A waft of cool air sent chills into the cage and I looked up at him with worried eyes.

"Brindt," I started. "I—"

"Codo, Lyris," he said. "Domodo."

I turned the piece of offered food in my hands and tried to figure out what it was. It had to be a fruit of some sort because it was cold and sticky in my fingers and had a citrusy smell like a cross between a grapefruit and an orange.

"Thanks," I said timidly. "Thank you, Brindt."

"Codo," he said along with some other words.

I wanted to roll my eyes at his coldness, but it was hardly the time to stand up for myself. I was hungry and after only a few hours I was lonely for Brindt's attention. I brought the bright blue chunk of food up to my mouth and took a tentative bite. Despite the smell, its texture matched its appearance of the inside of a watermelon and tasted like a tart grape. I couldn't help but let out a tiny sound of appreciation as the juice burst into my mouth and my hunger started to settle down. I easily polished off the tiny piece.

"Brindt—" I looked up and was surprised that he was already holding out another piece towards me, twice as big as the last one. I reached forward and took the fruit, and easily powered it down, feeling better and less angry. "Thank you," I said again.

He didn't answer, but instead held out a different looking piece of food towards me. It was hard not to focus on the degrading aspect of my situation. I was being fed like a hamster in a cage while sitting in a guy's lap, but I was too tired and too hungry to care. The new offering resembled something like bread and I quickly took down three or four pieces of this and then smacked my lips happily as my stomach started to swell. At least the food here was good and similar to ours in a certain aspect, but the bread had also dried out my throat. As I was trying to figure out a way to explain, another object entered the cage and between his fingers. A tiny glass filled with a liquid the color of the first piece of fruit. It was bright blue, but I could see tiny bubbles in the glass gave and this gave me the indication that it was pop of some sort.

"You giants have a lot of blue," I said as I reached for the glass. It was a shame that my words fell on deaf ears, but that was okay. At least Brindt was looking at me. He watched with the same sort of fascination I would have given to a new puppy who lapped up water from their dish. I frowned and just tried to focus on my drink.

A smile crossed my face as the bubbles hit my lips. "W-wow," I said with appreciation. "This is amazing. I don't think we have anything close to this back home." I dared to lift my head and show Brindt the same smile, and held up the large glass towards him with both hands. "It's good!" I called up to him.

He arched a brow.

"Good!" I said, smacking my lips and smiling wide so he could see.

He seemed to be fighting with himself as to whether to answer or not. After a few uncomfortable moments he finally tried out the word for himself.

"Gowd?" he said with a questioning look.

"Good," I said, gently correcting him. "This drink," I said, holding up the glass before taking another large gulp. "It's good! Tasty!"

"Tah-stee?" he tried.

"Tasty. Yum."

He smiled. "Yum?"

I smiled back. "Yes! Yum! Good!" I set down the glass and rubbed my stomach to get my point across. "Good! Yum yum!"

"Yum... yum," he tried, peering down at me.

His expression was softening, but he made no move to take me out of the cage. I supposed I might have blown that for a while, but at least we were talking. Maybe to win him over I would have to sing for my meal. Be cute like the pet he thought I was. It wasn't like Brindt was all bad. He was actually kind of cute for a giant with large pointy ears. *Speaking of which...*

"Brindt?" I took care to make my voice sound like I was asking a question. He arched a brow and peered down at me. It was a little unnerving to arch my neck to look up at him, but anything was better than being locked in the silence and darkness. I pointed to my ears, and then at his. "Why are your ears like that?"

"That?" he tried, tilting his head.

"Your ears!" I said, pointing at my ears and then up at him again. "They're pointed. We look so much alike except for size and those things. I was just wondering why..." I trailed off and realized that I was saying entirely too much and instead reached up to push my hair away from my ears so I could make my point. "Ears!" I shouted. "Mine are round," I went on, touching them for effect. I then pointed up at him. "Your ears are pointed! Ears!"

His mouth opened and closed a few times, but he didn't repeat anything. I wondered if the word was too hard for him to get out. Ears didn't really sound like anything he had said so far.

"Errs," Brindt said suddenly. A frown formed and he shook his head.

I dared to chuckle. "Ears," I repeated, pointing to mine. "Ears."

"Err-ras," Brindt tried again. He reached towards his face, pushed aside some of his longer blond hair and confirmed what I

100

thought I had seen before. His ears were large compared to his face and they came up to a point. I looked carefully before his cheeks reddened and he released his hair, hiding all but the tip of those large ears behind his hair.

"Ears?" I said, touching mine. "Different?"

"Err-ras," he said back. "Dif...difen..."

"Different," I repeated. "Ears."

"Daubis," he said, touching the top of his ear. "Daubis."

"Dowbis," I said.

"Daubis."

"Ears."

"Err-ras."

As our eyes met we both smiled. It was hard not to get uncomfortable looking up at him like that so I quickly lowered my eyes.

"Lyris?" Brindt's voice quickly filled the cage. "Daubis... err-ras?"

I nodded, tapping my ears. "Y-yes. Dow-bis... ears. Different."

"Dif-ernt," he said, frowning as he tried out another word.

The cage shifted a bit and I noticed that Brindt was slowly lowering his hand towards me. I thought he was going to pick me up, but instead his fingers shifted and started to drift towards my face. I flinched a bit and they stopped coming. I looked up and gave him a little nod, encouraging him to keep going and just as I suspected his fingers went towards my hair and brushed a bit aside to inspect my ears. I doubt he could see very well at that point, but he could feel, so his fingertips stopped on the top of my ears and he gasped.

"Daubis," he said in a hushed voice. His hand quickly pulled out and he touched his own ear before his eyes widened. "Dif-ernt," he said. "Ahhh..." His smile grew. "Lyris—" His hand started to come back into the cage when a woman's voice filled the air. I didn't recognize the words other than Brindt's name and he flinched.

"Ahhh..." He seemed to grumble before he turned back to me.

"Brindt!" The woman's voice was louder and more insistent.

"Nadentun!" he shouted back angrily. I held my ears as the voice pounded against them and he turned back. "Disellus, Lyris." He quickly seemed to explain something before his hand pulled away completely and he rose to his feet.

"Wait! What? Are you leaving?" I called out to him from inside the cage. He either didn't want to answer or he didn't hear because he only continued to stand. Rushed in his actions, he shoved my cage back onto the shelf. He shot me a helpless expression.

"Disellus," he said. "En—"

"Brindt!" the woman screamed.

He didn't waste another moment and quickly fled from the room and shut the door behind him. His steps pounded against the floor and another door opened and shut with a strange clank and then he was gone.

At least he left the light on.

Alone in the cage I was at least able to gather my thoughts. Thank hell Brindt didn't really seem to be too upset anymore. I made a mental note to not always assume that my complaints would fall on deaf ears. It had only been a day and we were already able to communicate with each other pretty well. Maybe I could even make an effort to start learning more of his language while I was there.

Wait.

What the hell was I talking about?

I didn't want to stay there. I wanted to get out of there and at that point I was actually planning to learn his language? I must have been losing my damn mind.

Really though, it wouldn't have been so terrible to learn a little bit about what the hell was going on. How many people got to say they traveled to a different world and made it back home? *If* I made it back home.

I looked down at my leg and the memory of Brindt bandaging me up was still fresh in my mind. Whatever was happening, he didn't seem like he was planning to return me to that blue lit room. Maybe I was going to be his personal pet – or maybe he was the guy who 'trained' people to behave before they were put in that little room. The people in the cages there certainly seemed to be a lot more resigned to their fate than I was.

Still... I slowly reached for my ear, and remembered how gentle Brindt had been when he touched it. Barely the tips of his fingers skimmed the area, but he realized immediately that they were different than his own. I wondered what else was different. What else was similar?

My thoughts wandered over to my family for the next few hours as there was nothing else to do with such a large, empty amount of time. I wondered if my mom and dad even realized I was gone yet or just assumed I was 'acting out' and were waiting for another few hours before they called the cops. I wondered if they were worried about calling anyone because it could affect their reputation as professors. How good could they be if they couldn't even keep their own damn kid from disappearing?

And then I thought of Wyatt.

I still didn't want to believe that he wanted to take me here to sell me off as a pet, but nothing else seemed to make sense. When he

103

didn't know me very well, he had been so insistent on bringing me to the portal, but when he got to know me, he suddenly didn't want me to have anything to do with the Shaw place.

He called me a target.

He had money, but he wouldn't explain why.

Dammit. He even said seventeen was the perfect age.

Everything he said had a double meaning looking back on it. He wanted to bring me here. He wanted to give me to the giants. Most likely he wanted to make some sort of profit. He had to. Nothing else made sense. The thought of being targeted took my breath away. Some women were kidnapped and sold into prostitution, but I never imagined there was someone living near my house who sold people to be pets for giants.

It was too messed up to think about so I decided there was no other way to pass the time with an injured leg so I laid down on my side and waited for Brindt. I would simply have to be patient and let my leg heal and my understanding of his language grow. I figured the more time he talked to me, the more he would learn that I couldn't be a pet. I had a family and friends. I had a life back home. He couldn't possibly want to take that all away from just so he could pet my hair and feed me fruit. He had plenty of other people he could keep to himself... so why me?

I closed my eyes. Those were all questions I could get answers to with patience.

I had to learn Brindt's language.

Ten

The next few days were tough because each day that went by meant another day that my parents had no idea where I was or what happened to me. They didn't know anything about Wyatt or the house next door other than my cryptic conversation with my father so at that point I just tried to focus on learning Brindt's language. It was slow going at first because he seemed to be just as interested in learning mine and for some reason he just wouldn't stop bringing up that stupid collar.

"Lyris, domodo," he said as he held up the collar. *Yet. Again.* At that point I knew he was begging and that 'domodo' meant please.

"Talk! Lyris! Brindt! Talk. This!" He held up the collar and lowered it in front of my face. My nose curled up at the sight of it as it nestled in the center of his palm and he looked as though he expected that I would willingly take it and strap it to my neck. *Like a good little hamster.*

"Brindt, no." I pushed his fingers away with all my strength. His hand didn't even move, but his fingers curled around the collar, brought it up to his chest and held it tightly. "Why are you so obsessed with me being a damn pet? Don't you think we've gotten past this? At all?"

"No—" he started.

"You're impossible!" I stood up on the bed. My leg had almost healed, but the comforter offered hardly any purchase as I tried to make my point by rising up to a staggering six inches by his enormous standards. "No collar! No pet! No collar, Brindt—"

"Talk!" His easily rose above mine. "Lyris..."

"Ugh, never mind." I sat back down on the comforter. The blankets sunk slightly under my weight and Brindt looked larger than ever as he also slouched sulkily. "Brindt, why can't you understand this one little thing? I don't want to wear that. You don't understand what it means."

"Talk, means," Brindt said.

"I can talk to you just fine without the collar. It's been four days. I've been learning your language. Can't we get past this?"

"One," he said, holding up a single finger.

"Huh?" I turned to look up at him and tilted my head - our universal signal of 'I can't understand what the hell you're talking about'. "What is it now?"

"One," he said again, pinching the collar between two hands. He stretched it out and started to lower it in my direction.

"No!" I shouted. "One? One what?"

"One..." He just jerked the collar out towards me. "One... Lyris. One!"

My face changed. *Once.*

"Once?" I asked, pointing up at the collar and then holding up one finger as he had done. "Are you asking me to wear it one time?" He tilted his head. "Uh... um..." I trailed off and pretended to lock the collar around my neck. "Once?" I tried, mocking the immediate removal of the collar and then tossing it aside before smiling. "Once?"

His face brightened. "Domodo!" He nodded hard. "Wun...ss?"

"Once?" I tried, mimicking the whole action of putting on and taking off the collar. "One time? Once?"

He nodded. "Wun-ss."

I smiled at his broken tongue. Despite speaking beautifully in his own language, the way he said my words made me laugh most of the time. He tried so hard to say things that I did that, in fact, trying to learn his language had turned more into his trying to learn mine. I

106

had to say it made things a little easier, sometimes. It was the one thing I could hold onto while I waited for my leg to heal.

"Fine." I stiffened slightly. "One time, Brindt." Excited fingers started to lower towards me. "Once!" I screamed up at him again.

"Wun-ss," he said. "Oh!" He stopped lowering the collar and reached for something in his pocket and secured it into his ear. "Ahhh... Lyris," he said, turning back to me. "One."

"One time." I swallowed nervously as those huge fingers started to come close. As the collar loomed dangerously close I pinched my eyes shut and stretched my neck. The thick material hit my skin and I instinctively flinched back. It was like one hundred little bees had started to sting my throat.

"Disellus," Brindt said quickly as he pulled it away.

"What the hell was that?" I hissed.

"Wun-ss, Lyris," he said. "Domodo."

My eyes narrowed and I could feel his nervousness as he brought the collar around my neck. I was a fool for trusting him. Wearing a collar. Maybe I had just sealed my fate as his pet forever. But he had promised, and like him, I wanted to give him the chance to prove he could be trusted. I swallowed as his fingers secured something into place and a loud click filled my ears. The stinging of the bees came and passed.

"Better?" he asked.

"Yeah, that's better—" I stopped short and my eyes flashed open.

Brindt looked just as surprised as me.

"Say something in your language!" I commanded.

"In your language," he said. His eyes grew wide and he started to smile.

"Holy hell!" I screamed as I sat up and touched the collar. "I can understand you!"

***

After a few moments of crazy intense silence, Brindt smiled. "I told you we could talk with the collar," he insisted.

"That's what you were trying to say?" I blinked hard. "Holy crap mother, this is really real. I can understand you. I can talk to you. You can understand me. I don't believe this! And to think we've gone days like idiots just trading words back and forth! Why the hell didn't you say anything?"

"Don't you think I tried?" he asked. "I asked you every day—
"

"You should have made it clearer!" I shouted. "Oh my God!" I touched the collar, and tried to understand. "But I don't get it. How is this possible? How can you understand me? How can I understand you?"

"It's the collar—"

"I know it's the damn collar!" I tried smile to soften the harshness of my screaming, but it was almost impossible. "This whole time we could have been talking. I could have told you everything instead of acting like a complete idiot. Oh man, this is unreal. This collar. It makes it so we can talk to each other." I looked up at him. "You can still understand me, right?"

"Every word," he said, smiling fondly.

"How old are you?"

"Fifteen."

"How tall are you?"

"Almost six feet."

"Who else lives here?"

"It's just me and my mom."

"This is so unreal!" I shouted at the top of my lungs. I collapsed on my back and stared up at the ceiling. "I still can't believe this. I'm here, wearing a collar, talking to a giant and he can finally understand me."

A large face loomed overhead. Brindt was smiling. Suddenly, hearing him talk normally and understanding every word... he didn't seem so much like a monster and I really began to regret my words.

"This is wild," he said softly as he peered down at me. "It's awesome to hear you talk and actually get what you're saying."

"Tell me about it. So tell me, how the hell does this thing work?" I tugged on the collar for effect. "I have to give credit to you giants, you certainly know how to make people feel like pets."

He arched a brow. "Giants?" he asked.

"Yeah. You." I pointed at him. "You're a giant."

"So what does that make you?"

"A person," I said with a laugh. "What the hell else would I be?"

"I'm a person, too." He started to frown. "Which reminds me..."

"Wait." I sat up straight on the comforter. "You think you're a person?"

"Of course I do!" I could hear the anger seep into his voice. "I

109

don't understand why I'm not."

"Because you're huge!"

"In your eyes. To me, I'm normal. You're the weird one for being so small."

"So that means you get to put a collar on me?"

He flinched. "It helps us talk, doesn't it?"

"It's the principle of the thing!" My cheeks grew hot as it became increasingly more obvious that he didn't understand. "Look, in my world, I'm the normal one. We don't have humungous monsters lumbering around—"

"There's that word again!"

Whoops. I stopped short and looked up at him only to notice that his cheeks were just as red as mine. "What word?" I tried to feign innocence.

"Monster," he said. "You called me that a few days ago."

I frowned, remembering how much that must have hurt. "Sorry—"

"Is that really what you think of me?" His nose scrunched up. "You kept making all these scary faces at me when you tried to describe it. A monster in your language is something to be feared."

"Of course it is."

"And you think that's what I am? Something to be feared?"

"Of course I do! Look at you! I mean..." I grew defensive as I trailed off and walked up to his hand resting on the comforter, but didn't dare touch it. "Your hand is almost larger than I am!"

"But that doesn't mean—"

"You put me in a cage!"

"That was just so you wouldn't get hurt."

"You put a collar on me."

"So we could talk to each other."

"You pet me! You talk down to me. You call me that word..."
I flinched for a moment as something occurred to me. Brindt was
stuttering out some lame excuse, but I was searching my memory.
"Before you learned my name, what did you call me?" I asked,
ignoring his protests about petting me. I didn't have time.

"Huh?"

"You called me something before Lyris," I said, growing
exasperated. "What was it?"

His eyes widened. "Oh that. Insignificant."

My face blanched. "W-what? What was it?"

"It's what your race is called. We call you Insignificants." He
shrugged it off. "What's wrong with that?"

"Are you out of your damn..." I trailed off and tried to
remember that this was a giant I was dealing with. Screaming at him
at the top of my lungs certainly wasn't going to help things, but my
mind fumed. That's what those people – those giants – called us? I
ran a hand through my hair. "Insignificants," I muttered.

"Lyris?" Brindt's voice came timidly and I shot my head up to
look at him. I was still surprised at how sometimes I could just give
him a look and he would shy away.

"What?" I asked irritably. I wanted to rip off the collar and
throw it in his stupid face for even having the gall to look so
concerned. Like somehow I was hurting him. Like *he* was the one

111

being called a name that meant 'didn't matter'. But without the collar we wouldn't be able to communicate at all, or we'd have to go back to uttering one and two syllable words at each other and that probably made me seem even more like a pet in his eyes. I absentmindedly tugged at the collar instead. "What is it?" I snapped.

"I don't understand why that word pisses you off so much."

"Of course you wouldn't," I grumbled.

"If it bothers you, I won't call you that. I haven't since I figured out your name."

"Whatever."

"Come on," Brindt said, still sounding hurt. "When was the last time I even called you that?"

I frowned. "It's been awhile."

"So I'll just keep not calling you that," he said. His shadow fell as he loomed closer. "But there's also something you can do for me."

"What is it now? You want me to learn how to 'sit' and 'stay'?" I growled.

"What? N-no," he said. His shadow shifted. "Can you at least look at me when I'm trying to talk to you? I thought the collar would make things easier."

"The collar makes things clearer," I corrected him.

"How's that?"

"Because," I said as I tried only to focus on the blankets in front of me. One of Brindt's hands shifted on the comforter, but at that point he didn't dare try to reach out. I probably would have bit him – pet or not. "You people... we're really nothing to you, aren't we?" I shook my head. "Insignificants. Nothings. Pets. Toys.

112

Animals. It doesn't matter what the word is, the message is the same." I touched the collar. "That's what's clearer."

Silence fell as Brindt didn't respond. There was probably nothing he could say. It was obvious he felt that way.

"It's harder." He spoke quietly, tentatively at first.

"What is?"

"To see you that way. It's harder now that I can hear you talk."

"Good."

"Lyris, I don't want you to be scared of me. I don't want you to see me as a monster."

"Why not?" I asked, already forgetting my promise to stop calling him that. "You are one."

His cheeks grew pink. "I'm not! I'm not scary—"

"You're scary to me," I huffed.

"So look at me and see that I'm not."

"Looking at you only makes me more scared."

"Lyris."

"Brindt. Seriously, get over it. You see me as a pet and I see you as a monster. That's just how it is." I shrugged. "Get over it."

More silence.

Brindt shifted away a few inches, but I didn't lift my head. How could he not see that it was impossible not to be scared of him? He was huge and his race thought humans were nothing more than tiny pets. And even though technology existed so that we could

113

communicate with the giants, it was clear that not every person in his world was allowed to wear one.

"I wonder why," I whispered to myself.

"What?"

I changed my question. "How does the collar work?"

"I honestly don't know all the details, Lyris. I just know that if I wear this earpiece and you wear the collar we're able to talk."

"And how do you know that?"

"Because the Targeter needs it to talk to my mom."

My eyes darted back and forth, but I kept my head down. "The Targeter?"

"Y-yes. He's the one..." He trailed off and finally I looked up at him. Our eyes met and he shifted uncomfortably on the comforter, trying to avoid eye contact. Honestly, it probably couldn't have been too hard – all he had to do was lift his chin and suddenly he was out of my range.

"Tell me." I don't know how my voice came out like such a command, but it seemed as though the rules still applied. "Brindt," I said. "Please. Tell me. What's the Targeter?"

"He's the Insignificant... er... the person who brings your kind here."

"Brings them here?" I tilted my head curiously. "What do you mean he brings them here?"

He jutted his chin towards the bedroom door and licked his lips. "That room you arrived in when you first got here. There's a portal that connects your world to ours, I guess. That's how the Targeter brings people here. He needs to be able to talk to my mom so the collar was created so they could communicate. Him and other

114

Targeters."

"Are there more than one?"

"Yes."

"Why isn't the Targeter a pet?"

He flinched. "Well, I think he was, but then he worked out a deal. My mom pays the Targeter and he brings more people like you here."

"Thus, that blue room."

His eyes flickered back over to me. "Blue room?"

"Don't play dumb," I hissed. "I saw that room – the one with all the cages and blue lights. The ones that were filled with people who aren't wearing collars."

He shifted. "Oh... uh... yeah. That's where they're kept until they're picked up."

"Picked up?"

He nodded. "My mom collects them and then sells them off to people who will take them."

"Like who?" My heart was already filling with dread to hear the answer.

"Pet stores, families, laboratories, things like that. Basically once a month people will come and buy them off her."

"Pet stores?" I hissed. "Like with dogs and cats?"

He nodded. "Yeah. My mom collects the money and she gives a part of it to the Targeter in the form of gold or silver or something." He shrugged. "She doesn't tell me too much, but I've seen her interacting with the Targeter."

I swallowed hard. "And what does the Targeter look like?"

He shrugged. "He's a guy. Your age. Maybe older."

I frowned. "What else?"

"Dark hair, light skin. He doesn't look very tall. Not for a guy – even an Insignificant guy."

I let the curse pass. "Have you ever heard his name? This guy who brings people here to be sold off as pets for profit?"

Brindt nodded. "It's a weird name."

"Try saying it."

"Y..." he trailed off, trying to form the syllables. "Y something."

My heart hiccupped. "Wyatt?" I tried.

"Yes!" Brindt smiled. "That's it. Y-at. Wyatt."

"I see." I was shocked. Since I stumbled through the portal I had a feeling that Wyatt was somehow involved in bringing others here, but to hear Brindt confirm it shook me to the core. To hear Brindt actually say his name – to know that Wyatt was planning to bring me here just to sell me off to those monsters.

"Brindt?" I asked.

"Hmm?"

"I need to be left alone for a little while."

"What? Why? Are you okay?" His face grew concerned. "Is your leg alright? Do you want me to bandage it?"

Fingers started to fill my vision and I pulled away from them

116

like fire. Brindt's face crumbled, but he lowered his hand, having enough decency to respect my fear of him. It wasn't like I had any idea what he was going to do anyway – probably just pet me again.

"Lyris, seriously, you're freaking me out. Is this about the Targeter? Do you know him or something?"

"Can you please, seriously just leave me alone for a bit, Brindt?"

"We should talk—"

"No." I shook my head. "No talking." My eyes watered with frustration. "Just leave me alone."

"But—"

"Leave me alone!" I shrieked and tried to rip off the collar. "What? What the hell is with this thing?"

"You can't take it off—"

"Then you take it off! Now!" I screamed and tried to reach behind to find the clasp. "Take this stupid thing off me!"

"But we should talk."

"I don't want to talk to you."

"Lyris."

"No." I shook my head until my red hair whipped back and forth across my face. "Brindt, no." I pinched my eyes shut, and only opened them for a moment to show Brindt how serious I was. Weight shifted and he finally reached behind my neck and sprung the collar free. The cool air hit my skin and for once, it was a welcome chill. The bed shifted and I noticed he was starting to leave.

"Lyris... demano?" he tried once more as he set the collar on his desk. "Domodo?"

I nodded pathetically. Where could I go? And like this? "Lyris, demano," I said weakly. "Now please just leave me alone." I waved him off and the door opened and shut, leaving me alone to process.

Eleven

Another day or two passed, but things hadn't really gotten any better. I suppose Brindt hoped things would change since we could talk and I would just embrace my new role as his pet – isolated to a single room. It was only then that I came to understand that Brindt's mom didn't want him to own a 'pet'. I wondered why the woman was so against the idea of Brindt having his own person as a pet, but clearly had no qualms about keeping twenty or thirty in cages to be sold off.

It was just another thing about Brindt's world that made no sense.

For those days I hardly spoke to Brindt, but he kept his schedule about feeding me, offering the collar, and trying to talk in my language. I played my role well because I didn't want him to get rid of me because at least with him, there was safety and security. Brindt would never hurt me and though he saw me like a pet, I was rarely treated like one. Sometimes it really was like I was getting through to him and other times... not so much. Finally, on a rainy day, Brindt was able to get me to open up.

I hated everything that damn collar represented, but I hated not being able to communicate with my kind and clueless captor even more.

"So you knew him?" Brindt asked once the collar was snapped snugly around my neck.

My ears rang with the change of him speaking clearly and smoothly and my throat muscles contorted so I could speak back to him properly. He pushed the cage off the desk so I wouldn't have to look at it while we spoke. At that point, I only slept in there at night.

"The Targeter?" Brindt tried again. "Wyatt? You knew him."

"I was dating him." It was a bit of an exaggeration, but I certainly thought that's where Wyatt and I were headed.

119

Brindt's eyebrows shot up. "Dating him? Insignificants—"

"Please don't call me that." I palmed my face with irritation. "You don't even know how much it hurts."

"S-sorry," Brindt stuttered. I could tell he meant it. "It's just, what should I call you?"

"How about people? Like you? We're like you only smaller." My eyes flashed to his. "Is it so hard to see me as a person?"

For some reason he blushed. "No, I guess not. You're a person to me." He smiled tentatively.

"Yeah right," I grumbled. "Whatever."

"So your people can date each other," he mused. "And he was your boyfriend?"

"Something like that." I noticed he still looked confused and I had to wonder why. "What is it? You can't picture us dating either? You think we just want to sit around all day in kennels and eat?"

"I didn't say that about you."

"About people in general," I snapped back. "Yes, Brindt. I was dating him. People date. I was dating Wyatt and I had no idea that all he actually wanted was to sell me off to you giants." I shook my head. "He dropped so many clues that he was weird, but I never expected this." I blew a raspberry and slumped. "I sure can pick 'em."

"Wow," was all Brindt said at first.

It was hard not to snort. "I'm sure it's hard for you to comprehend, but I *am* attractive in my world, Brindt."

His eyes widened. "That... that wasn't what I meant, Lyris. I think you're—"

120

"Just keep it yourself. I don't want to hear how you feel about people dating." I shrugged it off. "Can we move on? This subject is making me mad for some reason." When I looked up at him, I was sure he could sense the desperation in my voice and in my eyes.

To my relief, he nodded. "What's it like, then?"

"What's what like?"

"Your world," he said in a breathy voice. "What's it like to be a person in your world?"

"Honestly, this world doesn't seem that much different than mine. Only in my world we don't keep little beings as pets," I huffed.

He tilted his head and pushed some stray blond hairs away from his eyes. His one eye looked particularly teal because of the dreariness outside. I wondered how that worked.

"You mean there are people like you even smaller than you?" He sounded surprised.

"Ugh, no," I said. "It's just us in our world."

"You don't have pets?"

"Not that look like us!" I shouted. "Geezus, Brindt. What the hell is wrong with you?"

He frowned. "Is your world really like this?"

I frowned right back. "I don't really have a lot to go on, do I?" And I didn't. How could I say so confidently that my world was just like his when I didn't know anything beyond his room? "I guess I can't say for sure that our worlds are actually similar," I admitted.

"Why not?"

"Because I've been trapped in this damn room since I got here, you idiot." I rolled my eyes, and tried to will myself to calm down. "Look, I'm sorry. I don't mean to be a bitch. This is just hard for me, okay? The only guy who's ever really thought I was cute turned out to want to sell me off to the highest bidder in a land filled with monsters."

"We're not monsters, Lyris."

"You don't have to bite off my head to be a monster."

"I thought you said you were attractive in your own world."

Grateful for the change of subject, I stood up on the desk to stretch my legs. Brindt watched carefully, but he didn't dare bring a hand towards me. I didn't think about it much at the time, but he rarely grabbed without permission or a warning of some sort. I limped around and avoided discarded colored pencils and paintbrushes.

I bit back the idea of being ugly in Brindt's eyes, but I was too tired to lie about it. "So I lied. So what?"

"Well... for what it's worth..." Brindt began slowly as I turned around to look at him. He stopped talking when our eyes met.

"What?" I asked. "What were you going to say?"

"Nothing. It probably wouldn't matter to you anyway."

"Probably not." I continued to limp around on the desk, willing my leg to grow stronger. With the way things were going, I could probably try to make my escape by the end of the week. I tested my leg, walking faster and even faster still until I was able to jog slowly in a circle.

"Your leg's getting better," Brindt said as he observed. "That's good, right?"

"I suppose so," I muttered, still giving no indication that I planned to run away from him the first moment I could.

"Lyris?"

"What is it?" I asked, sounding a bit exasperated. I didn't know what it was, but when Brindt said my name like that, I always worried about what wild and humiliating question he was going to ask next.

"The Targeter..."

"What about him?"

"Was he really your boyfriend? Your first boyfriend?"

I chuckled darkly. "Why are you asking me that again? Aren't you a little young?"

"I'm fifteen, dammit," he retorted. "I'm only two years younger than you. Not to mention I'm a lot bigger."

My expression darkened. "Because you're a giant."

"I bet I'd still be taller than you."

"You're a guy. That makes sense."

"Answer my question," Brindt huffed. He didn't seem to be in the mood to banter. "Didn't other guys in your world want to date you?"

"Why do you care?"

"Because I'm curious."

His voice sounded more mature than usual so I stopped jogging for a moment to look at him. It was strange. The longer I was with him, the less I was able to see him as a monster and more of as a guy who just happened to be fifty feet taller than me. I shook my head of the thoughts because they were silly and wasteful.

"No, Brindt. No other guys wanted to date me."

"Why?"

"Because I'm too tall." He smirked. "In my world, you idiot."

"You don't look that tall to me."

"I'm too tall and my hair is weird."

"I like your hair."

"The same way a judge likes the puffs on a poodle's ass," I said, turning away from him.

"I'm serious. I really like your red hair. It's pretty. I don't see hair like that very often."

"No?" I turned around.

He shook his head. "People here don't have hair that color. There's brown and black, blond, but not hair like that. It... it's pretty. Unique."

My cheeks grew hot. "Whatever. Thanks, I guess." As rain started to fall harder outside, I turned towards the window. "From what I've seen so far, this world really does seem very similar to mine," I said, vaguely answering his question from before. "At least from what I've seen from your room."

"Do you want to see more?"

I mulled his question over while continuing to look out the window. "It wouldn't be the worst thing in the world," I started slowly, "but it's raining. Where could we go?"

"You know, it's not uncommon for Insig—er, little people to be seen. No one would bother us, but if you're really worried about seeing others—"

"I don't want to see anymore giants."

124

"Then we can to the park or something." His voice started to grow hopeful. "They have gazebos."

"Gazebos?" I snorted out a laugh. "This place really is just like home."

"So how about it?" he asked. "Do you want to see more than my bedroom?"

I thought it over. "I don't want anyone else to touch me."

He shook his head. "No. You're mine, Lyris."

"I don't belong to anyone," I snapped back. "I told you, I'm not your damn pet."

Brindt fell silent and for a few moments all I could hear was the pattering of rain outside. I could tell Brindt was a bit hurt with how snappy I was with him, but I couldn't help myself. I just needed him to understand that I wasn't a pet. I wasn't his pet and I never would be. The less attached he got to me, the better because I wasn't planning to stay.

"Look Brindt, I'm sorry—"

"I see you as more than a pet, Lyris." Brindt's voice came out a bit awkward and shy. "All I meant was that I wouldn't let anyone touch you when we're out. You're... you're safe with me."

I frowned. "S-safe with you? Whatever."

"Well, how else should I say it? You will be safe with me. Safer than you'd be alone. Safer than you'd be with someone else."

"Maybe someone else wouldn't have put me in a cage."

He huffed. "You're hardly ever in there anymore." He took in a heavy sigh and I swear his voice trembled. "Lyris... are you... are you still scared of me?"

125

"How are we going to get to the park?" It was cruel to change the subject, but I just couldn't take the seriousness of it any longer. The idea of Brindt liking my hair, thinking it was pretty and wanting to protect me... the sentiment was alright, but it didn't take away from the fact that I still wore a collar. And of course I was still scared of him. But he didn't need to hear that.

"You're too young to drive a car, aren't you?" I tried.

To my relief, he let the subject of my fear drop. "I have my bike."

"And..." I trailed off and finally looked over at him. He was wearing black jeans and a navy hoodie with a bright red shirt underneath. I didn't exactly see my traveling options. "How is that going to work?" My voice grew louder. "I'm not going in that stupid cage!"

He shook his head hard. "I know. I know that." He stumbled over his words. "You'll be okay in my pocket until we get there, won't you?"

"Your pocket?" My face turned white and then grew hot. "You want me to ride in your pocket?"

"I can't think of anywhere else," he said with a shrug. "It's too warm for me to wear a scarf, but I could wear one for you—"

"As if I'd be that close to you."

His eyes lowered. "You are still scared of me, aren't you?" he asked softly. "In your eyes, no matter what I do, I'm still a monster."

"Of course you—" I stopped short when I realized this wasn't another one of Brindt's attempts at banter. He actually looked hurt. He pulled away from the desk to stand up and walked into his closet without another word. I wondered if maybe I had gone too far. Despite his size and despite only being two years younger than me, it appeared that my words were starting to affect him somehow. And

126

even though he was a giant – and a monster for that matter – in my eyes, I didn't want to see him hurt.

I had no idea why his hurt face bothered me so much.

"Listen," I started in a loud enough voice that I hoped it would reach the closet. "I don't actually think you're a monster, okay? I just want to go home and I feel totally betrayed about what Wyatt might have done to me, okay? Can you understand that? You're really not that bad. In fact..." I started to flush, "... you're really—"

"Did you say something to me?" Brindt's face poked out from the closet with a clueless expression. He started to smile. "I heard something, but I wasn't sure if you were just muttering to yourself."

"You didn't hear anything?" I asked. I didn't know whether to be pissed or relieved that he hadn't heard. "Nothing?"

He shook his head. "Just something about that Wyatt guy. By the way, do you still like him?"

"That's none of your business."

"Tell me what you were saying. I'm sorry I couldn't hear you."

"It's nothing. I just..." I trailed off when Brindt emerged from the closet in a different shirt. No longer was he wearing the hoodie but a gray plaid button-down. It looked way too good on his frame and from a distance I could actually see him as a person and not just bits and pieces. His jeans clung to his long legs and he was wearing the same black belt with the silver buckle from before. From there I could see that he was wearing a pair of red sneakers.

"Not bad?" Brindt's voice called over. I glanced up and saw him smiling. "I just thought it might be easier for you to travel if I wore one of my holiday shirts."

"Holiday shirts?"

"Yeah, they're too fancy to wear anywhere except to holiday events where I have to be with my family. It's stupid, I know, but I thought this pocket," he said, patting a pocket on the right side of his chest, "would be a little more comfortable than the one in my hoodie."

"But it's raining." I was surprised at how flustered I was looking at that pocket against his chest.

"I can wear a coat," he said with a shrug. "You said you wanted to go out and this will make things easier for you." He started to walk over to the desk and extended his hand towards me, palm up. "Maybe once we're outside you won't be such a grouch and you can tell me about your world. I'm still curious, you know. Especially about this Wyatt guy."

"Why are you so interested in Wyatt?" I asked, eying up his hand.

"Because you are." He beckoned me to climb aboard his hand with one finger. "Come on."

"But I..." I swallowed deeply and looked up at him. I didn't understand him. I didn't understand why he was being so accommodating despite how awful I'd been to him for the past few days. I didn't understand his curiosity with Wyatt, either. *Interested in him because I'm interested*? How the hell did that make sense?

As thunder rumbled outside, I jumped with surprise and practically landed in Brindt's palm. Fingers instinctively curled around and my body rose in the air and gray plaid filled my vision and a hint of a spicy scent hit my nostrils. Was he actually wearing cologne? With his free hand, he opened the lip of the pocket and I was slowly deposited inside.

"Are you sure this is a good idea?" I asked as he started to move.

"I think we'll be okay," he said before smiling down from his

128

terribly awkward and humiliating angle. "I'll keep you safe."

I blinked and faced forward. After he realized I wasn't going to answer him, Brindt turned forward and all I could see was the underside of his jaw. I could see the beginnings of scruff, reminding me that despite his demeanor, we were only two years apart. And despite how he treated me like a personal belonging sometimes, I could tell that he genuinely cared and I would be safe while we were out. A strange warm feeling bubbled up as he walked, but all I could think about were his words.

He was interested in Wyatt because I was.

It didn't make sense.

***

"What's so great about the Targeter?" Brindt asked when we were settled. He was right about one thing. Because of the weather, no one was at the park that day. He parked his bike under the gazebo. I felt relieved because under the wooden canopy we were out in the open, but still alone. It was great not to see other giants roaming around because I still wasn't sure how I would react to them. Brindt was kind, but were all giants?

Would they pet me? Grab me or try to take me away from Brindt?

"Lyris? Did you hear me?"

"Why are your ears pointed again?" I was still desperate to avoid the topic of Wyatt. I didn't know why, but it still stung so much to be betrayed by him.

"My ears?" He reached up to touch his own. I smirked from the railing and looked up at him. From there, I was only down to his chest level so I didn't feel nearly as small and it was hard not to giggle as he tried to figure out what I was talking about. He looked down with red cheeks. "Aren't your ears pointed?"

"No," I said. "We talked about this a few days ago. Or at least we tried to." I pushed some of my hair aside so he could see my ears. "Remember? Mine are round at the top and yours are pointed." My breath hitched as Brindt leaned in for a closer look. "Uh..." I took a step back to give myself some room from his incoming face.

"S-sorry," he muttered as he pulled away. "I just wanted a closer look. They're so small."

"Maybe you're just so big."

He smiled. "Maybe."

"But seriously, why are they pointed?"

"Why are yours rounded?"

I flinched before laughing. "Touché. I don't really know."

His eyes were still focused on the side of my head. "Would you mind, though?" Brindt asked next.

"Would I mind, what?"

"Could I please maybe... take a closer look?"

As I took another step back I wobbled on the damp wood and Brindt's eyes flashed with worry. "Don't worry, I'm okay," I promised him. "I swear, I'm actually quite steady on my feet." I started to laugh, but Brindt was still focused. "You were serious?" I asked. "I thought we already looked at each other's ears."

"I asked permission, at least." He lowered his voice a bit as he started to come closer. "That has to be better than just doing it."

"You wouldn't, though."

"I could."

"But you wouldn't," I said, surprised at how sure of myself I

130

sounded.

Brindt arched a brow. "How can you be so sure?" he asked as he lifted his hand and brought it towards me.

"Because you're not like that."

His expression softened as his fingers curled. "I thought you were scared of me," Brindt said. He brought his hand even closer and warmth radiated from his skin along with the familiar scent of citrus and spice. I think it was starmelon. "Aren't you?"

"Not as much," I admitted. I wished he had heard my speech from earlier. That would have hopefully made the moment a whole lot less awkward, but I doubted it. "You're like me... only bigger."

"So you're like me, only smaller," Brindt reasoned back. His fingers outstretched. "Uh... hold still," he warned quietly. "I'm still not very good at this."

I sucked in a gasp and pinched my eyes shut. "I'll let you know if I'm freaked out."

Brindt didn't answer right away and for a moment I thought maybe he had changed his mind about touching me, but then something brushed against my temple. I gasped in surprise and the feeling went away.

"It's okay," I said. I still kept my eyes closed. "Just surprised me."

"You're okay?"

I nodded. "It's okay. I'm okay. You're fine."

"Alright..." His voice fell into silence as his hand approached again.

The only way I could tell his hand was still coming was the warmth because I refused to open my eyes. It was just too much to

131

handle, but there was something about Brindt which made it almost tolerable. I didn't gasp as his fingers brushed against my hair and started to push it aside to reveal my ear to him. The rainy air was cool against the newly exposed skin and I tried to focus on the pattering of rain outside the gazebo so my eyes wouldn't water under such careful attention. Something grazed the top of my ear and sloppily dragged all the way down to my neck and then back again.

"Now I remember," Brindt said in a hushed voice. His face was so close that I swore his breath moved my hair. The all too familiar scent of spice and citrus was almost overpowering. "They're different."

"But it's not a bad thing." I kept my eyes closed.

"No," he said immediately. His voice was still low. "It's not bad at all, actually."

The warmth pulled away from my ears and I was finally able to open my eyes. It was strange, but Brindt still wore that soft expression on his face.

"What's with you today?" I asked, still surprised at how gentle he could be.

He tilted his head. "What do you mean?"

"You're being so nice to me."

"I'm just happy because you're finally talking to me again. Like *really* talking to me."

"*Really* talking to you?" I asked as I tilted my head. "How else was I talking to you?"

"You were talking through me," Brindt said without hesitation. "I would say something and you would respond, but it was always so hollow. I just..." he choked out an embarrassed laugh, "... I guess I'm still getting used to the idea of someone being frightened of me." His eyes flickered down to mine. "It's weird being seen as a monster."

"Oh." I lowered my head, but I didn't correct him. I had tried to tell him that he wasn't a monster, but my voice was so small that it didn't even reach his ears from across a room. I didn't feel like saying it twice. Maybe it was a good time to bring up something else. "Brindt... you know I have a home, right? Back through the portal?"

He looked surprised by the change of subject, but quickly tried to compose himself. "I know."

"I have a life. I have friends. Family. My mom and dad are probably missing me like crazy. They probably called the cops."

"Your kind has a law enforcement?"

"Yes," I said in an exasperated tone. "We have all of that. Think of it this way. Most of what you have in your world, I'll bet we have in ours. And I miss it, Brindt. I miss home. I want to go—"

"Do you miss the Targeter?" he blurted out before I could get in my last word.

"Who? Wyatt?"

He nodded. "Yes. Do you miss him too?"

"I..." I looked away, "... hell, I don't know. I don't know how I feel about Wyatt right now. I need to hear his explanation."

"What can there be to explain? I told you he's the Targeter. If he wanted to bring you here, he obviously wanted to give you to my mom." He frowned. "To be someone's pet to a monster."

"That's just how he used to feel." I wasn't really sure why I was defending him. I guess I felt that I had to defend all people over giants or I would feel like I was betraying my entire race. "I'm pretty sure he changed his mind after he got to know me."

133

"Why do you think he did that?"

"Didn't your opinion of me change after you got to know me?" I snapped. "You certainly seem to have trouble seeing me as a pet sometimes, even when I'm wearing a collar."

"You're only wearing the collar so we can talk."

"So I'm only wearing this so we can talk? You wouldn't make me wear it otherwise?"

"That's exactly what I'm saying."

I frowned. "I just need to talk to him," I said. "I'm sure there's a good explanation for all of this. Maybe I can even talk him out of it."

"He's the Targeter, Lyris. It doesn't work that way."

"How do you know?"

"I just know. He..." Brindt looked away, "... he betrayed you, Lyris. How can you even want to talk to him?"

"He didn't betray me."

"Because you didn't give him the chance to."

"He changed his mind."

"Temporarily. If he hadn't it would have been too late."

"Shut up. The only reason I don't know is because I'm stuck here with you. Serving as your pet."

"You're not my damn pet!" His voice rose so quickly that I stumbled away from him and landed on my butt. It wasn't a big fall, but I could tell that it bothered Brindt. He turned back with that concerned look on his face.

"I'm fine," I said, holding up my hand. "Don't bother."

"I'm sorry—"

"Don't be."

"Lyris, I..." His eyes grew worried as I stood up and leaned heavily on my good leg.

Just because I was healing didn't mean I was 100%. I met his expression with a steely gaze, still angry at him for accusing Wyatt of betraying me... probably because he was right.

"Lyris, I don't see you as my pet."

"How do you see me?"

"I don't know," he said honestly, rubbing the back of his neck. "But getting to know you, talking to you, interacting with you and learning about your home, I just can't think of you that way. It seems..." he shuddered for effect, "... wrong."

"So let me go—"

"But I do know this," he said firmly. His voice carried over mine with such ease that I closed my mouth without thinking so he could get out what he wanted to say. "I know that hearing about this Wyatt guy makes me mad. I don't like to think about how he betrayed you and I don't like hearing that you don't think you're pretty or whatever. It really pisses me off for some reason."

"He didn't betray me."

"I would never betray you," Brindt spoke over me again.

"That's because I'm your—"

"The Targeter betrays your kind, Lyris. Haven't you realized that, yet? He collects people and he brings them to our world. Yes, they're pets and yes that's wrong, but the Targeter is a major part of it. He's not excluded because he's an Insignificant. He knows what's happening and he still does it. And he was going to do it to you. He betrayed you and if someone you were dating betrayed you then I bet there are other people in your world who would do the same. And that pisses me off."

"You don't know what Wyatt would have done." My voice trembled.

"Wyatt – the Targeter – whatever you want to call him," Brindt said, flushed with emotion. "He betrayed you. He wanted to sell you to my mom so she could sell you to the highest bidder. You said you're seventeen, right?" I nodded. "Well, that's a good age here. Buyers and sellers love teenagers. It's the perfect age."

Seventeen is the perfect age.

Wyatt's words rang heavily in my ears and my eyes started to water. "That has nothing to do with Wyatt," I croaked.

"I'll bet." Brindt snorted. "Your world sounds horrible if it has people who would betray their own kind for money. How could he look at you when he wanted to bring you here? How could he date you while wanting to bring you here?"

"So you're admitting your world is terrible?" I said, trying to hurt him.

"After seeing the way you look at me, I guess it is," Brindt shot back, silencing me. "If your world has people in it like Wyatt who would betray you like that, I don't know why you would want to go back. If your world has people in it who can't see how pretty you are, I don't know why you would want to go back. Lyris, your world sounds disgusting."

My lower lip trembled. "It's not that bad," I said, trying not to cry. "I love my life. I miss it—"

"You miss being betrayed? You miss being around people who would sell you out?"

"It's better than being around someone like you!" I said as a tear escaped my eye. "It's not so bad! I miss my home! I want to go home! Don't you get it? I don't want to be here with you! I don't like you! You're a monster and the only reason I'm tolerating you is so that when leg gets better and I can run away and go back home—" I stopped and immediately realized that I had said too much. Brindt looked down as I cursed myself through my tears.

"Is... is that true?" Brindt asked, frowning deeply. "It's so bad that you would run away? You wouldn't even ask—"

"What do you think I've been trying to do the whole time?" I asked, tears streaming openly down my face.

"This is the first I've heard of it," Brindt said. "I didn't know it was so bad for you that you couldn't even talk to me about it."

"That's not it," I said. "You called my world disgusting—"

"Because it is."

"It's not! You're disgusting. You stupid, overgrown, ugly giant, monster!" I could barely see Brindt through my tears, but I struck a nerve because for once, he was the one who had fallen silent. I sniffed loudly and tried to calm my crying. "I didn't mean that," I started, trying to remember that it wasn't exactly Brindt's fault.

"I never once betrayed your trust," Brindt said. "In fact, I've built trust when you were the one who broke it. You betrayed me. Just like your people do to each other."

"It was to save myself."

"I've never hurt you. I've done everything I could to learn more about you... to the point where I knew you'd be pissed. But I've tried."

"I know you have—"

137

"And yet you still look at me like I'm some monster. You're still so afraid of me."

"I'm not. I—" Brindt lifted up his hand and instinctively I flinched and backed away. His hand lowered.

"See what I mean?"

"Brindt, I'm sorry. I didn't mean it."

"You weren't planning to run away?"

I flinched. "That part's true."

"Ask me."

I glanced up and wiped my nose and eyes with the back of my sleeve like a lost and frightened child. "What?"

"Ask me what you were afraid to ask me earlier."

"Huh?"

"Ask me if you can go home!"

I flinched. "Really?"

"You're so frightened of the answer to a question you never even bothered to ask. Ask me."

I clenched my hands into fists, annoyed because Brindt had a point. Not once had I tried to ask him about going home again – not seriously, at least. I was so convinced that it wasn't an option that I had written off Brindt so easily. I actually felt a little bad about lumping him with other giants who I had never even met. "Brindt, can I please go home?"

"I think you're making a mistake."

138

"What?" I shouted as I started to lose my cool. "You said I could just ask you—"

"Let me finish," he said, holding up his hand. I didn't flinch back. "I think you're making a mistake. Your world sounds like a weird place – even though you say it's so similar to mine. You want to go back to a place that doesn't appreciate how cute you are. You're going back to a place which sounds like it's filled with guys who would betray you. I never would."

"Brindt..." I said slowly. "It's not about that. I know you wouldn't ever betray me—"

"Do you?"

I swallowed hard. "Y-yes," I stuttered. "I know that now."

"But you're still miserable," Brindt went on. "I don't want to be a part of that. I like having you around, but not if you're going to look at me like that all the time. If you really can't get over feeling like a pet here – with me – then I won't keep you here against your will. I'm... I'm not a monster, dammit."

"Brindt, I know—"

"You can go home."

My face contorted. "You're serious? Are you being serious, Brindt? Just like that?"

He nodded. "Just like that. I don't want you to feel trapped here. To be honest, I just wanted to learn a little more about your kind. I haven't had the chance since..." His words hung in the air a moment before he continued, "I wanted an Insignificant of my own for a few days so I could learn more about them. I certainly didn't want to get too attached again. And I really didn't want to find out how similar we actually were."

"So you wanted proof that humans can be like pets." The words were like acid against my lips.

139

"Yeah," Brindt said. "And I just wanted something of my own for a little while. I wanted something to take care of. But you don't need that from me." He laughed. "You don't even like me."

"That's not true, Brindt."

"And it's okay," he interrupted. "I think I finally get it. Because of you, I finally get how your kind sees us. I guess we would be monsters in your eyes." He shook his head.

"But you don't want to be a monster," I reminded him. "It drives you nuts."

"I thought maybe I could be different when I started to get to know you," Brindt said. "But I guess it's all the same with your kind. We're... we're monsters."

"Brindt, that's not fair," I stuttered. "I didn't say any of that."

"Come on," he said. "Let's just go home."

"Brindt, let me say something—"

"Just do me one favor." He scooped his hand around me.

"What?" I asked, growing exasperated because he kept talking over me. "What is it?"

"Can you promise to stay until your leg's healed? I'd feel better knowing you're going back to your world healthy."

"I'm fine. I can take care of myself—"

"Please? Please, Lyris?"

I was brought closer to his face and in that moment I realized that not only was Brindt not a monster, but he was a good person. He was kind and sweet and he tried his best not to see me as what had been drilled into his brain for most of his life. Despite everything his

140

race believed and had done to my race, Brindt deserved more than what I was giving him. Words bubbled in my throat.

An apology.

A compliment.

An admission of a feeling I didn't quite know how to place.

"Please, Lyris?" Brindt asked a second time.

His voice shattered any concentration I had about saying any of those things. "I'll stay until my leg heals."

"Promise?" His face was too hopeful and cute for his own good.

I nodded. "I promise."

The look on his face instilled more complicated feelings.

Despite my fear of him and hatred of his world... I trusted him.

**

I expected Brindt to be in a bad mood as he cycled back home, but his mood was surprisingly light – almost as if he expected me to change my mind and stay with him.

"There are places where your kind are treated well," he said through the rain as he pedaled. "You wouldn't have to just stay hidden away or ashamed."

"I'm not ashamed," I said. "Brindt, you're missing the point."

"So what is the point? You think I wouldn't stand up for you? That I wouldn't protect you?"

"It's not about that," I said, looking down into the depths of his pocket. A few scattered crumbs were at my feet and I kicked them away, despite losing some of my footing. I didn't want to talk about staying, especially not from this angle, but Brindt seemed to grow chattier as the rain slowed up.

"We could travel," he said, growing excited. "It wouldn't cost you anything to travel, you know. You could see my entire world and then you could decide if you wanted to stay. You don't have to go back just because your leg is healed."

"That's what I'm doing, Brindt," I said. "I want to go home and you promised."

"I'm just saying," he continued on with a shrug. "We could do so much more—oh crap."

I looked up. "What is it?"

He was still staring straight ahead, and his bike came to an abrupt stop. "My mom's home."

"So?"

"She's not usually home around this time..." He seemed to be thinking something over and I started to stand in the pocket so I could look at what had his attention. He glanced down after I moved. "My mom usually works all day unless there's..."

"A what?"

"A delivery," he said softly.

"Wyatt?" My face grew a little excited. "Well, that's good then! Let's go!"

"No," Brindt said. He remained still in the parking lot.

"What? Why not?"

"Because if my mom sees you, she'll take you away from

142

me." He frowned.

"Why would she care so much?"

"Because of your hair. We should just wait here until she leaves. She'll go back to work." He checked his watch. "Yeah... it's still pretty early in the day. She'll go back and then we can..." he trailed off as a door opened and a small, chubby woman waddled out from the door. Even as a giant, I could tell she was short and Brindt winced openly when the woman turned in his direction.

"Brindt!" she shouted. "Brindt, is that you?"

His eyes widened and he glanced around, trying to pretend that it wasn't him, but the woman wasn't stupid and took several steps towards him.

"Brindt, what are you doing out here? The weather's terrible. Come here!"

"Crap," Brindt whispered, looking in my direction. "You have to hide. She can't find you. Oh... she can't find you. She'll take you away."

"So I'll hide." I started to duck back into the pocket.

"Brindt!"

"No," Brindt hushed down to me. "She'll know. She has a sixth sense about your kind." He shook his head. "You'll have to wait here."

"Huh?" My face blanched. "You think she won't notice if you reach in here and put me down on the ground?"

"Now, Brindt!"

"You're right," Brindt said. "Oh..." His face grew more worried. "We'll just have to hope she doesn't see you. Duck down. Don't move. Don't do anything. Don't even breathe too loudly if you can help it, Lyris."

"I'm sure it's not a big deal..."

"Brindt Elinas, if you don't come over here right now—"

"I'm coming!" Brindt shouted loudly. I ducked deep into the pocket and held my ears as he started to walk. "Please, Lyris. Please don't let her find out about you. If you only knew what she would do if she saw your..." His voice trailed off to a whisper.

"As if I'd want to be with another giant..."

"Shhh, please," Brindt hissed. "I don't want to lose you." He pat the pocket and I pressed up against his chest and froze as that woman's voice filled the air.

"Why didn't you come when I called, Brindt?" Her voice was low and raspy and I wondered what kind of emotion it stirred in other people. I knew I was getting the chills because here was the woman who trapped and sold people.

With Wyatt's help.

I tried not to think about that part.

As the two talked, I wondered how long it took Wyatt to bring a new shipment of people. Did he try to bring more than one at a time? How did he convince people to go with him to that house? How did it work once they were here? Did Brindt's mom grab them up in her fist and just throw them in the cage?

I swallowed as more questions bubbled.

Did Wyatt wonder about me?

Did Wyatt ask about me?

Did he even care that I was gone?

"What are you doing out in the rain anyway? It's freezing. I won't have you getting sick over break. If you're upset about camp—"

"It's not that cold, mom," Brindt huffed. "Seriously, I was just heading back to the house."

"Why did you leave in the first place?"

"I wanted to go for a bike ride."

"In the middle of a storm?"

"It's barely thundering," Brindt said back. "Mom, please. Aren't you late for work?"

"I'm going..." she trailed off and I could almost picture her skeptical face.

Brindt's heart rate picked up and thundered in my ears. I tried not to move.

"The Targeter boy mentioned something to me today."

"Oh?" Brindt's heart pounded loudly. The temperature rose in the pocket. "I didn't know today was a delivery day."

"Just one," she said offhandedly. "Some girl. Another young one. Not with red hair, though. You know the red heads are the best. This one's not very pretty, but I'm going to sell her separately – see what kind of price she can fetch."

"Okay?" Brindt said, shifting a bit. "What does that have to do with me?"

"He asked me if one had slipped through the portal without him," she said. More loud pounding. I resisted the urge to cover my ears. "He wouldn't give me any details, but he asked if another Insignificant had arrived that he hadn't been credited for."

"You know I don't know anything about that."

"I know you're interested, Brindt," his mother continued. "And you know how I feel about you owning one of those things."

"Y-yes." I sensed worry in his voice, but I wasn't exactly sure why.

"After your accident a few years ago, I just don't think you can handle—"

"Mom, stop. I don't know anything about another person coming into the house, okay?"

"Person?"

"Insignificant," he quickly clarified.

My heart raced. Accident? What accident? I swallowed my worries and tried to focus on just staying still.

"Did he mention anything about the one who might have slipped in?" Brindt asked. His voice sounded desperate to change the subject.

"He just wants his money," she huffed. "Greedy little rats, those things are. He'll be lucky if I pay him anything next time if he keeps bringing dark haired girls."

"Then he'll stop bringing anyone," Brindt said. "He's the reason..."

"I'm sure another greedy being like him will come through who's much more reasonable. I swear, if he could have just found that redhead."

"Mom, I should go back inside before it starts raining again. And you should go back to work."

"Yes, I should."

146

We were almost home free, but my mind still raced not only with questions about Wyatt, but worries about him. And Brindt! The accident. What the hell happened that he was so desperate for me not to hear?

"Brindt, I don't want you getting close to one of those things again. What happened—"

"That was years ago! Dammit, mom. Can you just let it go?"

"If I find out you're taking what isn't yours—"

"I'm not. Please. Can I go now?" As if nature herself was bailing us out, a loud rumble of thunder sounded overhead with a flash of lightening. I pressed myself closer to Brindt's chest and he jumped slightly in surprise.

"Since when are you scared of storms?" his mother asked.

"I'm not."

"Huh."

I sucked in a breath and hoped that my reaction wouldn't be our demise, but it seemed Brindt's mom was finally moving away from him. Loud clacking came from below and her voice sounded more distant when she spoke for the last time.

"I'll be checking your room later, Brindt. So if you have something you shouldn't have, I would suggest you get rid of it now. I have a spare cage in the bathroom closet. If you give up whatever you have, then I won't punish you for taking it."

I only started to relax when a car started in the distance and Brindt's entire body slouched as though he had been holding his breath the entire time. He started to walk and after a few moments, something pressed against my back and I was even closer to him. My face flushed with embarrassment, but I was still too frightened to scream.

"She's gone," Brindt said, his voice coming out as a sigh of relief. "We're good." Doors opened and closed around us and his hand left my back. "You did great. You had me worried for a moment when you jumped at the thunder. You're not scared of storms, are you?"

"No," I said, keeping my voice low. "I was just surprised, is all."

"At least you jumped at a good time. Otherwise my mom would have read right through it."

"I wasn't the one who jumped," I reminded him.

"Right, right." He shifted slightly. "It still surprised me."

"What was she talking about earlier, Brindt?" I asked. He froze up as another door opened and was closed and I rocked against his body. The temperature rose to uncomfortable levels. His heart started to pound. I assumed we were back in his house. "About the accident? What was that about?"

"It's nothing," he said. He shifted and before I could react, fingers slid into the lip of the pocket and pulled me out. "My mom just worries too much. It's nothing."

"If it's nothing, then it wouldn't be a big deal to talk about it," I said. "Come on. What's up?"

"I told you, it's nothing," he snapped back. "Seriously, it was years ago!"

"What was years ago?"

"Nothing!" His voice grew angry as he started to stride through the house and various rooms and furniture flew past at such a speed that I couldn't even comprehend it.

"W-wait, wait!" I shouted at him. "Stop!"

148

"What?" he hissed. When I flinched in his hand, his features visibly softened. "I mean... what is it?"

"Do we have to go back to your bedroom?"

"What does it matter?" His voice and face hinted at exasperation. Something was up.

"Your mom just went back to work, right?" He nodded. "So why can't we do something else?"

"Because it's too dangerous," Brindt said as he started to walk. I glanced over the bottom of his hand as a blue light under the crack of a door caught my attention.

"So that's where we're kept," I whispered.

Brindt stopped in front of the door. "You'll never be kept in there," he said. "You belong to me."

"I don't belong to anyone," I hissed. "How can you just walk past that room every day and know that there are people in there just like me? Didn't you hear your mom? The Targeter brought another girl with him today."

"Yeah." Brindt snorted and looked down at the knob. "Maybe he betrayed her too. Your Wyatt guy sounds like a real winner."

"We don't know if it was Wyatt."

"The Targeter is Wyatt," Brindt said patiently, as though talking to a child.

"So there can't be any other Targeters?"

"Not at that portal."

I frowned and let him win that round. "You didn't answer my question."

"I didn't know you were asking one."

"How the hell can you walk past this door everyday knowing what's inside? How can you not think about how terrible it is that there are people just like me in cages who are being sold off?"

"Because they're not you," he said.

I flinched. "It could have easily been me."

"It's not."

"It still could be."

"But it's not!" Brindt said, growing angry. "I won't let her take you away from me. You're mine." He shook his head as though trying to work something through. "It bothers me more now, okay? Are you happy?"

"What bothers you?"

He groaned. "That the people in there have lives, friends, family... a life, as you said. I haven't thought about it in a long time, but since I met you, I think about it more. Maybe this isn't good for them. Yes, there's a chance things could work out great—"

"How can this be great?" I grumbled.

"Gee, let me think. Everything's provided for you, you don't have to work, you'd be safe and sometimes you'd end up with someone who would kill for you, who would die for you."

"As a pet." I was hardly moved when he got all white knight on me.

"You're impossible," Brindt said. "But yeah, like I said. Now that I've gotten to know you, it's harder to think about, okay? I'm not as comfortable as I was about what's behind that door as I used to be. Are you happy now?"

"No, not really," I snapped. "What was the accident?"

"You're still on about that? Seriously, Lyris, let it go."

He started to walk again and I jerked my head away from him. I hated it when he treated me like a child. Just because he was bigger he thought he could keep secrets and pamper me like some exotic dog. As I fumed in his hand, I wondered how hard it would be to free the others behind that door who had met the same fate as me. I wondered how many portals existed.

And then I wondered about the oddly familiar shape which caught my eye under the crack of the door.

"What the hell..." I trailed off as the shape shifted on the floor and emerged into the hallway.

Dark hair.

A slender, but masculine shape.

A familiar face.

Wyatt.

My eyes widened as I realized who I was looking at. Quickly, I glanced up at Brindt to see if he felt my reaction, but he was still focused on unlocking the door to his room. I turned back to the floor and realized Wyatt was staring up at him. I stole another quick glance at Brindt as the door opened and then turned back to Wyatt.

He waved.

I didn't know whether to feel relieved or pissed off, but I didn't even have a chance to respond as Brindt opened the door and walked inside. The door closed and locked again... along with any chance I had to figure out what Wyatt was doing here and what his wave meant.

Twelve

Thankfully, Brindt's mom didn't stay true to her promise about searching his room. It was almost a shame because Brindt had spent most of the afternoon preparing for it. From my spot on the bed, all I could do was stare at the spot under the door of his bedroom, and wonder if Wyatt would fill it.

Had he come to save me?

Had he come to check on me?

Or was he simply confirming that I was here so he could claim is pay?

The last option wasn't nearly as appealing, but I didn't really have to dwell on it. All through the afternoon and evening, Wyatt didn't reveal himself and other than a knock on Brindt's door to let him know dinner was ready, I didn't see the mom either. I was relieved, but still on edge when Brindt appeared late in the evening with a plate of food.

"Don't you ever eat meat?" I asked as I took in a large mouthful of some root vegetable. The taste was similar to a potato, but the flavor was smoky, almost spicy. "I mean, don't get me wrong the fruits and veggies are alright, but don't you ever want a burger?"

Brindt arched a brow and glanced over. "A burger?" he repeated. "What's that?"

"It's... it's a burger!" I huffed. "Cow? Meat? Two buns? A patty?" His confused expression almost was comical. "What about steak?"

He shook his head.

"Pork? Bacon?"

Another confused look.

"Anything?"

"Are you talking about animals?" he asked. He finally seemed to piece it together.

"Yes!" I exclaimed. "I'm sure you have animals here."

"Sure."

"Good."

"But we don't eat them."

"What?" I tilted my head and stood up straight with a large piece of the root vegetable between my hands. "You don't eat meat?"

"Animals? No... you... we don't eat animals. You don't eat animals, Lyris."

"Of course you do!" I couldn't hide my shock. "So let me get this straight. You're a giant, but you don't eat meat?"

"We don't eat animals, Lyris." He shuddered at the thought. "Gross."

"That's incredible." I smiled as I took my seat. "Giants. Vegetarian giants. And here I was worried about you eating me."

"What?" Brindt exclaimed. He dropped his colored pencil. "Did you just say you were worried I'd eat you?"

"Yeah!"

"Where would you get an awful idea like that?"

"It's in the stories. Giants grinding our bones to make bread and stuff." Brindt's face looked genuinely shocked and I tried not to laugh. "What? You never heard that before?"

"I haven't," he said, scrunching up his nose. "I never even

153

thought... well damn. No wonder your people are so scared."

"I'm sure it has nothing to do with being kept in cages."

"But, seriously? Eat you? Eat animals? Of all the crazy stuff you've said, that might be the worst by far." He turned back to his paper and started to return to his shading, still muttering. "Eating people... bizarre."

I shook my head and still tried to wrap my head around the idea that giants didn't eat meat. It was almost too weird to think about. My eyes trailed over to the door, wondering if Wyatt was still looking for me. If he cared.

"You've been looking there a lot," Brindt said, still focused on his work. "Expecting someone?"

I flushed with embarrassment of being caught. "No. I'm just worried about your mom."

"Don't worry about her. I'm sure she's occupied for the rest of the night."

"Occupied?"

"With the new Insignificant—er, little person."

He continued to sketch as though the idea of his mother hovering over a person didn't bother him, but I quickly polished off my dinner and strode to the edge of the bed.

"What?" he asked.

"What does she do with them?"

"I don't know," Brindt said, trying to focus on his sketch. His hand movements were surprisingly eloquent when he was focused on art. "I just know she'll be busy." He shrugged. "And before you ask me, yes... it's on my mind, too. It didn't used to be."

154

"What are you thinking about?"

He inhaled and exhaled and a flash of red went across his cheeks. "I wonder if the new girl is anything like you. I wonder how things would be different right now if I had found her instead of you."

"Different than what?" I asked quietly.

His cheeks grew redder. "Nothing."

I decided to let it go. "How long are you going to do that?"

"What?"

"The drawing. Are you going to be a while?"

"Why? Do you want to do something else?" He seemed dumbfounded as he set down his pencil. "Usually, you don't care."

"I have a lot on my mind," I admitted. "I wouldn't mind a little distraction."

"Do you want to talk about it?" he tried carefully.

"Only if you're willing to tell me about the accident," I said.

His expression darkened. "I'm not."

"Then I'm not, either."

He started to chew on his lower lip and glanced around his room, before his expression lightened again. "We could watch a movie," he said with a shrug.

"You have movies?"

"Of course," he said, chuckling at the idea. "I thought you were the one who said our worlds are similar."

"And they are! I just didn't think..."

"Well, I guess we could find out if our movies are similar," he went on. "Do you have scary movies back home?"

"Of course!" I said, beaming. "Those are some of my favorites."

"Mine too. Our movies are pretty scary here," Brindt said. He pushed aside his paper and pencil so he could rest his arms on the desk table. His chin settled on top of his arms. "You might not be able to handle it."

"Anything you can handle, I'm sure I can too."

"I doubt it."

"Bring it on."

"Fine," Brindt said, smiling wide as he reached ahead. I gasped loudly as his hand quickly grasped around my frame, but it didn't bother me as much as it used to. He walked to another part of his room, mulling quietly. "I have to warn you, Lyris. I have some messed up tastes. Are you sure this is something you want to try?"

"Do your worst," I said as he reached for a case. It was actually closer to something resembling a VHS tape, and I wondered if they worked the same. "Wait..."

"What?"

"Your movies aren't about torturing people or anything like that, are they?"

"I thought you said I should do my worst – oh, you mean *your* people, right?" I nodded. "No... I don't have anything like that, but I'm pretty sure they exist. But *Chasing Girls to Death* won't be like that. It doesn't even have Insignificants in it." He shot me a look. "That make you feel better?"

156

"With a room filled with people trapped in cages waiting to be sold next door? Not really," I said. "But I'm still willing to give your movie a fair chance."

His face changed slightly. "We can talk about that later."

"Talk about what?" I asked, looking up at him. He was already focused on another task. "Brindt? Talk about what?"

"Get ready to be scared," Brindt said instead as he grabbed an oblong black box. He settled on the bed and looked around before giving me one last glance. "Where do you want to sit during this?"

"Just set me on the bed," I said, pointing down at the comforter below me.

"What if you get scared?" he asked, smirking as I settled in.

"Don't make me laugh."

***

Giants' horror movies are ten thousands kinds more of 'messedupness' than the horror movies I'd seen back home.

I stared at the screen with a frightened expression as another young woman completely lost her head at the hand of the killer. With a huge, evil grin, he bent over to retrieve the dismembered skull and tossed it into the lake and watched it float with a serene expression. As though he had created art. He turned to the camera, still smiling and it looked as though he was walking right towards me and I leaned back in my seated position before Brindt chuckled.

"I thought you said you could handle horror movies," he said. "I'm not very impressed."

"I'm not trying to impress you," I huffed. I turned away from the screen so I wouldn't have to watch that horrible man heading right at me for a moment longer. "Your special effects are a lot better than the ones back home."

157

"Special effects?" he asked, tilting his head. "What do you mean?"

I froze and my eyes grew wider. "You do use special effects, don't you?" Another confused head tilt. "Those people!" I screamed. I pointed at the screen without looking. "Those aren't real people who died, are they?"

"Why do you think it looks so realistic?" he asked with a cold expression. "You can't get that same effect if you don't use real people."

I swear to God my heart stopped.

"They're just convicts," Brindt continued as though he was describing what a starmelon was. "They were being sentenced to death anyway. Why not use their bodies to make art?"

"Make. Art?" I sucked in a gasp, ready to start screaming, but Brindt's face suddenly lost that stoic look and he burst into laughter. "What?" I growled. "What the hell is so funny?"

"Are you kidding? You thought I was being serious?" He burst into even louder laughter, further infuriating me.

"Wait, you were kidding?"

"Of course I was kidding! Oh man! Convicts? Actually killing people on screen? Are you nuts?" More thunderous laughter came and I wanted to scream. "Lyris, come on. Of course it's special effects. You didn't actually think I was serious?"

I lowered my head.

"Oh, come on Lyris," Brindt said as his laughter started to die down. "You couldn't have actually thought..."

"It wasn't funny. Not at all."

158

"Well, it's your own fault. Geez, you have to stop thinking of us as monsters. We use special effects, okay? It's not a big deal."

"I don't know anything about your stupid world," I said, still angry. "How was I to know?"

"You should know that obviously we wouldn't kill people on screen just to make some tacky horror movie more realistic—"

"It's not tacky to me!"

Brindt narrowed his eyes. "That's just because you're sitting too close," he said in that stupid matter-of-fact tone.

"What?"

"You're sitting so close to the screen and it's already big. I bet it's scarier because of that. Why don't you lean back a little... or even... I dunno," he shrugged, "sit with me?"

"I'm not *sitting* with you."

"Why not?"

My eyes widened and I looked away. I had no idea why I was so embarrassed. "Because!"

"Because why?"

"Because it's weird, dammit!" I shrieked. "You're like... and I'm like... no. Just no."

"Are you worried you'll be too heavy?" A smirk crossed his features and annoyance surged inside of me.

"Are you kidding?"

"Because you're probably fine. I can't imagine you'd be too heavy sitting on me."

159

"That's not it!"

"Come on, I don't mind," Brindt said, leaning forward. "It's not a big deal. You're the one making it that way."

"W-wait, stop!" I yelled. "Brindt!" I held up my hands as his started to curve around and to my relief they stopped before they actually touched my skin.

"What?" he asked, looking a bit huffy. "You're not only scared of a stupid movie, but you're still scared of me? Tell me, what the hell is so bad about me? What am I doing so wrong that you still treat me like I'm going to take you back to that room?" He paused the movie and fixed his blue and teal eyes on mine.

"You're not doing anything wrong," I stammered. "Come on. You know I'm not that scared of you."

"Yeah?" he asked. "Prove it."

"I don't have to prove anything to you." I started to turn away but Brindt's next word was the last one I expected.

"Please?"

Frowning, I turned my chin up to meet his gaze. "You're serious," I said.

"As convict on death row," he said with a smirk. "Come on, I bet the movie will be a lot less scary if you're not sitting so close to the screen."

"But then I'll have to be close to you."

"Anything but that," Brindt said, no longer asking permission and scooping me up into his hands.

I lost my breath for a moment, but before I even had a chance to gather my strength to yell at him, I was deposited on his shoulder.

160

"See? No big deal."

"But—"

"Watch the movie, Lyris."

I fell silent as Brindt un-paused the movie and I lost myself in the screen. I had to admit he was right. The movie was much less scary hovering above the screen and not directly in front of it. From there, I could smirk at the characters and I finally understood what Brindt was talking about when he said the movie was cheesy. It was entirely too long and the plot kept dragging on and on – revealing one crazier piece of background information after another.

After almost two more hours the credits were rolling and I leaned back against the headboard behind Brindt.

"Alright, alright," I sighed. "Maybe you were right. It wasn't that scary." When he didn't answer me, I tried again. "Hey, did you hear me? Brindt?" I nudged his neck. "Are you actually asleep?" I dared to smile as his breathing remained slow and steady.

"Oh my God, you're totally sleeping. You big idiot." Affection accidentally laced my tone as I realized that his eyes really were closed. "If you're pretending to be asleep just to freak me out, I would suggest you stop right now, or I'm not going to talk to you," I threatened.

Silence.

"Seriously? You're sleeping?" I don't know why, but I was a little disappointed. It was kind of quiet and lonely without his annoying chipper voice. I mused quietly for a few moments before I decided that waking him up probably wasn't the best decision. Shrugging it off, I leaned against the headboard when I noticed a tiny bit of movement and sat up straighter.

Was his mom coming? Brindt said he locked the door, but what mother didn't have a key to their son's bedroom? I started to duck down behind Brindt's hair when another noise followed. A voice.

"Is he really asleep?"

My eyes widened and I sat up, straining to see over the bed... and towards the floor... right at the crack of Brindt's bedroom door.

"Wyatt?" I whispered.

The person waved and began walking towards Brindt's bed.

Thirteen

"Wyatt!" Relief washed over me as the familiar face appeared over the edge of the bed. He pulled himself up onto the bed.

"Shh!" He hissed loudly as Brindt started to stir.

I quickly settled myself down and tried to carefully move off Brindt's shoulder. "Is it really you?" I asked. "Wyatt?"

"Yessss..." the voice hissed back. "Now be quiet. If he's really asleep, I don't want him to wake up."

I nodded.

"Can you get down from there?" Wyatt asked.

"My leg," I started before I shook my head hard. "I'm gonna try."

"Be careful."

Painstakingly slowly, I began the descent down Brindt's shoulder. He stirred several more times, but to my relief I was able to get down his chest. I crashed softly into his lap and looked back at him, but he only yawned and slid a bit further so he was practically lying down on his back.

Wyatt ran up and embraced me in a hug. It was tighter than it should have been considering the circumstances. However, it was such a relief to be in the arms of someone my height that I hugged him back smiling wide and practically crying.

"Oh my God," I said. "You're here. You're actually here."

"Are you alright?" he asked. He pulled away and held me by the shoulders. He shook me gently. "Are you alright, Lyris?"

"I'm fine," I said, reaching to hug him for a second time. "I just can't believe it. It's so great to see someone my size."

"You're so lucky you don't even know," Wyatt muttered into my hair. "You're lucky the son found you before the hag did. Who knows where you'd be?" He gave another gentle squeeze. "The things I'd have to do to get you back."

I pinched my eyes shut, and held on to him like my life depended on it. As he pulled me away, his eyes fell to my neck.

"You let him collar you?" he asked, touching the stiff material.

"Just so we could talk," I said defensively.

"You shouldn't have done that," he muttered, shaking his head. "Ugh, I suppose it can't be helped. At least he wanted to hear you speak."

"How long have I been gone?" I asked.

"Three weeks and two days," Wyatt said. "Your family's been going crazy. It's only by luck that they don't know me. Otherwise I would have been connected to your disappearance."

"So they don't know about you? You didn't tell them?"

"What would I tell them?" Wyatt asked, pulling away slightly. "You came here despite me specifically telling you not to."

"How was I supposed to know *this* was behind the door? I thought you had some kind of perverted red room, not a portal filled with giants!"

"Lower your voice," Wyatt hissed. He looked past my shoulder towards the bed and shook his head. He reached out and grabbed my wrist. "Lyris, you should know, I didn't want this for you. Not after getting to know you."

"What about before you knew me?" I challenged, suddenly remembering I was supposed to be angry with him. "Was I only approached so you could bring me here? To be sold off as a pet?"

"How much do you know about this world, exactly?" he asked, arching a brow.

"Enough to know you're some sort of human-trafficker," I said in an accusing voice. Brindt stirred behind me, but it wasn't like I was frightened of him like that. If anything, Wyatt was the one who looked worried.

"We should go," he said, going to reach for my wrist.

I snapped away from his grasp. "Seriously, Wyatt, I need to know. Were you planning to sell me after getting me here?"

"I'll tell you everything you need to know once we get back home. We need to go. Now."

"Why would you only show up now?"

"You think I haven't been looking for an opening?" Wyatt tried to grab me again and came up empty. "Are you kidding, Lyris? You think I can just waltz in here, find you and take you home? It takes time!"

"Almost a month?"

"You don't know what it's like!" Wyatt hissed. "Come on. Please, we need to go."

"Are you a human-trafficker or not?"

"I am!" he yelled. More shifting came from Brindt's bed, but Wyatt wasn't looking. His green eyes were locked on mine. Pleading. Begging for understanding. "Alright? I am."

"So the money?"

"I get gold from the kid's mom and I sell it back home, okay? I get paid to do it. Alright? And yes! Yes, I was planning to sell you,

165

but once I got to know you I realized I couldn't do it."

"But you could do it to other people?"

"Yes." He flushed for a moment and started to scuff his sneaker against the hardwood floor. "That's different."

"Why's it different?"

"Because *you're* different, Lyris. Okay? What the hell do you want me to say? I came here to get you. I came to bring you back. I'm risking everything on a girl I've only known for a few days. What the hell does that tell you?"

"That I'm a good kisser?" I tried to hide the fact that I was flattered beyond imagination. I stepped forward. "Seriously though? You came back for me?"

"I'm here, aren't I?" His chin lifted to meet my eyes and he seemed surprised to see that mine had softened. "I'm not gonna say something stupid like I'm in love with you or anything like that."

"Of course not."

"But I do know you're different. I liked you. A lot. I still do." He shook his head and ran a frustrated hand through his messy black mane. "So I came to get you back, but I never imagined the boy taking you—"

"He's not a boy," I said softly. "He's—"

"He's one of them, Lyris. And I've got to get you home. Let's go." He tugged on my arm again.

I faltered and glanced over my shoulder. Brindt was sleeping so peacefully. I couldn't bear to think of how he would react if he woke up and I was gone without a trace – without a warning. Nothing. He would blame himself for my disappearance and wonder what he had done wrong. "I should at least tell Brindt—"

"*What?*" Wyatt hissed. "Tell him what? That you're leaving him? That you're asking permission? Lyris, it doesn't work that way. You need to come. Now."

"He's not like the others," I said, pulling back. "I should just tell him."

"You're wearing a collar from him. He sees you as his."

"So?"

"So?" Wyatt looked exasperated. "We need to go."

"The collar doesn't mean things like that to him."

"We should go before your new owner wakes up," he said drily.

"He's not my owner! He doesn't see me that way!" I tugged back a little more. "Please, just wait. Let me say goodbye. He'll let me go. I promise."

"Not if you're wearing that!" Wyatt hissed and pulled me back to him. I crashed against his chest and before I could let out another sound, his lips pressed against mine and kissed hungrily. I lost myself in the moment as I remembered just how well our kisses came together and I wrapped my arms around his neck. For a few moments there was nothing else. Just us.

We were so lost in our world that we didn't realize we were being watched.

"Lyris?" Brindt's voice sounded cloudy. I felt Wyatt pull away from me as I turned towards the giant. As I looked into his still-sleepy eyes, a sudden soft thump from below announced that Wyatt had reached the floor. At the sound, Brindt's eyes went wide and the sleepiness vanished. "You!" he roared. He stood up to his full height. "The Targeter! What are you doing?" He stood up quickly, casting the comforter aside and nearly knocking me off the bed. He took a few steps toward the sprinting Wyatt, who slid under the door a few seconds later before Brindt reached it.

"What are you doing here?" Brindt shouted in a voice I had never heard before. Ignoring me, he threw the door open and ran down the hall. His steps rumbled and I wondered what the hell was happening and if Wyatt was safe.

"Brindt, no!" I screamed. I slid down the comforter to the floor and limped as quickly as I could to the open doorway.

Out of the corner of my eye, something scrambled under a door – not the blue lit room and Brindt sloppily followed. For a few moments all was silent and I could only watch and listen helplessly, frozen with my fear of Brindt's mom coming out to see what was going on.

"Dammit!" Brindt shouted suddenly.

I jumped with surprise and my heart pounded heavily in my chest as Brindt re-emerged from the room, hair disheveled and pink faced. His eyes searched the floor and when they spotted me, I felt even smaller than I already did and immediately shrunk against the frame, ducking back a bit as his steps pounded towards me.

"You," he growled, storming up to me. His knees crashed right in front of me and his hand came forward at such a speed that I stumbled backwards. Brindt was relentless and scooped me up without permission. My eyes started to water and my stomach fell to my knees as I rose into the air at a dizzying page, possible excuses rattling around in my brain. I had to explain myself. Brindt's loud breathing slowed down and as I peeked out to look at him, he licked his lips.

I was already starting to shake. "I can explain—"

"Are you alright?" Brindt asked. He was still slightly out of breath.

I lowered my hands, surprised by his words.

"Seriously, Lyris," he said, concern still written all over his large features. "Are you okay? Did he hurt you?"

I shook my head, stunned into silence.

He licked his lips. "Good..." He trailed off and frowned before he turned back to me. "What did he want?"

I shook my head, still trying to find my words as I stupidly looked up at him. "I thought you were mad," I said as I finally found my voice.

"I am mad," he growled. "Not at you. At him."

"Why are you mad at him?"

"Why am I mad..." Brindt trailed off. He almost looked too pissed to answer, but instead he shook his head and his face softened. "Seriously, you're okay?"

"I'm fine," I said. "The question is, are you okay?"

"I thought I was going to lose you."

His words brought a frown to my face. "You *are* going to lose me," I said carefully. "Eventually, at least." He turned to me with an annoyed expression. "When my leg's better?" I asked, reminding him of the promise he'd made. The very statement which held together the entire concept of trust between the two of us.

He nodded distractedly. "Oh yeah. That."

"You *are* going to let me go, aren't you?"

"Of course I am!" he said, angry. "I just didn't think..."

"What?"

"I didn't think you'd run to him."

169

"I didn't run to him. He came to me," I explained as Brindt stood up. Possessively, he cradled me close to his chest as he closed the door.

"Thank hell my mom sleeps like she's in a coffin," he said distractedly.

"She does?" I squeaked. I could have gone after them. "Brindt," I said loudly, making sure he could hear me. He turned his chin down, but I could see in his eyes he was still upset for some reason. "I didn't run to him. I wasn't trying to run away—"

"You promise?" he interrupted.

I was surprised by how upset he seemed. I nodded hard. "Yes, I promise. He came to me. He wanted to take me home."

"Why?"

"Because I want to go?" I said, trying to laugh.

"No, I mean, why him? Why did he come back for you? Why now?"

I shook my head, still not completely sure myself. "I don't know, Brindt."

"I saw what he did."

"I'm still here, aren't I?" I asked.

"No, I mean. I saw what he did. To you."

"What are you talking about?" I started to look up, but I realized his cheeks were pink and his eyes wouldn't meet mine. If I didn't know better, he looked down right mortified. "What is it?" I asked.

"He... he kissed you."

"So what?" I retorted. "What does that have to do with anything?"

"It just..." He shrugged it off, seemingly fighting some inner turmoil.

"Did it weird you out or something? Two people my size kissing?"

"That's not it."

"Were you disgusted?"

"No! I mean... I don't know." He shrugged his shoulders. "I don't know, Lyris."

"Well, then if you don't know, there's nothing to talk about. Let it go. I kept my promise, I'm still here. I didn't leave, did I?"

"You will."

"When my leg is completely healed, yes."

"And you forgive that guy? The Targeter?"

I flushed and remembered the kiss. "What does that have to do with anything?"

He seemed annoyed and flustered at the same time. "I don't know. You just always make me feel like I'm going to eat you or something, but this guy wanted to sell you out and suddenly you're kissing him." He frowned. "Insignificants don't make sense."

My eyes widened. That word angered me beyond anything else and yet Brindt had said it – *yet again* – in front of me. "What did you call me?" I asked in a challenging voice.

"Well, you don't!" he grumbled, not apologizing. "I don't understand how you can kiss some guy—"

171

"First off, junior, he kissed me. I didn't kiss him."

"You didn't stop him."

"So what? He said he was sorry and I believe him. He warned me not to come to this world without him. I should have listened."

"So all is forgiven?"

"That's none of your business, Brindt!"

"Yes it is!"

"Why?"

"Because you're mine, Lyris! You belong to me!" The words tumbled out from his sloppy mouth before he had the chance to censor himself and I could tell he was worried he had gone too far. "I don't mean it like that, Lyris—"

"I don't belong to anyone, Brindt," I said, keeping my voice low and patient when actually I was seething. "I've told you that over and over again."

"I know."

"And I've also told you to never call me that word. Ever."

"I know."

"And yet here we are."

"And yet here we are," Brindt repeated. "I do everything I can to make things comfortable for you, and you treat me like a monster while this other little person shows up and you'll forgive him just because he's the same size as you. Does size really matter that much? You're willing to forgive everything he did to you—"

"He didn't do anything."

172

"Are you freaking kidding me right now? He would have if he didn't think you were so great after getting to know you."

"But he did."

"So he's the only one who can think you're great?" he snapped.

"What the hell are you talking about?"

"Nothing. Never mind." He maneuvered himself on the bed with a frown and started to lay down. "Can I trust you to sleep on my pillow like you usually do, or am I going to wake up tomorrow and you're gone?"

"I keep my promises," I said, still seething, "but you're being weird."

"No. You're just being impossible." He sloppily deposited me on the pillow next to his and turned his face away.

"Are we seriously not going to talk about this?"

"I have nothing else to say to you," Brindt huffed. "Go to sleep."

"Come on, Brindt. Don't be a baby."

"I'm not being a damn baby!" Violently, he sat up and hovered over me. He pressed each of his large hands on either side of me and I gasped and looked up at him. I felt lowly and helpless as his face contorted. "Seriously, just go to sleep. You don't understand. You can't understand. I don't even understand myself—"

"Understand what? What are you talking about?" I looked up at him with wide eyes, pleading with him to talk even as his fingers dangerously twitched on either side of me. I was frightened, but I didn't dare say it. Brindt seemed confused and vulnerable for some reason and whatever was eating him up inside, he clearly didn't want to talk about it.

His face crumbled and his hands lifted as he pulled away. "Just go to sleep. I believe you when you say you won't run away until your leg's healed, so for now... can we please just go to sleep?"

"Can we talk about this tomorrow?" He turned away and left me stranded and alone on the other pillow. "Brindt? Please?"

He shrugged. "I don't think it's anything I can talk about."

"Brindt—"

"Good night," he said. He reached over and turned out the light.

Darkness swept over the two of us just like the awkward silence and my lip trembled with anger. "Whatever," I grumbled, settling myself on the pillow. "I didn't do anything wrong."

"You're impossible," he muttered sleepily before his breathing slowed.

It took another few hours before I was able to settle down.

Fourteen

Wyatt didn't return the next day.

Or the one after that.

I kept telling myself that I shouldn't have been surprised. He had said it was difficult enough to find a good time to talk and that had taken almost an entire month. There were so many more things I wanted to ask him before our moment together had come to a screeching halt.

I didn't know when or if he was coming back.

The point was that something held me back from trying to escape that night. And though Wyatt's kiss was amazing and beautiful, I had to wonder what his motivation was behind it. How could I still like someone who sentenced people to a life of being pets for giants? Brindt had a point, though I would rarely admit it. At the end of the day, Wyatt had targeted me. He had all but tossed me through the portal for his payday when a combination of charm and dumb luck had saved me.

I had to wonder how many others had not been as lucky.

Despite Brindt's strange behavior the night Wyatt showed up, it only took a few days for him to get back into his normal routine. I still wore the collar so we could talk, but after I spoke with Wyatt, I started to have reservations about it and how it seemed to affect Brindt. How he seemed to think that it made me his personal belonging.

"How many people are in that blue light room?" I asked my giant captive/friend on a late afternoon. His mom was down the hall working on something so I had to keep my voice down. Brindt actually thought it made more sense for the time being to just talk in his closet. So despite the stupidity of it, I didn't want to be found by his mother so I agreed. We both sat on the floor as he worked to make me another shirt despite my telling him that I didn't need it.

"You need clothes, don't you?" he asked fumbling with a large button over the chest.

"I'm going back soon."

"Just let me do this," he grumbled. He turned back to the needle and fabric.

I had to admit, it was kind of adorable to watch him work. With fingers as thick as my body, he carefully stitched to create a long-sleeved yellow top so I wouldn't freeze while I was there. I shook my head fondly for only a moment before I grew serious.

"How many, Brindt?" I asked again.

"I don't know." His tongue stuck out in concentration. "Twenty? Thirty?"

"And Wyatt brings them all here?" I didn't know why my voice dripped with skepticism, but it was just so hard to picture Wyatt being able to bring people here.

"Wyatt's the Targeter," Brindt said simply.

"Are they all girls?"

I finally caught his attention. "What?"

"The people he brings," I explained. "Are they all girls?"

"Most of them are," he said. "I think there's a few guys close to your age. Maybe even a few younger than me."

"Kids? Wyatt brings kids here?"

"Whatever's in demand," Brindt said. "He's quite a guy, isn't he?"

I frowned. "I'm sure he doesn't fully understand what he's doing."

176

"I'm quite sure he does."

The idea of Wyatt sneaking other girls into Brindt's world was almost as alarming as the idea of him bringing children here. I tried to picture him flirting with girls at the coffee shop just like he had done to me with witty banter and smoldering looks. I had fallen for him so easily and whatever he had done worked because I still couldn't stop myself from defending him to Brindt despite how his words really were starting to sink in.

I couldn't help myself by asking. "You really think he's a bad person?" I kept my tone low.

Brindt stopped working on my sweater momentarily to glance up. "What do you think?"

"I'm serious."

"So am I," Brindt said. "I know in your eyes that I'm not any better, but I wouldn't do that to you." He shook his head. "I don't even see you as a pet, so how could I ever betray you?"

"I never said he's better than you."

"You didn't have to."

"Well, it's true," I said. My voice rose slightly and my cheeks grew hot. "It's true, dammit. You've been nothing but super nice to me and you didn't have to be. I have to wear this stupid collar, but when I'm talking to you I honestly don't even think about it. There are times when I completely forget that we speak different languages because you don't make me feel so... small... so alien, I mean." I lowered my head, embarrassed that I had even said it out loud.

"Hey."

Brindt's voice was soft enough that I almost couldn't catch it so I kept my head lowered. I was convinced that I had once again made a fool of myself. Only instead of a chuckle, Brindt's voice followed.

"Lyris, look at me."

As I lifted my head and our eyes met, it dawned on me just how kind Brindt had been. To my horror I realized that what I felt towards him wasn't just trust. I liked him. I genuinely liked *and* trusted him. I was safe with him.

"You're not small to me," he said, smiling a bit. "Not in the least."

I tried to play it off. "Yeah right."

"I'm serious." His hand started to come towards me, but instead he rested it back in his lap and continued his work on my sweater. I wondered what he would have done if he had kept reaching forward. "I haven't thought of you like a little person in days," he went on.

"Except when you said you didn't understand Insignificants."

"I'm sorry about that," he grumbled. "That's not what I meant."

"What did you mean?"

"Nothing."

His voice grew huffy and needles started to loudly clack against each other as he furiously started to sew again. My face grew thoughtful and I stood up on the carpet with ease, noting that my leg had actually been in good shape since Wyatt left. I didn't point it out to Brindt, but I walked up to him with ease and stretched my hand towards his bent knee. Needles stopped working and my hand froze in the air. My fingers shook and I curled them back into my palm, and chose to look up at him instead. He seemed as surprised as me that I was so close by choice.

"Tell me what you meant when Wyatt came up," I said.

178

"About how you don't understand Insignificants."

"I don't think you're—"

"Brindt," I said firmly. "Tell me what you meant."

He sighed loudly overhead and set the needles and thread next to him on the floor. I watched him closely and waited to see if he would speak on his own, but I obviously was going to have to keep working him in order to find out what was going on in that busy brain of his.

I tried to soften my voice. "What did you mean?"

When he finally turned to look down at me, his eyes were surprisingly tormented.

"What is it?" I asked.

He bit his lower lip. "Are you sure you want to know?"

I froze up. "Is it that serious?" I asked before I could censor myself.

Brindt started to pull away. "Ugh, no. Never mind, it's stupid—"

"No, no, stop Brindt!" I finally reached out to touch him. I tugged on his pant leg and he looked down with astonishment. I pulled back and continued to stare up at him. "S-sorry." I felt embarrassed for grabbing at him like a kid. "I didn't mean—"

He muttered something under his breath.

"What?" I tilted my head to the side.

"Jealous." He kept his voice low.

"Jealous?" I repeated. "What are you talking about?"

"When I said I didn't understand your kind." He lifted his head so I couldn't maintain eye contact. "When I said it that's not how I meant it. I was jealous, okay?"

"Jealous? Of what?" I still didn't understand how the two were connected.

"You really are impossible."

"You've really been saying that a lot lately."

"Because it's true."

"So then help me out. What are you jealous of?" His cheeks grew pink. *What the hell?* It hit like a ton of bricks straight to the face and then straight to the heart. "Oh my God," I murmured. I took a step away from him. "You can't... I mean... it's not..." I glanced up. "You're jealous of Wyatt?"

"Not in the way you think," he said. "I just don't... argh!" He jerked back, stood up, walked to the corner of the closet and sat back down so he didn't have to face me. "It doesn't make sense. You don't get it. I'm not making sense." He pulled his knees up to his chest and hid his face.

"Brindt, I—"

"It's weird, I know." He spoke into his knees. "You're you and I'm me, but I don't understand how else to explain it. I just know how much I hated seeing him kissing you and you just letting him. What else can it be other than jealousy?"

"Because you don't like him?"

"Because you *do* like him."

I stiffened and remained in the opposite corner of the closet. "Brindt, are you actually saying you like me?" His back stiffened just like mine had, but he didn't answer. "Is that why you're jealous?" I could hardly believe I was talking to a giant about Wyatt.

It didn't seem possible. What could he possibly see in me other than a pet?

That's what we were to giants, right? *Right?*

"Brindt..." I trailed off as I took a few steps closer to his massive hunched form. "Answer me."

"No."

"Why?"

"Because it's stupid. Just forget I said anything."

"I can't very well forget now!" I yelled, taking another few steps. "Is that seriously what this is all about? Do you like me? Like actually like me?"

He shrugged.

"Now you're the one who's being impossible," I groaned. I was finally close enough that I could touch him and as I reached out to grab the fabric of his shirt, he jumped. I yelped and took a few quick steps back as he turned around. His eyes were red and puffy and his cheeks matched. They looked sad which just about broke my heart.

"See? It's stupid and it doesn't make sense. Why would I like someone who's scared of me?" He shook his head angrily. "Dammit, I don't even know. I. Don't. Know."

"Brindt—"

"I just don't understand how you can think Wyatt is so great..."

"Brindt—"

"And he does this to people when I've been trying..."

"Brindt—"

"And yet you're still so damn scared—"

"BRINDT!" At the sound of my raised voice, he finally stopped blabbering and glanced down. I straightened my back, took a deep breath and approached his hand resting on the carpet. "I... I like you, too okay?" I lowered my chin so he couldn't look directly in my eye.

"Really?" His voice was soft.

"Not... not like that," I admitted quickly. "But I really like you a lot – as a friend. I trust you and I really have come to count on you. You're really great. If I didn't like you, don't you think I would have run home with Wyatt a few days ago? While you were sleeping?"

"I might have woken up."

"But you didn't. And I could have ran. But I didn't." I touched his knuckle. "Because I made a promise to stay with you until my leg is better."

"And it is," Brindt said. "And yet you're still here. Why do you think that is?"

I flinched. "I'm waiting for Wyatt."

"Or maybe... I'm not as bad as you want me to be," he said slowly. "Maybe you don't hate it here as much as you want to. Maybe you even like it here."

"That still doesn't mean I can stay."

"You'd never be a pet to me."

"But I'd be a pet to everyone else." I shook my head. "Brindt, I like you. As a friend..." I shrugged, "...maybe even more so, but that doesn't change things. I can't stay here. I have to go home."

Brindt's voice came as a hush, almost so soft that I couldn't catch his exact words. "You think you might like me as more than a friend?"

"Maybe, I don't know," I said truthfully. "That's not the point."

"I think it's a pretty big point."

"Maybe."

"Maybe, nothing," Brindt said.

As he shifted, I lifted up my head to see his hands coming towards me. He didn't slow down and I didn't tell him to. Entirely too easily, I was scooped up between his hands and brought up to his face. I shied away slightly, but I also grew curious of the new softer and calmer side of him.

"What?" I asked, when he didn't say anything right away.

"In your world, you said barely anyone thinks you're pretty."

I grew defensive. "Yeah? So what?"

"Well, for what's is worth. I think you're pretty. Beautiful. Gorgeous, actually."

"You mean cute."

"I already said what I meant."

"Even like this?"

One of his pale eyebrows arched. "Like what?"

"You know? Small?" My voice changed to a whisper as I was reminded just how little I was compared to him, but to my surprise his careful smile only grew wider.

"Even like this," he said. "You're gorgeous."

I couldn't hide my shock. "How is that even possible?"

"You don't have to look so appalled," Brindt said. "I didn't even think about it until I saw the Targeter. I can't think of why else I would feel this way." He tried to shrug it off. "But it's true, you know. You're beautiful."

As usual, my face grew hot. "Yes, well, I'm sure that's only because—"

"If you say the word 'pet' I'm going to scream," he interrupted. "Just stop with the 'pet' crap. You know I don't feel that way." His eyes locked on mine. "You know that, Lyris. Don't you?"

I looked away.

"You... you *do* know that, don't you?" he asked in a softer tone, losing some of his confidence. "Lyris, I—"

"I know you don't see me that way anymore," I admitted at last as I tried to look over the edge of his hands. "Can you uh... can you put me down now?"

"Why?"

"Because you're like right there." I waved towards his face. It was almost impossible to look at him when he was so close. I could see everything. Every tiny hair on his chin, every crinkle in the corner of his eyes, every trace of teal in his light brown eye and the depths of his bright blue one. I could see my reflection and I was so nervous to see how I looked in his eyes. His hand lowered a fraction, but I kept my back turned.

"You know... I know you're older than me, and you try to put up a front, but you're shy sometimes, Lyris."

"I'm not shy," I huffed.

184

"I called you pretty and now you can't even look at me."

"Because your face is too big."

"So what if it wasn't?"

I turned my head a bit so I could see him just slightly out of the corner of my eye. "What do you mean?"

"If I wasn't so big to you... would it really make a difference?" His eyes lowered. "Or would my words mean even less to you?"

"Brindt. You know they mean something."

"Even when they're from me?"

"Especially when they're from you."

Brindt fell silent for a moment and I was finally able to collect my thoughts. Brindt thought I was pretty. Beautiful. It didn't make sense. How could a giant think a pet was cute? *Was that all it was?* He that he didn't see me that way, but I couldn't help but wonder if it was even possible.

And then it dawned on me. What I felt for Brindt wasn't really that much different than how he felt about me. I trusted him. And when I could see him at a distance and really look at him as a person, he was attractive. Even two years younger than me, I knew that if he would have been the guy to approach me at the coffee shop, I would have been interested. And though Brindt was huge in my eyes, I did more than trust him.

I liked talking to him.

I liked arguing with him.

I just enjoyed being around him.

I liked him too... but I wasn't a fool.

185

Of course it wouldn't work.

It couldn't work.

"Brindt..." I started. "That still doesn't mean—"

"Her name was Kennedy." Brindt's voice came at a rushed pace.

When I turned around to look at him, he looked more uncomfortable than usual. *Why was he bringing up another girl?*

"She belonged to one of my friends."

"Belonged?" I asked, trying to understand where he was going with this new information. "So she was..."

He nodded. "She was like you. She was a few years younger than me. I was eleven, I think and she was eight or nine. It was hard to figure out because she didn't have a collar. My friend didn't want her wearing one." He shrugged it off. "She used to live a few apartments down from this one. Her owner's name was Sarice. She was okay, I guess. She wasn't really ever mean to me, but she was to Kennedy. It pissed me off." His expression darkened.

"Why are you telling me this?"

"Because you keep asking me about the accident," he said, frowning as he looked down into his lap where the yellow sweater lay on his thigh, unfinished. "And you're having a hard time understanding how I can see you as a person and not as a pet. Maybe if I tell you about Kennedy and Sarice it will make a bit more sense."

My voice faltered. "Is this what your mom was talking about?" I swallowed hard. "The reason why she doesn't want you owning any more people?"

He nodded. "Y-yeah. Like I told her, it was years ago, but I guess it's something that some people can't really forget." His eyes

186

flickered over to mine. "She didn't look anything like you, you know. I want to make that clear. She was really, really pale. Paler than you." He chuckled at the idea of it. "And even though she had black hair, if I held her up really close to my face, I noticed that she had freckles across her nose. Her eyes were blue, but not as blue as mine. She would laugh at me sometimes because my eyes are two different colors." He smiled at an unspoken memory. "She had the best laugh. I guess it was because she was so small."

He held up his free hand. "I remember she wasn't even as tall as my finger. She was young and tiny for an Insignificant, but she was so cute. She was sweet. She would always get in a better mood when I came over." He shrugged. "Sarice didn't really care about what I did. My mom and her mom just got along so it only made sense that we had to hang around each other a lot. She didn't really like me and I guess I didn't really like her."

"But you liked Kennedy?" I guessed.

"I think 'like' is a strong word to describe how I felt. I was only eleven." He shrugged. "But I cared about her. I wanted to protect her from Sarice. I knew she didn't take good care of her."

"How did you know?"

"The bruises," he admitted. "Sarice would play with her too rough sometimes and since her skin was so light, she couldn't hide them from me." He smirked. "I guess in that regard you two were a lot alike."

"You keep talking about her and Sarice in the past tense," I said, still confused. "What happened? Did they move away?"

He nodded. "Yeah. About a year ago, Sarice and her parents moved out of the complex."

I swallowed. "And Kennedy? The girl? What happened to her?"

Brindt started to chew on his lower lip and I realized this story

187

wasn't going to have a happy ending. Brindt was struggling to reveal this part of his story so I wanted him to know that despite my worries, I wanted to hear more. I touched his thumb and ran my fingers over it. He looked down with a mixture of surprise and shame.

"What happened to her? Did Sarice do something?"

"Sarice was always doing something, but the whole thing was my fault. It was an accident, Lyris. You have to understand that. It was an accident. I was only trying to help..."

"What. Happened?"

"I stole her from Sarice one day when I went over there to play," he explained. "Kennedy had a large red mark on the side of her face and she said she slipped through Sarice's fingers while they were playing."

"I thought you said she didn't have a collar. How could she tell you all that?"

"We figured things out just like you and I did." He inhaled and exhaled loudly, building the courage to continue his story. "When she explained what happened I had a really hard time believing her. She was lying. Sarice barely played with Kennedy at that point." He shook his head. "Something snapped inside of me when I saw her crying. She said she didn't understand why she was treated this way. One time she even drew a picture of a large person and a smaller person side-by-side and then crossed it out. After that she drew one of two people of the same size next to each other. She looked so helpless as she tried to explain."

"She was probably trying to tell you about her past," I muttered. "How she didn't understand why she was so small."

"I guess that's what it was," Brindt said. "Anyway, all I knew was that I was so tired. I didn't like going to Sarice's house because she wouldn't let me touch her things. I honestly only agreed to keep going to so I could check on Kennedy. But that day something was really wrong. I decided then that I was going to steal her."

"And that worked out?" I guessed.

"I was riding my bike and it was raining. You know? Like a few days ago when my mom—"

"I know what rain is," I huffed. "Go on."

"I was wearing a hoodie and I didn't know any better. I was biking to my granddad's so he could keep an eye on Kennedy until I figured something else out. I assumed Sarice wouldn't even miss her. I had it all planned. I was going to save her. I was going to protect her. Ugh... but I wasn't being cautious enough..." He flinched.

"Stop."

His mouth locked shut. He blinked hard a few times before he could bring himself to look at me.

"You don't have to say any more," I said. "I got the basic idea."

"Are you sure?" he croaked. "I can tell you—"

"I got the gist."

"So you hate me even more now?"

"What?" I asked, surprised. "What are you talking about?"

"I killed one of your kind," Brindt said. "Now you know why my mom doesn't want me keeping people."

"You said it was an accident."

"And it was."

"And you were trying to save her. Brindt, you were doing a good thing," I offered, trying to comfort him. Honestly, it was a little terrifying knowing that he had accidentally killed a little girl, but I refused to look at him differently. Not after everything we had gone through until that point. "It was an accident. Accidents happen."

"If she wasn't so small it probably wouldn't have even been a big deal," he continued. "But I had to stop suddenly and she lost her grip on my pocket and—" His eyes watered. "I couldn't protect her. She was actually safer with Sarice. Sarice would have never actually killed her."

"Not on purpose."

"I don't know," Brindt said. "But it makes sense, doesn't it? You thought I was a monster from the get go and now you know I am. And I'm being so stupid – trying to save and protect you when obviously I can't do that for anyone."

"I don't need saving or protecting," I said.

"Here, you do."

"Brindt," I said, making my voice firm. It was proving to be the only way to get him to pay attention. He stopped sniffing and looked over. "You didn't do anything wrong. Like you said, it was an accident. It happens. I know you're a good person, Brindt."

He sniffed. "You do?"

I nodded. "Yes. I wished I had learned sooner, but I see it now, clear as day. You're a good person. You have a good heart. But I'm not Kennedy. I don't need saving. I need to go home. That's the best thing you can do for me."

"I know that. I know, okay?" he said. "It's not like I can spend much more time with you. I have to go back to school soon." He frowned. "I don't want you spending time in that cage or hiding when I go."

I dared to smile. "And see? That's why I know you have a good heart."

190

He returned the smile at last, though his eyes were watery. "I can let you go back home this weekend, but you have to promise me that you won't go with him."

"With who?"

"You know who. Don't go to him, Lyris. He's not good."

"Wyatt," I breathed.

"The Targeter. Don't. Lyris, please."

I didn't want to lie, but I wanted to go home more than anything. "I at least want to talk to him," I started.

"There's nothing to say," Brindt grumbled. "Seriously, Lyris. You deserve better than him. You're so pretty. You can do better."

"Like you?" I dared to smirk.

He flushed. "No, not like me. I'm just as bad as him."

"Why?"

His eyes flickered to find mine. "Because I don't want to let you go. I want you to stay here so I can keep you all to myself. I don't want to share you with anyone."

"That's not weird at all," I chided.

"It's the truth," he said. "I know you don't like it, but I do see you as mine. My Lyris."

The corner of my mouth crept upward in a smile. "Brindt," I said slowly. "I... you're..." I lowered my eyes. "You really are something."

"Not a monster?"

191

"Not a monster."

He sighed. "So alright, then. You go back home the day after tomorrow." He smiled. "That's not so bad, right? The end of all of this?"

"There are some parts I wished didn't have to end," I admitted. "You've been great. This could have ended so badly."

"It really could have. You have no idea." His eyes landed on the lower half of my face.

I flushed and reached up to touch my chin. "What are you looking at? Do I have starmelon juice on my face again?"

"Heh, no," he muttered, lifting me closer.

"Checking for freckles?" I asked, as his face grew larger and larger. "I don't have any."

"No," Brindt said. "Uh, hold still. There's something I want to try."

I frowned. "What's that exactly?"

"Just hold still and close your eyes, dammit," he whispered. His face was so close that his breath moved my hair. I pinched my eyes shut.

"I'm not doing this just because you told me to," I said. "It's just too weird when you're that close."

"It won't be for long..." His voice trailed off and warmth flooded my face as he grew even closer.

"Seriously, what the hell are you doing—"

"Shut up," Brindt said before something pressed against the side of my face.

I yelped in surprise and stumbled back a bit in Brindt's hand. I pressed myself against his curled fingers and reached up to touch my cheek, noticing that it was warm and a little damp. "What was that?"

"Just something I wanted to try," Brindt said. His cheeks were bright pink and he looked away.

"Did you kiss me?" I squeaked.

"I tried to, but you wouldn't shut your face," he said in a huffy voice.

"You could have just asked me."

"You would have just freaked out," he mocked back.

"You don't know that," I said, growing shy as he turned towards me. "You could have asked. It's not a big deal."

"It's not?"

"Well, of course it's a big deal like *that*," I said quickly, growing embarrassed for reasons I couldn't understand. "I mean..."

"So I can try again?" Brindt asked carefully.

"Do you want to?"

He nodded shyly. "I know it's weird. You're just so small and I—"

"You can try again," I said over him. "On one condition."

His smile grew wider. "Anything."

"Help me."

"What?"

I turned around and jutted my chin towards the closet door.

"Help me get the rest of those people back to their homes, Brindt. Together, I think we can do it. If you really don't think I should be a pet, then those people shouldn't be either. Let's set them free."

"But what if my mom catches me?"

"She won't."

"How do you know that?"

"We'll figure it out tomorrow," I said. "Do we have a deal or not?" I expected him to put up more of a fight, but to my surprise he only smiled.

"I did say I'd do anything." He rolled his eyes and brought me to his face again. I stiffened up slightly when his lips touched my face, but I didn't pull away. It wasn't so bad and if I didn't have a good life back at home, living here probably wouldn't have been so awful. Brindt was kind, and he liked me, and he even thought I was beautiful. As he started to pull his face back, I grabbed what skin I could find and planted a kiss on his lower lip.

He gasped in surprise and fully pulled away. "What was that..."

"Let's figure out how to get those people home," I said, growing business-like with a smirk.

Brindt smiled back and I swear my resolve to go home faltered for a moment.

"Yeah," he said softly. "Let's get them home."

Fifteen

That night, Brindt and I planned. It was actually kind of pleasant because I could finally see an end to my horrible accidental journey. Brindt turned out to be an amazing organizer, as he worked hard on his notes despite my assurances that he really didn't need to bother so much.

"How hard can it be?" I asked, stepping up beside him on the bed. He was sprawled out on his stomach, sketching away. "Wait a minute. Are you actually working on the plan or are you working on something else?"

"Why can't it be both?" he said, still focused on his work. "I have to talk to my mom tomorrow. Or maybe when she gets home tonight."

"What for?"

"I need to know if the Targeter is coming."

"Will your mom know that?"

"She usually does," he said. He continued to sketch softly on the paper. "He lets her know when he's planning to bring another person here. It usually works out." He shrugged.

"What about me?"

He stopped sketching for a moment. "What about you?"

"Did your mom know I was coming?"

"Ummm..." His voice trailed off and he tried to go back to his work, but I stepped on the notebook and captured his attention. He bit his lip and looked away. "Come on," he muttered. "Don't make me say it."

"I thought you didn't know a lot about what was going on here."

"I don't, but my mom tells me some things."

"Did she tell you I was coming?"

He frowned. "Maybe."

"What did she say, Brindt?"

"She was excited because the Targeter mentioned he had spotted a redhead," he explained. "Redheads are a big deal here. We don't have a lot of people with hair that color." He reached up with his pencil and flicked a few pieces away from my face and across my shoulder. "They bring the highest price."

"Highest. Price."

"Yeah. Most of the people here have hair like your race. Blond, black, and brown, but red is insancly rare here. One time the Targeter brought back a girl with blue hair and my mom freaked out with excitement. It turned out that the blue faded once she washed her."

"That's hair dye," I explained.

"So she found out. The man who wanted to buy her certainly wasn't happy about it."

"And what the hell do you mean, she washed her?"

"Just what I said. It's standard..." he trailed off, noticed my shocked expression and tried to turn back to his notes. "Maybe we shouldn't talk about this tonight."

"Then when?"

"You're going back tomorrow, aren't you? I would say never."

I frowned. "Never?"

196

"It's not like you're ever going to come back."

"I..." My voice caught in my throat as I tried to choose my next words carefully. Was I really not planning on ever coming back? Could I leave Brindt? "I don't know. There's always a chance I could come."

"What for?" Brindt asked.

"You."

His head shot up, eyes surprised and cheeks pink. It really was hard not to find him cute when my words flustered him so much. I was used to being flirtatious with guys, but sincerity seemed to have the most disconcerting effect on Brindt.

"Don't lie to me," he said.

"There's more people stranded in this world, Brindt," I went on. "I don't know how comfortable I'll be going home and knowing this is still going on. Wyatt could still bring people—"

"Ugh."

"What?"

"So you really haven't thought about it?" He set down his pencil and pushed his notebook aside. Resting his crossed arms on the blanket, he looked at me with a curious expression before he lowered his chin to his arms. We were almost looking at each other eye-to-eye – a rare experience. His bi-colored eyes searched mine carefully. He came to a conclusion. "You haven't thought about it."

"Thought about what?"

"What's going to happen to your precious Wyatt if you take all those people back with you?"

"Stop being an ass and don't call him my 'precious'. He's not a damn ring." I snickered at my attempt at lame humor, but Brindt just

197

looked at me wordlessly. "Ugh, human joke. Never mind. What's the problem, though? We're taking the people back home. This is a good thing."

"Lyris, those people were kidnapped from their homes," Brindt explained. "The Targeter specifically brought them here with the intention of them never being able to go back home."

"Yes... and?"

He rolled his eyes. "So what do you think is going to happen when thirty people magically appear back in your world all with one thing in common?"

"And what thing is that?"

"The Targeter."

I frowned as it dawned on me. "Wyatt."

"Yes. Wyatt. He's the one who took them to our world. He's the one who shoved them into the portal and gave them to my mom. They'll all be able to point him out. And if I recall, you were the one who said your world has law enforcement."

"It does."

"So what do you think is going to happen to the Targeter after all those people point him out? What do you think is going to happen to the Portal if people figure it out?"

I frowned. "I'm sure we could explain—"

"Explain what? That he didn't have a choice? Lyris, the Targeter—"

"Wyatt," I said, picking the stupidest thing to argue about. "His name's Wyatt."

"Wyatt, then. Wyatt chose to bring people here. When all

198

those people go back to their world, they're going to blame Wyatt. Hell, they may even blame you."

"I'm the one bringing them back!"

"Your kind is cruel. They won't care."

"They're not cruel. It's going to be fine."

"And then what happens?" Brindt went on. "You go back home, Wyatt gets in trouble and then what happens to the portal?" His brow furrowed for a moment. "By the way, what is the portal back in your world?"

"It's a closet in a house."

"So what do you think will happen to the house?"

"I... I don't know." I began to crumble as I realized that Brindt's doodles weren't all nonsense. He actually was thinking things through and looking beyond what I could see. I wouldn't be a hero. I'd save some people, but I'd also be getting Wyatt into trouble. I didn't know what would happen to him if something like the portal became public news. Maybe it already was – Area 51 and all that nonsense.

"I'll talk to the people before I take them back," I started.

"Heh... good luck with that. Your race sounds really reasonable."

"Can you blame them right now if they're not? Boxed and caged like animals."

"Sometimes I wonder if that's the best way."

"Shut up. So what else can we do?" I asked, growing helpless. "I can't just leave innocent people here to save myself, but I don't want Wyatt to get into trouble either..."

199

"Don't worry about me, I'll be fine," Brindt muttered.

"Of course you will be—"

"Why can't you just stay here?" Brindt asked, silencing me for a few moments. "I mean... well... can't you?"

"We talked about this."

"No. You talked. I listened."

"You talked too, Brindt. It's final. I'm going tomorrow. You promised."

"I know. I just..." he lifted his chin slightly and looked down at me. "I don't know what I would have done without you this past month. Things would have really sucked."

"I'm sure you could have gone out with your friends more."

"Yeah," Brindt said, sounding a bit bitter. "I'm sure you've noticed how many of them have been around this past month."

I tilted my head. Come to think about it, Brindt really didn't seem to have a lot of visitors. On the few times he went out, he was back within an hour. "Why is that?" I asked. "I mean, you seem decent enough."

"Thanks."

"You know what I mean," I huffed. "Seriously, what's up? Don't you have any friends?"

"I'm not so pathetic," he grumbled. "All my friends went to sports camp during school break."

"So what?" I asked. "So you're not athletic? You're just really into art?"

"I'm good enough. That's not it."

200

"So what is it?"

He shook his head. "You know what? It's nothing. Don't worry about it. Let's plan for tomorrow night. My mom is probably going to be working—"

"What is it?" I asked, ignoring him. "Why aren't you at camp with your friends?"

"I don't think there's a delivery tomorrow and I don't think anyone's getting picked up—"

"Brindt."

"What?" He stopped fumbling around.

"Answer me."

"You're awfully bossy for being so little," he grumbled.

"You're awfully cranky for being so young."

"Shut up," Brindt huffed. "Don't call me young."

"Don't call me little. Now, what's going on?"

"It just would have cost too much," Brindt said. "Okay? It's not like my mom couldn't afford it, but it was an expense that really wasn't necessary. It would have stretched my mom too thin." He shrugged it off. "I don't mind, though. Not really. Not since I got you."

I frowned. "I thought money was okay for you. I mean, it's just you and your mom."

"My mom makes ends meet. She has a crappy day job that pays the bills, but the money she gets from selling... that's where expendable money comes from."

201

"And what?" I snapped. "Money's not good on people selling?"

"No, actually. It's not," Brindt snapped back. "That's why I'm so happy to be here and planning to take even more of her money away."

I blinked. Despite having spent a month with Brindt, I realized that I didn't know that much about him. He was kind, but I didn't know how his family life was. I knew he was kind and he liked me, but I didn't know that there was a sacrifice involved with him helping me out.

"How tight are things?" I asked quietly.

"Tight enough that I couldn't even go to camp with my friends," he said back. "It's not a big deal."

"Will it be?"

"Will *what* be?"

"Will it be a big deal if I take all those people back?" Brindt looked away and I stood up and walked up close to him. His eyes lowered into a sad expression. "Is it really that bad?"

"Well, there's about twenty or thirty people in there right now," Brindt said. "My mom has to pay the Targeter for each one he brings back, but she doesn't sell them as soon as she gets them unless they're in high demand."

"Like redheads."

He nodded. "Like redheads. Young girls. Pretty girls. Children are also pretty popular." He shrugged it off. "I know you don't want to hear this stuff—"

"Go on," I said, despite the lump forming in my throat. It was hard to hear people being discussed this way, but I wanted him to proceed.

"She doesn't always get her money back for it, but that Targeter. He's the only one who can bring people back and he demands a lot. My mom's right for calling him a greedy little rat. Whatever."

"Well, what if Wyatt gave some of the stuff back?" I asked hopefully. "You said she gives him gold, right? Maybe he can give some of that stuff back to your mom until—"

"The Targeter doesn't work that way, Lyris. Trust me."

"So what happens, then?"

Another shrug. "She pays him off and she tries to sell what she gets. Sometimes people are really interested and will pay right away. My mom will advertise what she has at work, but these days it's pretty easy to get a person like you. You just go to the pet store and—" He stopped short. "What makes the Targeter special is that he can specifically get what's popular at the time. Some Targeters don't care..."

"So there's more than one Targeter?" I squeaked. "There's more than one portal?"

Brindt nodded. "Yeah, but they're not... it's not the same. Not according to my mom, anyway. The Targeter she works with is different because he doesn't just take anyone. My mom makes a request and he does his best to get what she wants. That way he gets more money and my mom is more likely to sell quickly."

"It sounds like she's putting in an order at a fast food drive thru."

"Yeah, well the Targeter is the one who fills and delivers the bag," Wyatt said. "Things were going well, but apparently the Targeter was having trouble bringing what my mom wanted. It's easy to get women in their mid-twenties, apparently. Men were popular for a time..." he flushed, "... I don't really want to talk about that."

203

"Please don't," I said. I tried not to think about why a giant would want a grown guy as a pet.

"And then children were popular. They don't always remember their past and they can adapt more quickly. Plus it's easier to see them as pets, I guess." He frowned. "But mom's Targeter wasn't very comfortable stealing children."

. "He wasn't?" I tried to hide a smile.

"Don't get excited. He definitely brought back his fair share, but it was getting hard for him. Plus, since apparently this portal is in such a small town, he was worried people would notice something. So my mom had to change tactics. It definitely took a hit to her business when she couldn't offer Insignificant children. She had to find a type of person that was hard to get in other places, but her Targeter would have easy access to."

"Teenagers."

He nodded. "Yeah, and not just any teenagers." His eyes flickered to my head.

The words almost took my breath away. "Redheads."

"There's nothing rarer than hair that color."

For a few moments, I fell silent and tried to understand what was going on. Wyatt had specifically hit on me because I was a redhead. Honestly, if my hair was brown, I wondered if he would have shown much interest. And going beyond Wyatt, I had to think of Brindt.

Brindt was at home and not with his friends because the sales of people had gone down. Wyatt wasn't delivering what was popular. It was so hard to imagine him kidnapping children and though Brindt had said he had done it, it was comforting to know he had a harder time delivering what was needed.

"Is my hair color really so great?" I asked Brindt in a low voice.

"Yes." He swallowed. "Not only are you a redhead, but you're seventeen. Seventeen's the perfect age."

"So I keep hearing," I muttered.

"When the Targeter told my mom he had found a young woman with red hair, she was actually so excited she told me about it. If she managed to get a redhead and sell her in time, the money would have been good enough that I could have went to camp with my friends for the second half of vacation." He sighed. "And then suddenly it was like the topic was closed."

"Wyatt changed his mind," I filled in for Brindt.

"I guess so. Whatever it was, my mom was pissed. It's probably the reason the Targeter was so worried about coming here for a while. He had backed out on his word to deliver a young redhead."

Wyatt's words ran through my mind. The idea that things were more complicated than I could understand and why it had taken him so long to come and find me. He was worried that Brindt's mom would take him or who knows what else. Suddenly, Wyatt didn't seem like such a great guy who had just gone down the wrong road. He seemed greedy. He knew he could have come to find me, but he was so worried about breaking his promise to Brindt's mom and losing his income that he had stayed away.

"And the girl he just brought..."

"She's sixteen, I think," Brindt said. "Dark hair, though. Not as special."

I wanted to argue, but something started to change inside me. I looked at Brindt. Not only was he kind, but he had sacrificed a lot by not immediately handing me over to his mom. "So when you first saw me, you must have noticed my red hair."

205

"I noticed it." He looked off to the side.

"So then, why?"

"Why what?"

"Why didn't you just hand me over to your mom right away?" I frowned and started to fumble nervously with my hands. "You could have gone to camp with your friends. You could have had a good break. Your money situation wouldn't have been so bad." I finally looked up at him almost wild and desperate for an explanation. "Why didn't you just get rid of me? Why keep me around when it's obviously causing you problems?"

"Causing me problems?" Brindt repeated, looking a bit surprised. "Lyris, you're the greatest thing that's happened to me this vacation... or... I don't even know."

"But you didn't even know me right away. We couldn't even talk to each other!"

"I wanted to get to know you. I told you, your people interest me."

"Because of Kennedy."

He flushed. "Yeah. Because of her. Not to mention..."

"Oh God. What now?"

"I never saw an Insignificant quite like you. Eh, I mean a person. You were pretty... you are pretty. I guess I figured if things got really bad I could have given you to my mom, but it just never came to that." He shrugged it off.

"But you could have—"

"I couldn't," Brindt insisted. "Not you." My eyes watered with embarrassment and Brindt looked a little shocked and lifted his head.

206

"Whoa. Wait. Why are you crying? Did I say something wrong?" Worry laced his features and I shook my head hard.

"No, you've actually always been saying things right," I said, chuckling at my horrible grammar. "I didn't know you were giving up so much. I thought you just saw me as a pet. I didn't realize how much better things could have been for you. I didn't know..."

"Hey..." Brindt started. "Look at me for a second." As I lifted my chin to face him, his face lowered. I froze up, expecting another awkward kiss, but instead his chin kept lowering until his forehead practically touched mine. His skin was warm and I blushed even more as his lips moved so close to my face. "You're the best thing to happen to me this break," he whispered. "Not once did it ever occur to me to give you away after I saw you."

"I don't know why you think I'm so special."

His face pulled away. "Because you are."

I sniffed loudly and wiped my nose with my sleeve. "You... you're..."

He arched a brow and dared to smile. "Impossible?"

"Yes. Seriously."

***

"When I see him, I'll warn him," I said to Brindt the following afternoon. As he came into the bedroom with a small plate filled with fruit and bread I had to smirk. I still couldn't get over the fact that the giants didn't eat meat. Hell, I didn't even know how much I missed meat at that point. The fruits there were pretty incredible and I had no idea that bread could taste like something other than salt and fluff. He took a seat at the desk and shot me a curious expression.

"Who? The Targeter?"

207

I nodded. "He needs to know that he has a chance to escape. You're right. If I bring back a bunch of people who can identify Wyatt as the one who led them to the portal, he'll be in so much trouble. But I can't just let him be ignorant. I'll warn him."

"You're too innocent for your own good," Brindt said as he broke up a piece of bluemelon. I took it greedily in two hands and started to eat. Brindt watched for a moment before he focused on his lunch. "As far as I know, there won't be any deliveries tomorrow so my mom will be at work."

"On the weekend?" I asked between bites.

"She works a lot because... well... you know why." He flushed for a moment before plucking up a roll and taking a large bite.

"And you're sure about this?"

He stopped chewing. "You're asking me? I thought I didn't have a choice."

"You don't, but if you don't want to get in trouble maybe I could figure out a way to do this myself. It's bad enough that I'm taking away all those people, but I can't leave them here in good conscience even if it will help you get some money. Brindt, they could take away the portal."

"I'm aware of that."

"They could burn the house down. You could lose any chance of getting another person to come to this world."

"I thought about that, Lyris. One of us actually mapped things out last night."

"But..." I trailed off, "... aren't you worried?"

"About what?"

208

"About money." I didn't really understand the concept of not having everything I ever wanted. If I wanted something, I nagged my mom to buy it. And if my mom didn't buy it, I cried to my dad. And hell, if my dad and mom were both being lame, I would just wait until they let me use their credit card for emergencies to pick up what I wanted. They were always too worried about pissing me off to make a big deal about anything.

I really had it too good and it was a shame that it took being captured by a giant to make me realize that.

"I'll probably have to get a job," Brindt said. "But I know this is important to you. I will admit there's one thing that bothers me."

"Thank God. What? Tell me."

"The possibility that I'll never see you again," he said.

"That bothers me too, Brindt."

He rolled his eyes. "Yeah right."

"No. It really does. But you never know. There's other portals."

Brindt smirked. "Yeah and I'm sure you'll just be dying to find one and come back here."

"To see you again? Hell yeah."

"Really?" He tried to hide his surprise, but it was hard for him to hide his facial expressions when his face was the size of a billboard.

"Really," I said, smiling up at him. "Besides, the people in that room aren't the only people trapped in this world. I'll have to come back eventually to free some more."

"I could help."

"We could change the world!" I declared dramatically.

"We could save all the Insignificants! I mean people!"

"Humans!" I corrected.

"Humans! We could save all the little humans. Brindt and Lyris." His eyes softened. "Partners. You and me. Seriously, we could do it."

"If I come back you'll be the first person I come to."

His eyes softened. "I believe you."

For a few moments we both fell silent and I wondered if such a thing could really happen. Honestly, I could see it. I tugged at my collar and wondered how different things would or could have been if I didn't have one. I wondered if things could change if more people could wear them and giants could see just how similar we were to one another.

I could come back.

Brindt would wait.

I shook my head and tried to focus on freeing twenty people before trying to free my entire race from a world filled with giants.

"So your mom will be at work tomorrow," I said, growing serious. Brindt nodded. "And you know where she keeps the emergency key to get into the blue room?"

He nodded. "Under a loose tile in the bathroom."

"Crafty." I nodded with approval. "How the hell did you find it?"

"I have my ways," Brindt said.

"I'll bet you do." I shook my head fondly. "So we wait until your mom is at work and then go get the key."

"Yup. We unlock the door and I'll send you in to talk to the people so they don't freak out. Explain everything you can to them... what happened. Who you are and how I won't hurt them."

"Yeah, and then we'll lead them back to the room with the portal and send them back to their families."

"And then you go back."

"Yeah." I wasn't sure if I liked that part of the plan so much at the time. "And then I go back. I try to find Wyatt to let him know."

"He may come back here," Brindt said.

"Why would he do that?"

"I dunno. It's what I would do. It's probably the safest place for him. I can't think of many people who would want to come here, and I'm sure my mom would find a way for him to get more people. All she cares about is money. It sounds like that's all he cares about, too. You should just let him get caught, Lyris."

"There's always a chance that no one would believe anything," I said. "I'm still going to give him a chance. Maybe he can start over."

"Or maybe he can find a new portal and start all over and my mom will get evicted."

I froze up. I couldn't take the guilt. "I'll ask you one more time, Brindt. Are you sure you want to be involved in this?"

"I already told you. I don't have a choice now." A small smile crept on his features.

He was good. Much more than I deserved. "You know Brindt, if things were different it really wouldn't be so bad coming here. To see you. Like more often."

"Yeah?" His smile grew wider. "Despite everything?"

I nodded. "Not everything," I said with a chuckle. "But yeah. For the most part."

I stood there and stared at him for a little while longer to just enjoy the warm comfort he provided. With Brindt I was safe. Even with a collar around my neck I felt like an equal, and despite his size, I found him attractive. It was hard to look past his heart and good intentions.

"If things work out that I can still use the portal, I'd like to come—" I stopped short as a new sound hit my ears for the first time since arriving there.

Someone was coming into Brindt's room. As I started to turn around, the massive door flew open and a woman, who was somehow huge and short at the same time filled the doorway. Her large eyes bulged out as they landed on me.

"The redhead," she whispered, stepping forward.

And then all hell broke loose.

Sixteen

"The redhead!" the woman shouted again as she came closer to the desk. A loud screeching sound erupted as Brindt slid out from his chair and stood up to block me from her sight. I ducked behind some books on his desktop as the woman shuffled close by. "What is going on here?" she shouted.

"Mom, it's nothing. You didn't see anything."

"I saw a redhead! The one with red hair!" she shouted as she tried to push past Brindt. I saw their massive bodies collide from behind the safety of some art books as the woman worked her way past him.

"You didn't see anything. That's just a toy. I made her for class."

"You don't have class," the woman huffed. She panted loudly as she started to wiggle, and arms and hands flailed past Brindt's back as she continued her search despite his attempt to block her. "I told you! I told you not to take one of those things as your own. Not only did you not listen to me, but you took the redhead? Are you out of your mind?"

"There's no redhead," Brindt said. He held up his arms so she would stop knocking things over. A large book fell over above me, but was luckily caught on a cup of paintbrushes. I was too scared to move, but I feared the brushes couldn't hold up the book for long. "You're losing your mind. There's no redhead."

"She's there!" she shouted. "I saw her. The Targeter boy was right. She snuck in! And you stole her from me. Brindt, you can't keep that one. If you want a new one—"

"I don't want a new one!"

"Ahh! So there is something there! You crafty little... I thought you learned your lesson after you hurt the other one..."

213

"That's... there's... there's nothing there, mom. Now get out."

"Get out of my way," the woman huffed loudly. "I saw her. I saw that hair. Do you have any idea what kind of price she'll fetch? Even the higher ups are interested in a girl like that. She's perfect... give her to me. I'll give you a new girl if you're so keen on having one of your own. Just give me that one."

"You can't have her."

"So you're admitting there's something there?"

"Yes, and she's mine. You can't have her."

"Give me the redhead, Brindt. You don't even know what you're playing with. Insignificants like that—"

"That's not even what they're called. They're humans, mom and—"

"They're rodents! Pests! I don't care what they are, all I know is that one...the one you're hiding from me? She's worth thousands. People will bid up to the rafters to get one like that. And you're keeping her? I won't punish you for this, but you have to give it to me now!"

"She's mine! You can't—"

Both voices stopped as the book that had been balanced over my head shifted and started to fall. I screamed in surprise and burst from the spot, dodging fallen paintbrushes as I sprinted towards the lamp at the edge of the desk. If I had escaped down the lamp cord before with a hurt leg, I was sure I could do it again.

"Lyris, no!" Brindt yelled, hurting my ears.

The desk shook even more violently as their struggle intensified. I grabbed the lamp cord and had swung myself over the side when suddenly a sweaty, grasping shadow filled my vision.

214

The woman yelled as thick fingers wrapped around my frame. "Gotcha! You little vermin!" I wailed in pain and surprise. Her touch was nothing like Brindt's and I hadn't realized until then just how gentle he had been. My healed leg cried out in renewed pain as I was hoisted into the air and Brindt's worried face rushed in and out of my sight.

"Mom, stop. No, please, you can't do this to her," Brindt pleaded. His footsteps easily kept pace and he stopped in front of her to block her path. "Please, just give her back. She's mine. I didn't take her from you. I found her outside."

"I don't believe you," she snapped. "And even if I did... she's still a redhead and she's worth too much for you to keep as a pet until you go back to school."

"She's mine," he insisted.

"Not anymore. Now move... I need to put her someplace safe."

"She's safe with me!" Brindt said as he reached his hand forward. I screamed as the pressure around my body increased. "Mom, stop! You're hurting her! She doesn't like being held like that!"

"Doesn't like being held like what? What does it matter? Are you her pet now?"

"I'm her friend," Brindt said. He lowered his hand. "Please. I won't try to grab her... just loosen your grip. She hurt her leg."

"You injured it already?" she yelped, pulling me towards her face. I pinched my eyes shut as those dark, beady eyes settled to look at me. "What is wrong with you, Brindt? Did you break it?"

"No, I didn't hurt her. It was an accident—"

"It always is," she muttered as she pinched my leg.

215

I screamed and writhed in the woman's sweaty grasp, but she didn't seem to care.

"Mom, please! Don't hurt her. She's mine. I'll take care of her. You won't even know..."

"Brindt," his mom started in a slow voice. "This isn't even about how you'll take care of her. It's more than that." She thrust me in front of his face and it took everything I had not to cry in front of him and his horrible mother. "This is more important than that. She's too valuable, Brindt. I'm sorry, but she can't stay with you. If it means that much, I'll get you another. I have a fresh one closer to your age than this one. Dark hair—"

"I don't care about hair! I don't want another one! I just want her! She's mine!"

"I'm sorry, Brindt," his mother continued in a firm voice.

All thoughts of going back home went down the drain as Brindt's face grew helpless. She had reached the door of the blue-lit room and pulled a key out from her pocket.

"Brindt, don't give me that look," she muttered as her son followed closely behind her. He stood next to her in front of the door.

"Mom, come on, please," he muttered, eyes watering. I couldn't believe he was starting to cry over me. "Not today, please don't take her away from me today. She's mine..." his eyes flickered down to me, "... I care about her. You have to let me keep her. She doesn't like anyone else."

"She'll learn," his mom said simply, throwing the door open. She didn't argue as Brindt followed her inside and she started to fumble around. "Clean out that cage for her," she instructed her son. "I can't risk any of the other ones messing her up. I'll take a picture and post her tonight. I wouldn't be surprised if she was sold by morning."

216

"Mom, don't make me do this," Brindt muttered. His eyes grew even more hopeless as he looked at me.

Everything was gone.

All of our planning.

Just a few hours away.

Gone.

"*Now*, Brindt," she said, squeezing me again. I squeaked in surprise and Brindt's face crumbled as he looked away and opened the lid of the nearest cage. With careful hands he gathered the four people inside and deposited them into another cage which already seemed a bit full. None of them shouted or cried out. None of them reacted. All that happened was that they ran to the corners of the new cage facing away from Brindt and his mother. The woman smiled triumphantly as she started to lift me towards my new cage.

"And what's this?" she asked, narrowing her eyes and pulling me close. I pinched my eyes shut and looked away. Something touched my neck. "Not only did you steal one of my Insignificants, but you also stole one of my collars? Brindt, what's gotten into you?"

"Don't take it off," Brindt said. "She needs it to talk."

"I know what they're for," she said. "She doesn't need it. Those who will pay for this little one will probably not want to hear her speak."

"Mom, don't..." he trailed off as the woman reached behind my neck and snapped the collar off. Brindt's once clear voice turned into a language I could no longer understand.

"Lyris," he muttered, stepping forward.

His mother tossed the collar on a desk and said something to Brindt before she thrust her hand out towards him. He frowned and his eyes locked on mine, saying something, but without the collar it

217

fell on deaf ears. My eyes watered and I finally started to cry and Brindt continued to beg and plead with his mom. He might as well been speaking English because she didn't seem to be listening, but instead, continued to thrust out her free hand towards him.

Brindt reached to his ear and pulled out a tiny mechanism and dumped it into his mother's palm. Fingers curled around it for a moment before she also deposited it on the desk. The two continued to talk for a few more moments and it was only after another horrible squeeze from my new captor that Brindt was forced to leave.

"Demano," he said, looking at her. More words flowed, but his mom shook her head and dangled me over the open, empty cage. She said something and Brindt reluctantly turned away.

He was leaving.

Leaving.

Fingers released and I fell into the empty cage covered with shredded paper. I curled up into a ball, truly and actually frightened. The lid above shut and I flinched as fear settled over and Brindt was ushered out from the room. His mom was saying things I'm sure were supposed to be reassuring, but Brindt's voice was what truly caught and captured my heart.

He was crying.

He sounded so helpless.

As a giant in my eyes, there was a part of me that thought Brindt was invincible, and that nothing would bother him. As I listened to him cry over me... it made things even more terrible as he lifted his chin one last time.

"Lyris..." he called as his mom gave him one last shove. "Disellus. Lyris..."

More words... no meaning.

The door shut and both Brindt and his mother were gone from my sight. I collapsed to the floor as my eyes adjusted to the only light in the room – the small blue lights set up in each of our cages. I pulled my knees up to my chest and released a few pained wails as the door locked. I could still hear Brindt arguing with his mother. I couldn't understand a damn thing without the collar.

"Why are you so important to the kid?" a new voice asked. It was clear and sharp in my ears.

I lifted my head with a sniff. "Who said that?"

"Down here."

I lowered my head to another shelf across from mine. A man in his early thirties stood there and cocked his head. His clothing and hair looked to be a mess and he was the only one standing in his cage with a few others curled in the corner.

"Answer me," he called across the chasm. "Why're you so important to the beast's kid?"

I blinked.

***

"Are you talking to me?" I squeaked across the chasm.

The older man tilted his head and looked around him with a weathered expression. "I don't see anyone else who seems interested in conversation, do you?"

I looked around. *No. He was right.* Save for the man talking to me, everyone else was huddled in corners or sleeping. It was actually kind of scary how depressing the room was. I pressed my hands up against the plastic so I could lean forward and get a closer look at the one talking to me. Despite his ragged appearance, I could tell he was dressed well. He was wearing khaki pants and those 'richie people' boater shoes and a button-down shirt with a vest. I wondered if he was a professor like my dad.

"Did you work at the university?" I asked. My head tilted with curiosity.

He actually looked surprised. "I... uh... yes, actually." He frowned. "That's quite a weird question. Why don't you answer mine?"

"About Brindt?"

"The beast's kid," he replied, nodding. "Was he your owner?"

"I don't have an owner."

"Right, right," the guy said, nodding with a smirk. "Of course not. None of us have owners, I suppose. I guess that's why we're here."

"It's not that he didn't want me," I said.

"I assumed as much," he said back. "Frankly, I've never heard or seen him that upset before about anything. You must have been quite the little doll for him."

"That's not what it was. He's my friend."

"Whatever you say." He waved me off. "My name's Isaiah."

"Lyris," I called back. He arched a brow, but didn't say anything else. "So how long have you been here, Isaiah?"

"About four months, I figure."

"Four months!" I shouted, surprised at how long that was. Just under a month there and I was already starting to feel like I had lost all sense of reality. And to think, he was here so much longer than that. "That's horrible. How can you stand it?"

"I guess I'm a fool," he said, shrugging. "I'm still holding on to the dream that I'll get to go home to my wife and son."

"You have a kid? You're married?"

"I was," he said. A hint of sadness crept up into his voice. "Who knows what she's doing now. She probably thinks I'm dead. Go away, dangerous thoughts." He tried to shake it off and turned back to me. "What about you? How long have you been living in this hell?"

"Almost a month," I said.

"And on the outside," Isaiah muttered. "At least it's something."

"The outside?"

"I'm assuming that you were with the beast's kid the entire time?" he asked.

I nodded. "Yes. His name's Brindt."

"Did he ever keep you in a place like this? Did he ever put you in a cage?"

"For the first few days," I admitted. "But he stopped seeing me as a pet—"

"That's a lie," Isaiah said. "They'll never change the way they see us. Especially if that kid's mom is the beast."

"Brindt's different," I said. "He's going to get me out of here."

"Is that what he told you?" he asked, arching a brow.

My face flushed with irritation. "He will come to save me. He promised. He even has the spare key to this room." I smiled proudly. "I'll be out of here by tonight, I bet."

"I bet you will be, too. Just not in the way you're thinking."

221

"What the hell is that supposed to mean?"

"How long has the kid known where the spare key is, huh? Why didn't he do anything earlier?"

"B-because..." I stumbled, "... he didn't think much about it."

"And I suppose you think you're different, huh?" Isaiah spat.

"I do."

"You're a fool. You're as screwed over as the rest of us now. The beast moves that spare key around all the time. I've heard her do it when the kid's at school." He shrugged and took a seat in the newspaper scraps. "Let's just hope some respectable guy buys you and treats you well. Honestly, girl, that's the best you can hope for."

"My name isn't 'girl'," I huffed angrily. "And I'm not going anywhere. Brindt will come here and he will let me go."

Isaiah chuckled to himself and shook his head. "You just don't understand anything. Your owner has been too kind to you. Which is actually cruel considering what's going to happen."

I swallowed hard. "And what exactly is going to happen?"

Isaiah pointed towards the large door. "In about an hour I'll be willing to bet the beast is going to come back into this room. Whenever she gets a new catch she gets excited and takes off from work to learn about them. She'll give you a collar for a little while so she can take down your name, age, measurements and history—"

"I'm not telling her anything!"

"She has ways to make us talk," Isaiah said with a shudder. "Trust me, do what she asks." He looked back towards the door. "After she gets your information, she'll take off the collar and prepare you for a picture. Now that is completely up to how you look... and it looks like the kid has been taking good care of you. You may be spared the worst."

222

He shuddered at some unspoken memory – one I didn't want to ask about.

"So she'll take a few pictures of you. Some to show how small you are, others close up so people can see your face." He grimaced. "Though with your hair color I'd be willing to bet that it doesn't matter. She's probably already calling interested parties and trying to start a bidding war."

"Redheads are popular," I said with growing worry.

"So the kid didn't completely keep you in the dark," Isaiah said. "So you know. Yeah, the beast has been waiting for a redhead even before I got here. And to think you're young on top of that. How young are you?"

"Seventeen."

"Seventeen is the perfect age."

"Ugh, I know that," I huffed as I finally sat down. Knowing that Brindt's mom was coming back took a hit on my stomach. What if Isaiah was right? What if Brindt didn't come back? Was I really just something fun for him to play with until his friends got back from camp?

No.

I couldn't allow myself to think that way. Because if I did it would mean that everything I did with Brindt over the past month was a lie. A joke. The idea of him laughing with his friends about how he tricked his Insignificant into liking him took my breath away. He couldn't be like that. He said he liked me. He said he couldn't see me as a pet. He wasn't a liar!

"He will come," I said in a hard voice. "I know Brindt."

"Whatever you say," Isaiah said in a bored voice. He turned around to look behind him, muttered something and turned back to me.

"What's going on in there?" I asked.

"Just people complaining that I'm talking too loudly. Don't worry about it. You won't be here much longer."

"Stop saying that," I said. Honestly, Isaiah's confidence was frightening. He'd been here so much longer than I had. He must have understood how things worked here better than I did. So if he said that I would be bought by the end of the day, I had to wonder if my fate was already sealed.

"How many others are in there with you?" I asked, desperate to change the subject. I could hear footsteps outside the door and I swore I could hear Brindt and his mom still arguing, but I didn't want to think about it. I didn't want to doubt Brindt. I had already been betrayed by Wyatt... and Brindt hated that. Brindt wouldn't allow me to confuse him with Wyatt. He couldn't.

"Seven or eight," Isaiah said with a shrug.

"Why aren't they talking?"

"They are. Just a lot of them don't speak English."

"Well, why not?"

"What an ignorant question. I thought the kid told you about how this whole thing works. Don't you know how we end up here?"

"The Targeter," I said.

He nodded. "That little psychopath picks out people who he thinks he can sell to the beast and then the beast sells them out. Everyone gets paid. And who do you think are the easiest people to target?"

"Kids?" I guessed.

"Well, I suppose that's true," Isaiah admitted. "But it's more than that. Those headpieces and collars are designed to work with the English language because that's the majority of who's brought here. But the Targeter got clever and decided to bring over people who couldn't communicate with the collar." He shook his head. "I'll kill that bastard if I ever get my hands on him."

My eyes widened. "Did Wyatt bring you here?"

"How the hell would I know?" Isaiah asked. "He told me his name was Riley." He shrugged it off. "I guess he tells everyone a different name so he isn't caught. He's such a cruel..." he trailed off. "It was my fault though. I shouldn't have been so stupid."

"What happened to you?" I asked softly. "How did he trick you into going there? If you're a professor—"

"Being a professor doesn't make me a genius," he snapped. "I was a fool just like you. That Targeter must have worked a number on a pretty girl like you. I'm assuming you didn't go to that house to look at first-edition copies of science-fiction novels."

"So that's how he got you?"

He nodded. "I was so stupid and greedy. My wife and I, we just moved to the area and I was all set to teach my first spring semester class. I met the guy at a coffee shop and he asked if I was the new Science-Fiction professor. When I told him yes, he got very excited and told me that he was clearing out his grandmother's closets and he found some old books with notes. He said he was willing to sell them for cheap to a good home and he thought who better to take science-fiction books than a science-fiction professor?" He chuckled darkly. "I should have known better. No one gives anything for cheap anymore."

"So what happened?" I asked, still watching shadows move under the crack of the door. Brindt was shouting loudly. I pinched my eyes shut.

"There's not really much to say," Isaiah continued. "The kid –

Riley or Wyatt or whatever his name is – brought me to the house. He told me it was his grandmother's. Honestly, there was a voice in the back of my head which tried to remind me that the house was abandoned, but the kid was just being so pleasant. And it's not often that you hear about first edition copies of *Dune*."

"We went upstairs and he started showing me the books and at first I could hardly believe it. They were real! All those old copies of books that people like me only dream of buying one day. I had a large stack of them picked out and we were negotiating the price... so then he mentioned..." his face darkened momentarily, "... that there were some others in the closet. He pointed it out. I walked over. Something shoved me from behind and then all of sudden I was in a bright room. I couldn't see anything."

I nodded. I remembered all too well what had happened when Brindt found me.

"Who was on the other side?" I asked.

"The beast."

I smirked. I had never heard a full grown man remain so intent on calling a woman a beast, but I supposed that due to the size difference it made sense.

"She grabbed me and started talking in a language I couldn't understand," Isaiah went on. "I was still having a hard time figuring out just what the hell was happening. I have to say, my first thought wasn't that I was in a world of giants. By the time I was able to gather what was going on, I couldn't see Riley. I was put in a cage with a few others and they tried to explain to me where I was and what was going on."

"Did you believe them?"

"How could I?" Isaiah groaned. "A portal? A world of giants? A world of giants who kept people as pets? No! I didn't want to believe it. I just kept waiting to wake up so I could get back to my wife and kid. Dammit, my wife. My son. They're back home all alone."

"They won't be for long," I said. I tried to be encouraging. "We'll get you back home."

"Who's we?"

"Brindt and I."

"The beast's son?" Isaiah said with a snort. "Dream on. Honey, I hate to break it to you, but your kid isn't coming to save us. No one's coming to save us. I've been here for four months and that kid hasn't done anything."

"It's different with me—"

"You're a fool to believe that," Isaiah snapped. "The kid won't betray his mother. Trust me."

"He has the key. He'll come. And when he does, I'll tell him to let you go. We'll both go back. We all will!"

"You're living in a fantasy. Those monsters will never see us as anything but pets and profit. I suggest you just hope and pray that you end up with a decent owner next. I'm sure whoever it is will be wealthy at the very least. That's got to be better than being here."

"I'm not going to have another owner because I never had one in the first place."

"Just be quiet," Isaiah said. "I'm trying to listen to what those two are saying now."

"You can understand them?" I asked. I lowered my voice so I could hear their voices too. I knew some of the words Brindt said, but his mother was talking so damn quickly that I could barely make out individual words.

"I've been here long enough to understand the basic idea," Isaiah huffed with an annoyed expression.

I looked towards the door and shadows filled the crack. "So, what are they saying?" I asked quietly.

"The kid's upset," Isaiah said immediately. "I can tell that right away. He keeps saying 'mine' and your name. He's begging."

I frowned. In earlier circumstances I would have been upset with Brindt referring to me as 'his', but if being his meant I had a chance to leave, or to at least get out of the cage, I gladly would have accepted the term. I couldn't help but smile as Isaiah explained that he was begging. Brindt really wanted me. He liked me. He wanted me back.

"What's the mom saying?" I asked, desperate to know how she was handling her son's pleading.

"She's not budging." Isaiah stood up in his cage and leaned forward. "She keeps talking about money and a better life." He shook his head. "It's hard to make out the exact wording, but her message is clear, Lyris."

"And what's that?"

"You're being prepared for sale tonight."

"You! That's not a message!" I yelped. "That's pretty specific to me!"

"Yes, I know. The beast—" He stopped short as Brindt roared something so loud that even from the blue lit room, several people stirred and woke up in their cages. I squeaked in surprise as Brindt yelled. I never heard him sound like that before.

"He's winning," I breathed. "She has to listen..." I trailed off as thudding footsteps started to leave the front of the room. "No," I said. Horror washed over as the steps grew further and further away. Brindt's voice. My hope. My only chance at getting home. I could hear him retreating. "Brindt, no. Don't give up."

There was another yell, but it was so far and faint I barely caught it.

A door opened and slammed shut.

And then there was silence.

For a few moments all I could hear was my breathing. The house had fallen silent except for Brindt's mother's footsteps rumbling over the carpet outside of the room. I inhaled and exhaled slowly and waited for Brindt's voice, but the halls remained silent. He was gone and Isaiah looked at me sadly.

"See?" he said in a low voice. "In the end, they just don't care."

"I'm sure he'll be back," I whispered, thought it was obvious I doubted my own words. "He's just pissed."

"Oh, he's pissed alright. But he's not going to do anything about it. I told you. The kid doesn't stand up to his mom." He chuckled darkly. "For a moment I thought he was going to..."

"It's not over yet. He must be planning something. I don't know. He's not going to give up so easily. He just needs time."

"Time? How many times do I have to tell you that that's something you don't have? You're not like us, honey. You're valuable. You're young. You're cute. You're a redhead. You won't last the night. In fact..." He trailed off and fell silent as Brindt's mom started to talk loudly and in a rushed voice. I swallowed hard and tried to picture her on the phone.

"What's she saying now?" I whispered.

"She's making arrangements," he said.

"For what?"

"For you, honey," Isaiah said. "I told you. She plans to start a bidding war. She's contacting all serious collectors and she's trying to drive up the price." His eyes widened as Brindt's mom said something else. "And you seem to be worth quite a bit. I'd imagine the kid will be going to lots of camps with the money you're going to bring in."

"Brindt?" I squeaked.

He nodded. "Oh yeah. That was a whole big thing less than a few months ago. The kid wanted to go to camp with his friends, but money was so tight that he couldn't go." He turned back with another deep frown. "That was the only time I saw the beast look even remotely human. She would come in here and lock the door after the kid was gone and cry her eyes out. It wasn't like we'd comfort her, but it was kind of humanizing just the same."

I returned the frown. Brindt had mentioned money problems, but I didn't know that it actually affected his mom, too.

"Am I really worth that much money?" I asked in a low voice.

"Think of it this way," Isaiah said. "In our world you would be like a one-of-a-kind purebred horse. People from all over the world would come to get their hands on you."

"But horses are worth—"

"A lot," Isaiah continued. "My younger sister wanted a horse when she was younger. My dad said he would have to sell the house and the two cars just to get it for her." He chuckled. "Do you understand now?"

I did. I tried to think of how much happier Brindt would be if he could do all the things he wanted with his friends. With that kind of money his life could change. Things could be comfortable and he wouldn't have to spend school breaks alone in his room doodling. Maybe he knew in the back of his mind that selling me was the best thing.

And if I really couldn't go back home maybe this was something I could give him.

I could always try to escape and find my way to Brindt's house.

231

I was still dumb enough to think that was a possibility.

"If I escaped from my new home, it's not like the person could take the money away from Brindt," I mused.

"*That's* what you're thinking about?" Isiah's face turned incredulous. "Man, you do care about the kid. That's weird."

"Answer me," I said hotly.

"I'm sure that if you escaped your precious Brindt wouldn't lose any money. It would be your new owner's fault for being stupid enough to let you escape. But building that kind of trust where you would even have that opportunity... that could take... weeks... months... maybe even longer than that."

"But it could happen," I said. "It would take time, but I could help out Brindt and maybe I could still get home."

"There you go again, talking about getting home." He rolled his eyes. "You're playing with the most dangerous concept of all."

"And what's that?"

"Hope."

I looked away. I didn't want to think about just how impossible it would be to get home. Not only would I not know where I was if I did somehow manage to escape, but I would be small and in a world where I wasn't only seen as a pet, but as a valuable one. The odds were not in my favor.

"I won't give up," I said.

"Good for you," Isaiah said, before jutting his head upward. "Uh-oh."

"What?" I asked, following where he looked. Brindt's mom no longer spoke, and her steps were growing closer to the room. I looked at Isaiah who had shrunk back into the shadows of his cage.

"What?" I asked. "What is it?"

"She's coming," he said. "Good luck."

"What..." My voice caught in my throat as the lock of the door started to rattle. Brindt's mother muttered something angrily under her breath and the sound of the doorknob ceased. My heart fell a few seconds later when tiles scraped together just outside the door.

Tiles.

The bathroom tiles.

The spare key.

A tear crested my eye as the footsteps returned and the door easily swung open to reveal the same large yet short woman from before. In the light of the doorway she looked like an angel of death. She was here to prepare me to be sold and despite my desire to be strong, I found myself creeping towards the back of the cage. The woman's mouth curled into a grotesque smile as she shut the door behind her and started to come right towards me.

"Lye-reeze," she said in a cool tone. She said my name the same way Brindt had done when he was learning. I was so used to hearing Brindt say my name correctly that I was actually a little surprised to hear someone else try it out. My eyes widened as I shrank back into the corner of the cage, but Brindt's mother was quick to pull open the lid and find me inside.

Struggling proved useless so I remained limp in her sweaty, thick fingers as she moved to another part of the room. It was a desk much like Brindt's and mine back at home, but not covered by homework or art supplies. She set me down on my back and asked a question as she used her free hand to grab some pins. Within moments, I was pinioned by my clothes to the desk, facing upwards as the triumphant face of Brindt's mother filled my vision.

"Ahh..." she said softly. She reached her finger out to touch my hair. I remembered how Brindt had done the same thing, but her touch was like that of a person rubbing a coin for luck and I flinched back with disgust. She smelled like fried food which was odd considering that the beings here didn't even eat meat. She frowned as I pulled away from her but was not deterred. Instead she smiled and muttered words which I couldn't understand. After a few moments, she pulled away and started to dig into a desk drawer before she pulled out something that looked familiar.

A collar.

She put something into her ear and tapped it a few times before she lowered the collar and secured it around my neck.

"There we are, pretty girl," she purred as her fingers left my skin. "Aren't you just divine?"

"Where's Brindt?" I asked. I couldn't believe I had the courage to snap at her. I didn't know where my bravery had come from, but there was no going back and even his mother looked surprised that I spoke so openly.

She smiled that same eerie smile which sent chills down my covered neck.

"Mouthy little thing, aren't you?" she asked. "I suppose he went out for a bike ride to calm down. He had quite the fit when I said you couldn't go back to him. He'll learn to understand once I can send him to those art classes he's been dying to go to for the past year. Finally..." Her smile changed from something demonic to that of a worried middle-aged woman – for the briefest of moments, I was almost sympathetic. Money had never been an issue for our family so I didn't quite understand the concept of 'want'. I was lucky and that made me sick to my stomach.

"Can't I see him?" I dared to ask in a timid voice.

She looked surprised. "No. No, you can't see him. If you see him he'll only get more attached and I can't have him doing anything stupid. He's old enough to understand. You're much too valuable to sit in his room." She reached down and brushed my hair with the tip of her finger. "Is this real?" she asked.

I narrowed my eyes and arched my back to get away from the incoming digits. "Is what real?"

"This hair," she said impatiently. "If I run your head under water with soap, will it run out? Or is this natural?"

"It's natural," I hissed.

"How can I be sure?"

"Ask Brindt," I grumbled. "It's not like I haven't wet my hair for a month."

"That's true," she mused. She lightly pinched the ends of my hair before she gave them a tug. I yelped in pain and surprise. "It's not a wig, at least." She hardly noticed my watering eyes as she reached around her and pulled out a tiny pointer. It reminded me of something my older teachers would use in class and she used it to poke at my stomach.

"Did my son make you this?" she asked, flipping up the fabric of my teal sweater.

I swallowed hard and tried not to envision what else could be done with that poker. It was as Isaiah had said. Just comply. "Yes."

"Huh, not bad," she muttered, running the pointer around my body. I shivered with disgust, but didn't snap at her. I didn't want her to tug on my hair again. With too much of a rough touch, I pictured my neck snapping. I swallowed as she continued to inspect my attire and dropped the pointer over a large button over my chest. "He really does have a talent for this," she muttered. "Does he make all your clothes?"

I nodded tentatively.

"And they're in his room, I expect?"

235

Another nod.

"Talented," she said with a soft smile. It was much too heartwarming to handle considering my situation. "My son has always been so talented, but I had no idea he could do this. Clothing for Insignificants." She shook her head. "We'll have our own store in no time."

"We're not Insignificants. We're people."

"Whatever you are, this is fantastic work," she continued, looking over my pants. "I'm assuming the shoes are from your world?"

"Y-yes."

"Hmm, well, I'll have to ask Wyatt to pick up a few pairs of shoes while he's out." She frowned. "They add such a richness to your outfit. I can't believe it, though. Such workmanship." There was true admiration in her tone. "What else has Brindt made for you?"

Though I was shocked by her choice of conversation topics, I swallowed hard and tried to make nice. "A few sweaters," I said. "It's colder here than it is at home. Uh, just a few pants. Simple shirts."

"And he made them all?"

I nodded.

"Fantastic," she murmured. "I'll have to make sure to include those when I put you to sell in a few hours."

My face lost all color. "Put me to sell?"

"Of course. You didn't think you were going to stay here? Do you have any idea how many parties are interested in you?" She smiled and reached into her pocket to hold up a large screen in front of my face. Using a pudgy finger, she scrolled through the screen and pictures of giants rolled through. Some young. Some older.

236

Some male. A female or two. One man looked to be over seventy. One looked to be not much older than I was. I swallowed nervously as numbers popped up next to their names.

"They're all bidding on you, my pretty girl," she said proudly as the screen left my view. "They haven't even seen your lovely picture and yet they're all bidding. Bidding for what I have!" She giggled like a school girl. "Wait till they see your face. You're so pretty. I can see why Brindt wanted you all for himself. My greedy, talented son. But if he can create work like this!" She thumbed my sweater. "Then he'll be getting his own Insignificant soon enough." She glanced around the room and her eyes settled on a specific cage. "I think I know just the girl. She has a similar shape to you... horrid fluffy, black hair, though. No matter, I just need the clothes."

"Please," I croaked. "Just let me see Brindt. Let me see him one more time."

"I'm afraid that's not an option," the woman clucked.

My face faltered and I started to lose all the grace of carrying a normal conversation. All I could think about were those faces. Those numbers. I was being auctioned off like a limited edition anime. Ugh, or like Isaiah said. A thoroughbred horse.

"Please," I tried as the woman's face pulled away and she started to shuffle through her desk. "Just one more time. I just want to say goodbye to him."

"Goodbye?" she repeated. "So you've accepted the fact..."

"I know that by selling me, Brindt can get more of the things he wants," I muttered. "I just want him to know I'm okay with that."

Her dark eyes narrowed and her jowl quivered. "Brindt talked to you about me? About his..."

"He told me a lot of things, ma'am. I just want to say goodbye and let him know I'm okay."

For a few moments, her stern expression faltered as she looked at me with curious eyes. I couldn't help but wonder what she was thinking in that moment. Was she beginning to understand that we weren't mindless animals, but people with thoughts and feelings like them? Was she beginning to understand just how important I was to Brindt? Did she even care?

Her expression turned hard. "That's out of the question," she snapped and held something over my head. A blinding light flashed and a loud clicking sound filled my ears for a few moments. I saw stars. "Try to smile, pretty girl. I'm trying to find your good angle."

More blinding light and clicking.

I didn't dare smile.

As the light turned to shadow and the stars started to fade, the woman's face appeared. She looked pouty.

"You're a grumpy little thing," she said. "No matter. I think these pictures should do just fine." She moved away and a different type of clicking filled the room. "Excellent," she mused softly. "You're seventeen, correct?"

"Ask Brindt," I huffed. I was no longer in the mood to play her stupid games. *Damn her.*

"Wyatt mentioned that the redhead was seventeen," she muttered. "I'm assuming that's you. No matter. You look seventeen – the perfect age." More clicking. "Beautiful pale skin without freckles. Lovely. Tall. Slim. Perhaps athletic. Recommending a leash and harness. Seems like a runner."

"A what?" I cried out. "I'm not a dog! You can't leash me up!"

The woman clucked her tongue. "Very spirited. No doubt my son's fault. No matter. Recommending no collar for at least six months. Needs to learn to respect her owners. Provide collar for this one at your own risk."

I couldn't believe my ears. She spoke like I was a dog! As though I wasn't screaming my head off in the background in a language she could obviously understand.

A leash.

A harness.

Losing the ability to communicate for six months.

I squirmed against my restraints.

"Oh, stop that now," she hissed and shot a look at me. "There's no escape and you said yourself that this was to help Brindt. So why don't you be a good girl and just settle yourself?" She returned to clacking. "Very devoted to owner if she gets to know you," she read out loud. "Dedicated and passionate. A fine and spunky specimen."

"Stop," I roared. I couldn't listen to her speak like that for another second. "I'm a person, dammit! We all are! We're not pets to sell!"

"Delusional at times," she went on. "Seems trainable. Not recommended for first time owners."

"I'm not trainable!" I yelled and tried to find her face. All I could see was her profile and the soft glow of the scree as she finished up.

"Overall, seems like a fun project for an experienced owner. Beautiful red hair and will come with a custom wardrobe." The clacking stopped and tears fell down my face as she appeared and hovered over with that horrible smile. I wished she was close enough that I could spit in her face, but she was too high above. It would only fall back onto me and cause further humiliation.

I bit back my tears.

"Now that wasn't so bad, was it? Tell you what. Just to show

239

you just how valuable you really are, I'll turn the screen so you can watch your numbers climb. I'll set it so that bidders can see your beautiful face and not your horrible scowls. Come now..." She trailed off as she sloppily pulled me out from the pins and set me back in my cage. I tumbled off her palm and into the shredded paper.

When she walked away, she then tilted the screen towards my direction and to my horror, I saw not only the numbers climbing on the screen next to each bidder, but my face.

My own defeated and humiliated expression.

"There we are," the woman said. "Now you just sit back and watch those numbers for me. And try to smile, eh pretty girl?" She patted the top of the cage before her face pulled away and she started to leave the room. "I'll be back to check on you," she said. "And Grace? I'll be back for you later. I want Brindt to re-create some of his lovely work."

She reached into the cage suddenly and removed my collar in one practiced motion, then closed the cage and strode out the door, closing and locking it behind her.

The screen dinged as another bidder raised his final offer.

Another ding.

I covered my ears.

***

"Is he really not so bad?"

A light voice caught my attention and I looked away from the screen. The voice didn't belong to Isaiah and I couldn't see him from there since Brindt's mom had moved the cage. I looked upward and realized I could see another kennel above mine with a dark-haired girl who was looking down at me.

"Grace?" I guessed.

240

She nodded. "I guess that makes me the one who's going to replace you."

Another few loud dings.

"Wow," Grace muttered. "I guess that means you're popular, eh?"

"I guess so," I said drily. I didn't want to think about those numbers and how they continued to rise. To my relief, I couldn't hear myself talking on the screen. I only saw myself on a slight delay. I guess Brindt's mom didn't want her bidders to hear me being 'spunky'. *Damn her!* Talking about me like a dog.

"Is he nice?" Grace repeated. Her dark, fluffy hair fell over her eyes as she tilted her head and I wondered how Brindt's mom could say she wasn't pretty. She looked gorgeous. A bit scruffy, but who wasn't after being kidnapped and thrown in a cage? She also looked young.

"How old are you?" I asked.

"Thirteen."

"Thirteen!" I gasped, surprised that she was so young. "But you look older—"

"It's because I'm tall and built like my mom," she huffed. "Guys always think I'm older than I actually am. But trust me, I'm thirteen. Seriously though, is he nice?"

"Who?"

"The blond guy," she whispered. "The one with two different color eyes. He's young, right? He's close to my age."

"He's close to my age, too," I said.

"Would you shut up?" a voice growled from behind Grace.

241

"Some of us are trying to sleep."

"Sorry," Grace whispered before she turned back to me. "He seemed nice. I hope she'll give me to him."

"You actually want to be here?" I asked.

"Of course not," she hissed. The man grumbled something else at her and her cheeks grew pink. "But it's just... if I have to stay... I rather it be with someone who will treat me well. Maybe he'll even let me go back home so I can start school on time." Her eyes lowered. "I know it sounds weird, but that would be a lot better than being home with my dad." Pain flickered across her features. "The blonde guy seems alright."

"He is," I said. "He's going to get us out of here."

"Even if he doesn't, I'd rather be with him than in here. It's scary."

"I'm telling you for the last time... SHUT UP!" a male voice roared.

Grace frowned. "I have to go," she whispered. "I hope we both end up with good people. It's the best we can hope for."

"Yes, but—" She ducked away before I had the chance to finish which forced me to turn back to the screen. I didn't understand just how much I was bringing in at that point, but I could see that my numbers had skyrocketed. To my relief several people had even pulled out.

The one scary looking woman's bid screen was blank.

So were two other guys.

Several men who looked Isiah's age were still bidding and the man in his seventies was in the lead. I frowned. That man looked even older than my grandfather, what could he possibly want with me? I turned away from the screen and tried not to listen to the horrible dinging sound as more people continued to bid.

I closed my eyes.

I guess that's why so many people slept there.

There was nothing else to do other than get trapped in your own thoughts.

"Brindt," I muttered my exhaustion suddenly caught up with me.

I missed him.

***

When I woke up, I was groggy and cold. I was used to Brindt letting me sleep with one of his sweatshirts, but in there all I had was the clothing he gave me, the warm glow of the cage's blue light and scraps of newspaper to keep warm. I picked out the few pieces which had gotten caught in my hair and strained my ears.

Brindt was home.

He sounded much calmer than before, but I could tell he was still upset with his mother. I wanted to know what they were talking about, but all I could hear was the tone and Isaiah wasn't there to translate.

The mom sounded excited.

Brindt sounded huffy, but not pissed.

I stood up in the cage, looked down at the floor below the door and watched a large shadow go past... and then another.

"Still convinced he's going to help you?" Isaiah called from somewhere out of sight below me.

"He's going to help," I said, growing firm. "I know he is."

"Not if you knew what I'm hearing." His voice was teasing.

"What's he saying?" I tried not to let my worry show. My eyes trailed over to the screen with the climbing numbers. Six people were still bidding. My face on the screen tilted curiously and one of the numbers spiked. I narrowed my eyes and turned away immediately. I didn't want to entertain some creep who thought my facial expressions had a price tag on them.

"Well, I don't think I need to tell you, but the key is gone," Isaiah explained. "The beast found it and was yelling at the kid earlier."

I remembered the sound of the tiles. "No," I muttered. "He can't... I mean... he can't."

"Just give up, honey," Isaiah said. "At least you get to look at your possible new owners." He let out a low whistle. "Damn, you're worth a lot. I wish I had red hair. At least then maybe I could get out of here."

"I don't want to think about it," I muttered.

"They're not half bad," Isaiah went on. "Some of them look like business men. I bet they're worth a lot of money. You'll probably end up more spoiled than you are now."

"I'm not spoiled."

"Oh please. I could tell you were spoiled the moment you were brought in here. Both in our world and in this one. I bet you live in that neighborhood with the house."

"What house?"

"You know what house. The house with the portal that brought us here. You live in that neighborhood, don't you?"

"Yeah? So what? My parents are professors."

244

"I'm a professor, too. That doesn't mean I'll throw all my money away to live on that street. Take a look at some of them, honey. They don't look all that bad. It'll probably be good for you."

"I don't want an owner."

"You already had one."

"He was my friend."

"He doesn't seem to think so."

"Shut up!" I shouted angrily. The shadows outside the room stopped moving and Brindt's voice started to plead.

"Man," Isaiah said. "You must have really worked a number on him."

"What's he saying now?"

"Same old, same old. He wants you back. You belong to him. It's not fair. Blah, blah, blah," Isaiah said in a bored voice before he chuckled. "Something about working. He wants to buy you."

Hope glimmered in my eyes. "And what does she say?"

"I think you know the answer. But wait..." He trailed off and listened intently to the conversation and I pressed my hands to the back of the cage. I wished I could see his face, and I wished that I had taken the time to learn more of the basics of Brindt's language when I had the chance.

"What?" I croaked. "What's she saying? Did she change her mind?"

"Shut up," Isaiah growled. "I'm just making sure..."

Their voices continued outside and someone raced from the door and returned. Brindt's voice grew even more panicked and the mother chuckled.

"What is it?" I hissed.

"Your boyfriend just found out about the key," Isaiah said. "He's upset to say the least." He laughed darkly. I wished I could see his smug little face so I could smack the hell out of it, but he was my only source of information. As usual, I was forced to play nice to get what I wanted.

"And what else?"

"I'm not sure..." Isaiah trailed off as though thinking. "Something about clothes?" He fell quiet for a few seconds as Brindt lowered his voice.

"He's admitting that he did something about clothes. I think?"

"Brindt makes all my outfits," I muttered.

"What was that?"

"I said he makes all my outfits!"

"Ahh," Isaiah said. "Well, that makes sense. Apparently the beast is very pleased with his work on clothes. She wants him to do more, or at least that's the gist I'm getting."

"So what?" I asked. "What does that mean for me?"

"It means she's leaving."

"Leaving?" I squeaked. "You can't be serious."

"I'm deathly serious," Isaiah said. "I don't quite understand it, either. But apparently the kid makes good clothes and she wants more. For your sale."

Brindt said something else.

"The kid's saying he needs more fabric."

"He's trying to get her out of the house," I said.

"The beast won't fall for it. She can't..."

"Now what?"

"Either the stuff that kid makes is really good, or the beast is losing her touch," Isaiah said. We both fell silent as Brindt said a few more things and the mother answered back. She yelled once more before her footsteps started to fade away.

"What did she say?" I asked.

"Something about keeping a promise," Isaiah said. "Damn. Your kid must be pretty damn talented to convince the beast to leave the day of a sale. I can't remember the last time there was an auction." He sniffed with distaste. "I didn't really get a good look at what you were wearing, but if the beast is impressed by it then it must be amazing."

"He's going to save me..."

"It's not like he has the key, honey. I'm sure she knows what shc's doing. She's left us alone in the house plenty of times and the kid's never shown any interest. You need to stop getting your hopes up."

The clanging of keys caused us all to fall silent. A shadow remained in front of the door and if it was Brindt, he wasn't saying anything quite yet.

The woman barked something else as a door flew open.

"What did she say?" I asked Isaiah. I wondered if he was getting tired of hearing me ask.

"I don't know," he admitted. "Something about..."

247

The door slammed shut.

The shadow in front of the door shifted.

A knock followed and I stood on my tip toes and leaned towards the shadow.

"Lye- ris?"

Eighteen

Brindt's voice was as loud and clear as I remembered it, but he sounded so far away from behind the door. With giants I didn't just hear voices, I felt them. And though Brindt still had a somewhat high pitched voice for a guy, it rumbled in my stomach and made something clench in my chest. From behind the door, he almost sounded normal.

"Are you going to answer him or not?" Isaiah asked.

Oh! Right!

"Brindt!" I shouted. "Brindt, I'm in here!"

"I think he knows that," Isaiah grumbled.

"Hey!" I shouted, pounding on the back of the cage. "Translate for me! You have to tell me what he's saying."

"He said your name," Isaiah said.

"Ugh! Would you stop being a prick and help me out here?" I shouted.

"Lye-ris?" Brindt tried from behind the door. He asked a question.

"Quick! What's he saying, Isaiah?"

"Seriously—"

"Tell me, please!" I screamed before turning around to look at the bidding war. My number was still climbing and another person had just backed out. It was down to five and they were all men.

"Something about 'are you okay'?" Isaiah repeated. He actually had the nerve to sound irritated.

"Do you know how to say 'I'm fine'?" I asked.

"You spent a month here and you don't even know—"

"Please!" I wailed. I no longer cared how desperate I sounded. "Tell me."

"Pomun means good," Isaiah said.

"Pomun!" I shouted. "Brindt! Lyris pomun!"

The shadow slumped forward a bit. Brindt was relieved. He was actually relieved I was okay. I'd never admit it to Brindt, but my heart soared at his joy that I was safe. He quickly started asking more things and I banged on the back of the cage.

"Come on, Isaiah! What's he saying?"

"Are you hurt?" Isaiah said.

"No!" I shouted, remembering that Brindt knew the word. "Lyris... uh... no..."

"Banum," Isaiah filled in.

"Thank you, Isaiah," I said in a low voice before shouting. "No Brindt! Lyris no banum!"

"Ahhh..." Brindt said from behind the door. I swear I could hear him smile. More words came.

"Quick, Isaiah. What did he say?"

"I can't make out everything," he grumbled. "Just something about..."

"What?" I asked. "What?"

"Getting you out."

My face lit up. "I told you!" I squealed. "I told you he

250

wouldn't let us stay here!" The dinging on the screen continued, almost taunting me to look, but I couldn't bear it. Brindt was right outside the door and he was going to save me.

"You shouldn't put so much faith in him," Isaiah warned.

"Lyris?" Brindt asked from behind the door. Another question followed.

I fell silent. Isaiah knew what I wanted.

"He's asking who I am," he said.

"So tell him!"

"There's nothing to tell," Isaiah snapped back. He barked a few words towards the door.

"Wait! What are you telling him?" I asked. I pounded on the cage. "Isaiah, dammit! What are you telling him?"

Brindt's voice came next.

Isaiah answered him.

"Wait, what? What's going on?" I shouted. I started to grow even more desperate. "Isaiah! Brindt? What's going on? What are you guys talking about? Please! DOMODO!" I shrieked out the last word because it would catch Brindt's attention. His voice finally came to a stop.

"Isaiah, please. What did you tell him?"

"About the bidding war. He needs to know."

"You... you were just telling him about that?"

"What did you think I was telling him, honey?"

"To leave? To go away?" I guessed.

"Why would you think I would do that?" Isaiah sounded offended.

"Because... I don't know. I just thought..."

"Don't get me wrong," Isaiah interrupted. "I think you're stupid for trusting some giant kid to set you free."

"He's not just a kid—"

"However," he continued. "I want to get out of here to get back to my wife and kid more than you know. And if working with the beast's kid is the only option I have, then dammit, I'm going to have to take it and deal with it. What did you think? Do I come off as such an ass that you assumed I'd just give up? I'm not like the others. I want to go home."

"I want to go home too," I said. My eyes watered. "So bad."

"Well, then I guess we're going to have to trust him," Isaiah said. "He wants to help. He just doesn't know how. His mom won't be out for long. And you..."

A loud dinging sound filled my ears. It was different than before. It had a certain finality to it.

"Dwan?" Brindt's voice came from behind the door.

I turned around to face the screen with a dreaded feeling that I already knew what awaited.

"It's official," Isaiah said. "The bidding war is over. You've been purchased."

***

"Eh?" Brindt called from outside the door. "Lyris?"

Isaiah snapped at him as I slowly turned around to face the

252

screen. It was true. The bidding was over and though I couldn't understand the writing on the screen, the red box flashing around one of the men told me everything. All the other bidders had backed out. Only one man remained and his smiling face tormented me.

"Not bad," Isaiah said with a chuckle. "At least he doesn't look like a serial killer."

He didn't. Honestly he didn't look that bad. Maybe a little younger than Isaiah with skin the color of dark chocolate. His teeth were blindingly white and though his eyes were dark, they were warm. Even his smile looked kind. Much too kind to be a person who would bid on a seventeen year old girl.

"Twenty-six," Isaiah said. "Not too terrible."

I jerked my head around. "That's how old he is?"

"Yup."

"How do you know that?"

"I can read numbers pretty well," he explained. "I think that information is from a business card of some sort. It says he's six foot three inches, one hundred and eighty pounds. At least I think that's what it says. Or maybe he's six hundred and three pounds and one foot, eight inches tall." He laughed to himself. "Seriously though, Lyris. It could be worse."

"What's his name?" I asked, looking at my future owner.

"Lyris?" Brindt asked. I couldn't bring myself to talk to him. My future seemed to be crumbling around me.

"What's his name?" I snapped at Isaiah.

"Names are always a little tougher. Uh... Cal-ash?" He tried sounding it out several times. "Damn, I really hate how much I can read and understand this language. Makes me feel like I've been here too long."

253

"Say it again," I demanded.

"Calash," Isaiah said. "Once again, I could be wrong. But the letters look right."

I frowned and turned back to the screen. His warm smile. He didn't look terrible and he looked like he might have been reasonable. Maybe even more reasonable than how things would have been if I stayed there. And Brindt would get the money his family needed. Maybe I could work on this Calash guy and convince him to let me go home. We could find another portal. I could escape. After all, despite Brindt's kindness, he never truly seemed to want to let me go.

Maybe my new owner would.

"Calash," I muttered, looking into his near-black eyes. They were so much different than Brindt's. Brindt's eyes were always fascinating because they were so different than anything I had seen at home. Calash's eyes reminded me of people I had seen before. However, despite being dark, they weren't cold. "Why would he want someone like me?"

"An accessory most likely," Isaiah called over.

"Tell him I'll be okay," I said quietly. I couldn't stop looking at my future owner. It could have been worse. "Tell Brindt."

"Excuse me, what?" Isaiah asked.

"Lyris?" Brindt tried. I could hear the hopelessness as it crept into his voice. Honestly, I was surprised he was still standing there.

"Tell Brindt," I said to Isaiah. "Tell him that I'll be okay."

"You're giving up?"

"No." My voice grew hard. "I'm taking a detour. Tell him I'll go with this guy and see what happens. He's a rich guy, maybe he'll

254

even let me visit. I imagine he'll have me on watch 24/7 so I can't escape right away, but maybe this won't be so bad."

"Honey, no," Isaiah said. "I can't... I don't even know the words."

"Just tell him to go," I hushed. "Tell him to ask his mom to let me to wear the collar before I'm taken away. I just have a few things I want to say to him." I trembled as I inhaled and exhaled. "Calash," I muttered.

"I'm not telling him that—"

"Tell him!" I shouted. "Tell him to go!"

"Lyris, domodo," Brindt started. He must have heard the desperation in my voice and was trying to figure out why. "Dea, Lyris."

"He says you're his," Isaiah said. "Seriously, honey, we shouldn't give up so easily."

"I don't belong to anyone!" I yelled. "I mean..." I trailed off and waved at the screen, "...I belong to Calash, now. I'm not his. No, Brindt."

"Honey..."

"Lyris... dea Lyris..."

"NO BRINDT!" I shouted through my watering eyes. "Lyris... no Brindt. Brindt no Lyris!"

"You can't," Isaiah started. "You shouldn't give up—"

"Go!" I shouted. "Tell him to go! To leave! It'll help him this way!"

Isaiah fell silent and the shadow behind the door shifted slightly out of the corner of my eye.

"Tell him," I said again.

The shadow behind the door moved and I finally turned away from the screen. Calash's warm smile was just as terrifying as a frown because I had no idea what it meant for someone like me in Brindt's world. Looks could be deceiving and humans were not viewed as equals. A smile on a business card didn't necessarily mean a smile for a tiny person, but the stranger was the only chance I had.

"Dwan..." Brindt said softly.

"What's he saying?" I asked Isaiah.

"Uh... 'what', I believe," Isaiah said. "I think he sees something."

"Ugh, his mom must be home," I grumbled. It really was over.

"I don't know about that," Isaiah said.

"Bu!" Brindt suddenly roared. His shadow pulled away from the door and a loud crashing sound filled my ears.

"Brindt!" I screamed. "What?"

He was already gone.

"What was it?" I asked Isaiah. "What the hell did he see?"

More loud rumblings came from behind the door.

"Bu!" Brindt shouted. The sound of a door wrenching open.

And then my heart stopped.

"Y!" Brindt shouted a second time as something crashed loudly in another room. "Y-at! Y-at!"

"Wyatt?" I yelped.

"The Targeter?" Isaiah asked. He shifted amongst the newspaper. "The Targeter?" he asked. "You said his name was Wyatt?"

I locked my lips together. Isaiah had already said that he wanted to kill the man who took him away from his wife and son and frankly, I couldn't say I blamed him. Why had he come back? Was he making a delivery?

"Y-At!" Brindt roared as a door slammed door shut.

A small voice was shouting as Brindt's steps moved closer to the blue-light room.

"Brindt?" I pounded on the back of my cage. "Brindt! Is that him? Do you have Wyatt?"

He didn't answer, but his voice continued on.

"Quick!" I screamed at Isaiah. "What's he saying?"

"I don't know," Isaiah said. "He's talking too fast. I can't make out the words, but that Wyatt guy sounds pissed. He's trying to explain himself."

"Well, get him to stop!" I yelled. "Brindt, please! Domodo! Stop! What are you doing? What's going on?"

A door opened and slammed shut.

The room fell silent.

"Well, so much for that," Isaiah groaned. "He's dead."

My eyes widened. "He would never hurt anyone," I said defensively.

"I'll admit the kid has a sweet spot for you, but don't think for

257

a second that he suddenly wants to set us all free. He's probably going to get rid of the Targeter. And good riddance. That ass is the reason I'm here."

"He's also the one who could get us back home," I said. "They both are."

"And you think they're going to work together?"

I frowned. *No.* I certainly didn't think that. Brindt hated Wyatt and Wyatt just wanted to get paid.

The voices fell silent.

My heart hiccupped as the minutes passed and the only sound was the beeping on the screen in front of me. Grace even tried to catch my attention, but I waved her off. She easily gave up and shuffled back to the corner of her cage.

What had seemed like hours passed, but there were no signs of Brindt or Wyatt. The room had fallen silent and I wondered if Isaiah really did know what he was talking about. Maybe Brindt did have a cruel side to him that just couldn't see something so small as an equal.

And then a new door opened.

I flinched.

Keys jangled in the distance and heels clacked across the hardwood.

"Showtime for you," Isaiah said drily.

Nineteen

The rumpling of newspaper was the only indication I had that Isaiah was scuttling to the back of his cage. I wanted to do the same, but there was no point. Brindt's mom was back and she was coming back to the blue light room. There was nothing I could do to stop anything.

"Brindt?" his mother asked. She knocked on a door.

I expected to hear Wyatt's voice, but another door only opened slowly and Brindt said something to his mom. Without Isaiah to translate I could only listen hopelessly and wonder what was happening to Wyatt inside. Would he give him back to Brindt's mom? He mentioned that she had a sixth sense about people, but so far I didn't hear anything that was cause for alarm.

"She's giving him the fabric."

I glanced up. "Isaiah?"

"She's telling him to get to work. She knows you've been bought. The bidding war is over."

I frowned. "So it's really happening."

"It's really happening," Isaiah said as the paper shifted. The door shut and I could no longer hear Brindt's voice. Footsteps approached the blue-light room and the sound of the door being unlocked rang heavily in my ears.

"Good luck," Isaiah said.

After the door opened, heels clacked loudly on the floor until she reached the carpet. I couldn't understand her words, but she sounded excited and it wasn't long before the cage shifted and she pulled me away from the screen and towards her face. I winced and fled to the far corner of the cage because I didn't want to look at that horrible face. She looked just like any other mother... well-meaning... just huge. Her thin red lips pulled up into a smile.

"Dendot," she said triumphantly. "Dendot!" More words flowed from her greedy mouth, but without Isaiah I couldn't make out a single one. She seemed overjoyed and tapped Calash's face on the screen several times before she tapped the number below it. It must have been what he paid. I wondered how much I was sold for.

The cage shifted and without warning the lid flew open and a pudgy hand darted inside. Brindt's mom grunted with frustration as I fled from her sweaty fingers, but I didn't want to make everything so easy for her. She had a redhead, she was going to go through hell for *this* redhead.

"No!" I screamed and kicked at the digits in hopes that she would get frustrated and give up.

No such luck.

Brindt didn't even respond as I yelled the word several times which usually caught his attention. Whatever he was doing with Wyatt kept him busy and in that moment I realized Isaiah might have been right. I truly was alone.

"Ugh," Brindt's mom growled as she finally grabbed onto me. She barked something angrily as I continued to squirm, but I wasn't about to give up. Fingers easily wrapped around and started to pull me out from the cage. She tossed the cage back on the shelf where it had originally been and I could no longer see the screen.

Once I was pinned on the desk, I was relieved to see her reach for the collar. I didn't like the damn thing, but at least I could understand what the hell was going on when I wore it. Isaiah had fallen completely silent and the cages I could see looked empty. No one dared to draw attention to themselves when the beast was in the room.

The beast. Not a bad nickname.

I dared to smile a bit as the collar hooked into my neck, manipulating my throat muscles. I didn't know if I would ever get used to the feeling.

"What's so funny?" the beast asked as she arched an overly plucked brow at me. "In case you haven't noticed, your time here is coming to an end."

"I know. Maybe that's why I'm able to laugh about it."

The woman smiled down at me with a strange look. Respect? Admiration? Annoyance? I never found out.

"You *are* a spunky one," she muttered. "I can see why my son wants you back."

"So give me back to him," I challenged.

She choked out a laugh. "Heh! Did you see what people were willing to pay for you? Far more than anything my son's going to earn in the next ten years." She nodded. "The things people will do for a special little pet." She clucked her tongue. "He'll be here in a few hours to make sure that you two get along."

"I have to do a damn meet and greet?"

"Despite your hair, people want to make sure they're not paying a fortune for trouble," the woman said in a huffy voice. With ginger hands she rolled up the cuff of my pants. "I'm sure you'll pass any inspection. I've already warned all buyers that you would be a handful." She chuckled a bit. "That man has no idea what he's in for."

"So what do I have to do?"

"Just be yourself," she said. I was surprised with the simplicity of her response. "He's read about your personality so I'm pretty sure he's prepared for you to be difficult. I'm sure it's nothing that a little training can't fix."

"I'm not a dog."

"No, you're worse. Dogs don't talk back."

I suppressed the growl that rose in my throat.

"We'll have to get you pretty for when he comes," the beast went on. "Brindt said he was making something for you before..." she chuckled, "... before I outed him." She reached next to her and held up a beautiful canary yellow sweater with a large black button in the center and I swallowed. Brindt had made it and yet he had given it over to his mom so easily so I could wear it in front of my new owner?

"You look surprised," the beast said. She smiled as she set down the sweater close to my head. "My son is an artist above all else. He wants to see his work get noticed. Don't look so shocked that he's giving this to you as a good bye gift."

Good bye gift? The words stuck in my ears like the thickest bluemelon pulp.

"You'll look lovely in this," she marveled. "Such a pretty color against your skin and hair. My son has such an eye. And look..." She trailed off a she revealed a long piece of lilac fabric. "A pretty little scarf. And if I recall..." another trail off as she reached into her drawer and pulled out a tiny leather jacket. It looked expensive and I hated to say it, but I liked it. I had wanted a leather jacket for a while, but it was one of the few things my parents refused to buy. They said only tattoos and motorcycles would follow. *Whatever that meant.*

"Like a little rebel doll," the beast said with too much affection for my liking.

"Did Brindt make the scarf?" I asked carefully.

"He did. In fact, when I go to call your owner to confirm a time to visit you, I'll be sure to remind him that my son makes one-of-a-kind custom clothes. He'll have a way to make some income of his own. He'll like that." She smiled that horrible motherly smile again and turned back to me.

262

"What's his name?" My voice hinted at defeat.

"Calash Reason," she said. "A very wealthy and young entrepreneur. He's in diamond sales. Makes some of the loveliest engagement rings you'll ever see." She poked me lightly on the nose which further embarrassed and humiliated me. "You're a very lucky girl. He'll probably deck you to the nines with gems and stones and he's very attractive. He's an artist like my son. Maybe one day the two of them could work together on a line for Insignificants. Can you imagine the headlines?" Her eyes glowed. "My son working with Calash Reason." Her eyes looked down to me. "You really were a God-send, pretty girl. You could change everything for my son."

I swallowed. It was hard to get mad at that statement.

Could my presence really change Brindt's life so much?

Was I the missing piece that could change everything for him?

I felt the pressure building heavily as I remembered Calash's smiling face. A diamond and ring designer. Wealthy beyond imagination. And young. Maybe he wasn't old fashioned. Maybe I would get him to see that I wasn't just some doll he could dress up and parade around.

"I wouldn't be surprised if that's the reason he purchased you, actually," Brindt's mom went on. When I looked up at her with a confused expression, she grinned. "There's been talk that Insignificants need more luxuries. The higher ups want you to sparkle and who better to find that sparkle than a diamond designer? He'll probably use you to create some masterpieces. Maybe he'll let you model. I can see it now. Diamond headpieces, diamond bracelets, diamond necklaces, diamond collars—"

"I'm not wearing a damn collar!"

"Sure you're not," the beast said as she tapped the tip of my

263

nose again. "You're certainly not wearing one right now." She reached into her pocket. "Enough of this. Stay there. I'll give Mr. Reason a call and see what time he'd like to stop by tonight. Probably an hour or so would give me more than enough time to get you ready."

"Get me ready?" I squeaked as she stood up and hovered over me.

"Yes. And plus I have to set up the money transfer... ugh, I'll have to stop at the bank. I have to make sure everything is ready." She held the device up to her ear. "I'll be right back... unless that is..." she held the device close as a rumbling voice came from it.

"Hello? This is Reason..."

"Unless you'd like to talk to him yourself?" the beast asked in a taunting voice.

I froze at the new voice. It sent chills through my stomach. I squirmed in my restraints. "That's okay," I squeaked.

"Ahh, as you say," the woman said as she winked and pulled away. She brought the device up to her ear. "Hmmm? Yes. This is Mrs. Elinas. And yes! That was her! Darling little thing, isn't she? I promise you she's even prettier in person." Her voice faded as she exited the room and I watched her go with a frightened expression. I had seen my captor and I had heard my captor.

And later that night... I was going to meet him.

***

An hour.

That was all I had left.

In one hour I was going to meet Calash Reason and if all went well, I would go home with him. All thoughts of him looking kind and being reasonable went flying out the window as the beast swept

264

past to deliver the news. In a painful flash, I was swept out of my old clothes and pushed into the new outfit. I hated that it looked so perfect. Brindt had taken such care over the past month to give me clothes that fit well.

The pants fit like leggings and the sweater fit snugly across my prominent chest and the scarf really did look great against my hair and skin. And the leather jacket... *oh God.* That leather jacket was to die for. My heart fell slightly when I realized it was actually a high-end brand from my world and not a Brindt original. *Who had once worn such an expensive garment?* It looked like it was custom work even though it couldn't close across my chest. Tiny knee high boots were slid over my feet and despite my squirming, the beast had me ready to go with forty-five minutes to spare.

She checked her watch and looked around anxiously.

"It won't be long," she said, smiling widely as I was dumped back in the cage. "I have to make sure that my account is set up for a transfer." A worried frown flickered across her face as she looked behind her and I could tell she was worried about Brindt. Why had he been so silent and compliant for the past hour? Both of us wondered what he was up to, but the beast's greed overtook her worries.

"If he doesn't bring his checkbook and he wants to take you tonight, I need to be ready," she said, almost as though trying to convince herself to leave. "It won't be long. The 24 hour market can take care of it. It should take ten, fifteen minutes, tops."

I frowned, relieved that she hadn't taken off my collar yet. Maybe she had forgotten in her excitement for her visitor. Frankly, I didn't care either way.

"Don't you dare ruin this for me," she warned as she stepped away from my cage. "You're worth more alive to me than dead, but I'm sure there are some people out there who would pay quite a bit for a stuffed and mounted seventeen-year old redhead."

I was silenced.

265

I nodded and she smiled at my fear.

"Good girl," she said in a cold, praising voice. "I'll see you soon."

After she shut the door behind her, my shoulders slumped. I hadn't expected a threat. I thought my whole Trump card was that I was valuable alive and worthless dead, but she had a point. I swallowed nervously as the minutes ticked by, took a seat on the floor and wondered what Brindt and Wyatt were up to.

"Won't be long now," Isaiah called over.

"I suppose not," I grumbled.

"And you're seriously giving up?"

"What else can I do? Calash is on his way and I'm decked out like a high-class escort. There's nothing I can do, Isaiah."

"The kid—"

"Since when do you believe in Brindt?"

"I don't. But there's nothing else I can believe in, is there? Besides..." his voice lingered in the air and I couldn't help but feel that he was baiting me.

"What?" I growled.

"Listen," he hissed.

I fell quiet and was surprised to hear a slight sound. No high heels. Light steps... almost like a mouse.

"What the..."

"Lyris?" A new voice pierced the air and I strained my neck to see who it belonged to. It wasn't Brindt, but there was still something familiar about it.

"Lyris, where are you?" the voice came.

I looked down and my eyes widened with surprise. "You're alive!" I yelped.

"Of course I am," Wyatt said back. His green eyes danced as he found my frame in the cage. "What the hell did you think happened?" He walked up to the shelf and peered up at me. Several others stirred in their cages, but I only had eyes for him.

"I thought he killed you."

"Killed me? Who? Him?" He jutted his thumb towards the door.

I nodded hard. "Yes, I heard him shout for you."

"You!" Isaiah roared suddenly. He pounded on the plastic cage. "How dare you show your face here!"

"Isaiah, please," I said as several others started to work their way to the edge of their cages. Angry faces were all around and people started to shout at Wyatt. Some spoke English, but not all of them.

"How could you do this to me?" Grace squealed. "Let me out! I want to go home!"

"I'll kill you, you bastard!" Isaiah shouted. "Just wait till I'm outta here! I'll put you in a damn cage for four months and see how you like it! You mother fu—"

"Please! Stop!" I yelled and hoped that my voice would carry over the rest. "Please, he's here to save us." I looked down. "Aren't you?"

"I'm here to save you," Wyatt admitted.

267

The shouts started up again, even those who couldn't have possibly understood him.

"Let me out! Let me out! Let me out!" Grace wailed. I could hear her crying. "Please! I miss my friends!"

"You didn't seem to mind getting away from your dad when I talked to you," Wyatt shot back.

"Shut up!" Grace shouted. "Please! My mom—"

"Wyatt, come on!" I shouted over everyone else. His eyes locked on mine. "You can't be serious? You can't come here and expect to just set me free and leave everyone else here to rot?"

"I can't..." Wyatt said. I finally detected some humanity in his normally cool and calm voice. "I'd go to prison."

"You're damn right, you would!" another man shouted from his cage. "Unless I kill you first!"

"Not if I get my hands on him," Isaiah went on. "My wife! My job! My son! You'll be lucky if I haven't lost everything you little—"

"You see?" Wyatt said. "I can't. I can't do it. I'm here to get you out. You're the only one of these people who's even worth a damn to me. Take my offer and just be grateful."

"You expect me to be grateful?"

"Kinda?" Wyatt sounded exasperated. "Do you have any idea how much you're worth? It should mean something that I'm planning to let you go."

"I won't leave unless you let out the others."

"Are you out of your damn mind?" Wyatt shouted. "Lyris! I don't think you understand. I'll let you out, but only you. I shouldn't even be doing that. Luckily the beast moved the spare key or her kid would be in here screwing things up."

"You're here – we don't need the key. Now you can let the others out!" I shouted.

"I can't risk it, Lyris! Do you understand that? I can't risk it! Do you know what will happen if I let all these people go?" Voices erupted into angry shouting. "There's nothing more to say about it, Lyris. I'm getting you out of here."

"And what about Brindt?"

"What about him?"

"I have to say goodbye! And..." I trailed off as I looked around. "And I'm not leaving the others!"

"Do you have any idea what I'm offering you? You can go back to life as usual... and as for me... we'll have to come to an understanding."

"I don't want anything to do with you!"

"I have a hard time believing that," Wyatt said smugly. "Come on. Let me take you back home."

"And what about the key? What about the others?"

"That's my business with the kid," Wyatt said.

"So you just plan on leaving the others?"

"What the hell do I care? Lyris, I can't give Brindt the key. He'll let everyone go!"

"That's the point!"

"No. Dammit, just no." Wyatt shook his head. "Look, the kid will forget about the others just like I have. He'll move on. In the end, I'm sure he just wants to see you safe. So let me take you back home. And then we can go from there."

"There is no we!" I fumed. Brindt was right. I still wanted to believe in Wyatt. I wanted to believe that there was something good inside of Wyatt, but he was letting me down and quickly. "Brindt knows how I feel. There's no way Brindt would just forget about everyone."

"Please," Wyatt said. "That's the reason he doesn't need the key. Once he finds out you're safe, I bet he won't even give a damn. That's why I lied to him."

I frowned. "You lied?"

"He said he wanted to see you get home before anything," Wyatt said. "The only reason he let me go and didn't try to sell me off himself is because of you and the key. He knows I'm the only one who can sneak in and get the key. He knows I can move around and not even the old hag herself can detect me. He lied too, Lyris. I bet once he knows you're home, he won't bother to come back and risk saving the others. Either way, I can't risk it. I'm not giving him the key."

"You have to!"

"I don't have to do anything, but I have decide to help you so I would recommend you stop reminding me of the payday I'm losing my doing this."

He shook his head and I didn't understand how he was so easily able to ignore Isaiah and so many other people's threats as he started to climb up the desk. It was amazing to see him move so smoothly in a world not built for him. I never pegged him as an athlete, but I saw that even though he was lean, he was strong. I swallowed and willed my body not to find him attractive as he climbed up the desk with a hook and thread and finally pulled himself onto the counter top with a smug expression.

"I guess you still like what you see," he said, waggling his eyebrows.

"I hate you," I growled. "I'm not going."

"Oh, come on, Lyris! You're the only one actually worth anything here," Wyatt grumbled as he jumped into a partially open desk drawer. After a few moments of digging, he emerged with a large key. It looked like it weighed as much as a case of pop in his hands and he quickly threw it over the side of the desk. It landed with a gentle thud in the thick carpet below.

"What are you doing with that?" I asked.

"I told you already. I'm gonna hide it someplace safe until this whole thing blows over," Wyatt explained.

"By thing, you mean me."

"Yes. I mean you." He shrugged it off. "If I give it to him now, the first thing he'll do is let everyone out."

"That's the idea," I growled.

"Once I get you back home, I'll tell him I can't find the key then hide it near his room. That way you can go home, he gets the credit or blame for letting you go like he wants and mine and his mother's business isn't destroyed. Stinking monsters."

"Brindt's not a monster."

Wyatt chuckled. "They're all monsters, Lyris. The sooner you realize that, the sooner you'll be better off. And hey! Now that you know about this place, maybe you and I can work together." He waggled his brows. "I bet you could lure some young guys here. They always give me a hard time and I'm sure you've met few who could do with being taken down a peg or two."

"I can't believe you're joking at a time like this!" I shouted. "You're talking about—"

"I'm talking about surviving," Wyatt said seriously. "Before I

271

found this place my life was shit. My dad was a loser, my mom was a cheater and we didn't have any money. They kicked me out when I was seventeen and I had nothing. And then this happened. Now I have my own place and the freedom to do whatever I want."

"The freedom to kidnap people," I huffed.

"The freedom to give people a slightly different life than they had planned," Wyatt clarified. He climbed over some books until he was standing on top my cage and he glanced up. "Oh... hello Grace. Still here, I see? Pity, I thought a pretty young thing like you would have been bought already."

"Shut up!" Grace screamed. "You call them monsters, but you're just as bad!"

"Oh stop, you're turning me on," Wyatt said with a laugh, as he unlatched my cage opening. "Come on now," he said as he turned on that charming smile which made me sick to my stomach. "We're getting out of here."

"I won't go," I said. I turned away from him and crossed my arms. "Let me give the key to Brindt."

"Are you kidding? Lyris, no. Just no. Get over it. Now come on." He flexed his fingers a few more times. "Let's get going! I'm got a schedule to keep here. Will you get a move on?"

"I don't think you heard me," I said. "I want the key. I want to give it to Brindt!"

"Not a chance."

"Do it or I'm not going anywhere with you!"

His expression darkened. "You really think you're special, don't you?" he asked. His voice almost came out like a growl. "Spoiled in one world and spoiled in the next. I shouldn't be surprised."

Isaiah had said the same thing so with a furrowed brow I looked up. "I may be spoiled, but I don't think it's such a wrong thing to want to save others from this hell."

"If it's such a hell then accept my gracious assistance. Though knowing you, you'll probably end up on top. Spoiled brats like you always get what you don't deserve in the end."

It was like I had been shot.

"What's wrong with you?" I hissed.

"Let's. Go." Wyatt said, growing impatient as voices started to shout loudly. His eyes were only on me, but they occasionally checked the floor. "I've gotta get you back and I need to hide this key. Now hurry up before I leave you here and tell him you were on a shelf that was too high and just go back alone."

I froze. "You wouldn't."

"You're not that special, Lyris," he said, warning. "You're hot and I love your body, but I know I'd be lucky if you gave me the time of day after this. I'm not expecting too much. So whether you stay here or not doesn't matter so much to me. I'll find a way to survive. The question is... will you?"

I remembered my buyer. Time was running out and there was no guarantee that Calash would even listen to me. Maybe the beast was right. Maybe he just wanted a doll to wear his product to further his career. To gain even more insurmountable wealth.

Could I really take that chance?

"Let's go," Wyatt said again. "Last call."

As I glanced around the blue lit room, I reluctantly realized what I had to do. I was only human after all, but as I looked at those tired and frightened faces it didn't make things any easier. I swallowed hard as I reached for Wyatt's outstretched hand.

273

"I'm sorry," I croaked, looking directly at Grace. "I'm so sorry."

Her eyes watered. She didn't say anything, but shook her head and turned away.

"I'm sorry, Isaiah," I said.

"Foul," he muttered from his cage as Wyatt pulled me free. The air was no longer stuffy and it didn't smell like ink. "You're disgusting! You both are!" He pounded on the cage. "If I ever get out of here... I'll kill you for doing this to me! I'll kill you both!"

My eyes watered. I only had one chance.

I felt terrible.

Wyatt pulled me to my feet above the cage and we began our descent to the floor down the rope.

"I know this hurts now," he muttered. "But it will get easier."

I nodded.

"At the end of the day, they're faceless," Wyatt said. "Faceless people. You learn to cut off that part of your emotions. I swear it gets easier."

I nodded again, eying the key as we continued to descend. I wasn't very fast. All I had was the element of surprise. Everything depended on how fast Wyatt could move. I blinked hard and tried to remember where Brindt's room was in relation to the blue-light one. I would only have one shot.

"They'll eventually get homes," Wyatt said. "Sometimes this life can be good."

"I'll bet," I said. The words tasted like acid on my tongue, but I tried not think about it.

274

The key. I had to focus on the key.

"Bitch," one man spat as we slid past.

I pinched my eyes shut.

Focus. Breathe.

"There we go," Wyatt said proudly as I was set on the thick carpet. I tested it out. It would be rough, but it would be manageable.

I took a slow step backward towards the large object and hoped and prayed that it wasn't as heavy as it looked. I lifted my head and noticed that Wyatt was focused on gathering his rope and hook.

No time to wait.

As silently as possible I grabbed the key and started to sprint towards the door. The carpet didn't cover the whole room so eventually I hit the hardwood and it became easier to run. And louder. Wyatt finally turned at the sound.

"Hey! You bitch! What the hell do you think you're doing?"

I ran.

I swear Isaiah cheered.

Twenty

"Brindt! Brindt!" I screamed. I ducked under the crack of the door and ran towards the hallway. *His voice.* I just needed to hear his voice one time so I could know for sure where to run. Wyatt's annoyed yelp came from the blue-lit room.

"Dammit!" he shouted. "What are you doing? Give that back!"

"Brindt!" I screamed, ignoring his pleas. "Brindt, please!"

"Lyris?" His voice rumbled from under the nearest door to my right and I was relieved that I wouldn't have to run far. The key weighed heavily in my arms and Wyatt was in such better shape than I was.

"You son of a bitch!" Wyatt yelled from the rapidly closing gap between us. "Give that back! You don't know what you're doing..."

"Brindt, hold on!" I shouted as my legs pounded towards the door. Wyatt was on my tail and my back groaned in agony as I stooped to get under the door.

"You... dammit!" Wyatt shouted. He lunged forward at the last moment to crawl under the door.

Once I got through the crack, I looked up and Brindt was seated at his desk with a shocked expression. "Lyris?" he asked. He pushed away from the table to look at me. "What are you—"

"Brindt! Here! Take the—OOF!" I let out a pained wail as Wyatt tackled me from behind. I cried out as my body hit the hardwood and the key clanged loudly under me.

"Give it to me!" Wyatt went on, trying to wrench the key from my arms.

"What are you doing?" Brindt's voice came, confused as ever.

276

Wyatt's attempt to take the key under me was making it difficult to breathe and I was beginning to see stars when suddenly Wyatt's weight was lifted from mine, along with the key. I blinked and looked upward to find that Brindt had Wyatt's shirt pinched between his two fingers as he brought him up to his face.

"What are you doing to Lyris?" he asked in an annoyed voice.

"Get the key!" I shouted from the floor.

"The key?"

"The key!" I shouted. "He tried to take it from me!"

"But he was supposed to get it," Brindt said. He easily removed the key from Wyatt's grasp. Wyatt writhed in Brindt's grip but he held him tight, and set the key on the desk next to him before knelt down. "I told him to let you go home and then come back with the key. He was going to take you back and then give the key to me so I could set the others free."

"But he wasn't going to do it!" I shouted. "He was going to try and just take me back and hide the key! He wasn't going to give it to you at all! He doesn't care about the others."

"I was going to let you go. What does the rest matter?" Wyatt spat.

"Those people matter! They have lives! Family! Friends!"

"It doesn't matter now!" Wyatt shouted angrily. "Who cares about them?"

"So he was just going to let you go?" Brindt asked. He looked relieved that he was able to follow the conversation. *When did he put in his earpiece?* Maybe he finally found a spare.

"Yes!" I shouted. "He just wanted to let me go and then hide the key. He had no intention to set anyone free! He just... he just wants to keep bringing people here to your mom."

"But..." his eyes narrowed as he looked at Wyatt. "But he was still letting you go."

"But I want to let the others go, too!" I wailed.

Brindt nodded in understanding. "Right." His expression darkened as he turned his attention to Wyatt. "You said you would take Lyris back first and then give me the key so I could let out the others. That's what you said."

"And you really think I would do that? Do you have any idea what I would lose? My livelihood. My freedom. Your mom's trust. Face it, kid. You need that money just as much as I do." Wyatt's voice sounded smug. "I did what I needed to do. I'm sorry. I can't stop bringing people here. It's my only income."

"So why let me go back?" I asked.

"A weakness for smartass redheads with nice racks," Wyatt said with a grimace. "A weakness that I am regretting more each passing moment. I should have left you in that cage."

"You *what*?" Brindt growled. "You... you said..."

"You dumb giants will believe anything," Wyatt said. "Just stop playing around before your mom gets home and sees you messing with her beloved Targeter and her redhead. You're going to be in quite a bit of trouble, Brindt."

Wyatt's voice was beginning to make me sick. "You son of a bi—"

"I'm living my life—"

"Shut up," Brindt said, finally silencing us both. "You said you would let Lyris go back home and bring back the key. I said you were disgusting and couldn't be trusted, but Lyris said you weren't so bad so I gave you a chance." His eyes narrowed as he spared me a

278

glance. "Do you see what I mean now? The Targeter will always betray others to get what he wants. The only person who matters to the Targeter is the Targeter."

I frowned. He was right. At the end of the day Wyatt had done exactly what Brindt said he would do.

He betrayed others to save himself.

"You're right," I muttered. "You're right."

"Oh, come on," Wyatt said. "I'm not so bad. I was going to let you go."

"Just me," I said. "Not the others."

"Lyris, you don't understand," Wyatt continued from his awkward position. "If those people go back then I can never show my face here again. The beast—er, the kid's mom will never trust me. And I can't go back home because all those people will know who I am. It's not black and white, darling. Try to understand that."

Despite how annoyed I was with Wyatt, I didn't like the idea of him being stuck in limbo – unable to go home but unable to stay here.

"But those people..." I muttered. I thought of Isaiah and Grace. "They need to get back to their families—"

"They've gone this long," Wyatt said. "They'll have a chance to build new ones."

"Under the watchful eye of a giant owner," I growled, looking at Brindt. "No offense."

"You're going home," Brindt said. He bit his lip. "We're wasting time."

"But... but, Brindt," I said. I could hardly believe how easily he had changed topics. "Maybe we could..."

279

"You're going home and that's final," Brindt said. He stood up and walked towards his desk.

"Hey!" Wyatt shouted. "What are you—"

"And you're staying here for the time being," Brindt said. He plucked up his old cage from the floor and set it on the desk. Despite Wyatt's squirms and struggles, Brindt kept his grip firm and slowly deposited him into the cage.

"What the hell do you think you're doing?" he wailed. "You can't do this, you little shit! I'm the Targeter. Do you have any idea how much your mom is going to—"

"I don't care," Brindt said as he picked up the cage and walked into the closet. I couldn't hear what he saying, but it sure didn't stop Wyatt from shouting. The sounds grew more muffled and for a split moment I actually felt bad for him. He'd never had the tables turned on him and I couldn't imagine anything more emasculating than having a kid five years younger than you pluck you up and put you in a cage. He was helpless. A helpless human.

When Brindt emerged from the closet, he was smiling.

"Brindt," I muttered as I took a step towards him. "You're not going to do anything..."

"I won't hurt him," he promised. "I just don't want to worry while I'm helping you."

My face brightened as he started to come close and knelt to hold his hand out.

"Once this blows over, I'll let him out. But for now..." he smiled and held up the key with his free hand, "... I think there's something you wanted to do."

"You mean it?" I croaked as I walked towards his outstretched hand. "Are you sure? What about your mom—"

"Lyris?" he asked, quirking a brow.

"Yes?"

"Shut up." Without another word, I was easily swept into his free hand. He walked over and opened the door to his bedroom and started towards the blue light room.

***

Getting everyone out from their cages and towards the portal turned out to be easier than expected. As soon as Isaiah climbed out of his cage, these lifeless, timid piles of rags suddenly became humans again. In short order, with Brindt's help everyone was out marveling at their freedom and looking for the portal. I swear I could still hear Wyatt yelling loudly as I ushered the last of everyone through the portal door. They all seemed wary of Brindt, but eventually some muttered a thank you.

Grace was in tears as she blushed up at Brindt.

"Thank... thank you... so much," she said as she wiped her eyes with her long sleeves. "My mom... I can't wait to see her. Thank you."

Brindt looked at her with a blank expression as I tried to elaborate. His cheeks turned red as he glanced down at Grace. "You're welcome. I'm glad to help you get back home."

She nodded before walking through the door. There was no way she could have understood his words without a collar, but the message was clear that he wasn't going to hurt anyone. I could see others standing around the office in the Shaw place. It was a breath of fresh air to see everything my size. I turned back.

"Brindt," I muttered.

"Lyris." He tried to smile, but his eyes were watering like mine. "You want me to remove the collar?" He started to lean forward, but I pulled away.

"No," I said. "I... I want to keep it."

"But what it means..."

"It means that I have something to remember you by."

"I don't want you to remember me that way." His face turned sad. "That collar was one of the main reasons you hated me so much."

"But now it's one of the reasons I'll miss you so much," I muttered. "Because I got to hear your voice. I got to know you. I got to like you." I smiled up at him.

"I don't want to let you go."

I shook my head. I couldn't let the words come. There was a part of me who didn't want to leave either. I shook my head hard before I could rethink my decision. "You promise you won't hurt him?" I whispered.

"I'm not a monster, Lyris," he said as tears welled up under his bi-colored eyes.

"I know," I said, "I know that now. You're not a monster. Not at all."

"So you're not scared of me anymore?" His voice was soft and tentative as he leaned forward.

"Let's go," Isaiah hissed from the closet door. "They're getting restless."

I heard a commotion starting behind us, but I wasn't sure what it could be about. They were home and Wyatt was trapped in Brindt's room. *Why did it sound like a fight was starting?*

Despite the noise, I smiled up at Brindt. "No," I whispered.

"I'm not scared of you anymore."

"You'll come back one day?" Brindt asked in a hopeful voice.

"Lyris, come on!" Isaiah shouted.

"Hold on!"

"You don't understand..." Isaiah trailed off as glass broke behind him. I spun around. "They're tearing the place apart! You have to come back..."

"But why?" I asked.

More glass broke. Pages ripped.

"You should get out of here," Brindt said in a rushed voice. "Don't waste this chance..."

"Brindt." I lunged towards his kneeling form and hugged his knee. "I'll miss you. If I can come back, I swear I will." My eyes watered, but the smell of something burning started to alarm me.

"I believe you," he said softly.

Something rested against my back and I smiled. "Are you sure you'll be alright?" I whispered.

"Lyris, please!" Isaiah coughed. I turned around. He stood in the closet with wisps of smoke on either side of him... *smoke?*

I pulled away from Brindt's knee. "What are they doing?"

"I told you! They're burning the place down!"

"Burning it down—"

"Lyris, go," Brindt said. He gently shoved me forward with his hand. "Before the portal breaks."

"What about Wyatt? What's going to happen to him?"

"Lyris!" Isaiah shouted. He thrust his hand out of the closet as more smoke filled the floor. He coughed violently. "Please!"

"Wyatt?" I looked up at Brindt. "I can't leave him."

"I'll try," Brindt said. "But you need to go. You have to go!" He shoved me towards Isaiah and a thick arm wrapped around my waist as I looked back.

"Brindt!" I screamed. "Are you sure you'll be okay?" I coughed loudly as more smoke filled my nose and Isaiah yanked me hard back into our world. All I could see was Brindt's face as he pressed it down into the carpet.

"I'll be okay, Lyris," he said. "Just get out of there."

"And Wyatt!" I screamed as I started to lose track of Brindt's face through the smoke. "Get Wyatt."

"Just get out safe," Brindt's voice called.

The sound of a door opening and two voices was the last thing I heard before Isaiah kicked the door shut.

Brindt's mom.

Calash.

"No!" I screamed as Isaiah pulled us through the smoke. "Wyatt!"

"Forget about him," Isaiah grunted. "We gotta get out of here!"

"But what about him?" I said, remembering Brindt's sad face. "I didn't get to say thank you! I never got to tell him!"

"He knows, Lyris," Isaiah said. "What he won't like is if you die in here right now! Then everything he did for you... and us... will be worth nothing! Dammit!" he groaned as his impatience grew and finally he slung me over his shoulder. "After all this... I'm not going to die now!"

I pinched my eyes shut as I was carried through the increasingly thick smoke and down the stairs. Voices continued to shout and smoke soon turned to fire as Isaiah landed sloppily on the first floor. He staggered through the open front door and clear air hit my nostrils which I inhaled greedily as Isaiah dropped me heavily on the grass.

"Damn you," he huffed as he collapsed to the ground next to me. "After all that... you still almost got me killed. I would kill you myself if not..." he coughed loudly and his eyes softened for the briefest of moments, "... if not for that weird relationship you had with that kid. It got me home." He smiled and coughed. "My wife," he muttered, "my son."

Despite my joy for Isaiah being able to see his family, it was hard not to think about what had been lost. Brindt. He was going to be blamed for setting all of us free... I was sure of it. And that Calash guy was going to be livid about losing his prize.

I worried about what was going to happen to Wyatt.

Would Brindt try to blame Wyatt for our escape to save himself?

No.

I shook my head. Brindt wasn't like that. He was never like that. Brindt would take the blame and probably think of some way to keep Wyatt safe or even get him back through the portal.

"Burn!" a man roared from the street. Others surrounded him and cheered. "Burn, you damn mother, burn!"

My eyes welled up as I focused on the house. The windows were filled with flames and smoke and ash filled my nostrils as the

285

place continued to blaze. Several people cheered from the streets while others who lived in the neighborhood started to leave their homes to find out what the commotion was – where the bedraggled cheering people had come from. Sirens pierced the air and I could only watch the house continue to fall apart in a sort of trance.

I would never see Brindt again.

I would never have the chance to save so many others who were trapped in that world with no one to help them.

The roof began to collapse as the firefighters arrived on the scene. I pulled my knees up to my chest as the house fell apart right before my eyes.

"Lyris, oh my God! Lyris, is that you?"

A new voice caught my attention while I was lost in thoughts of Brindt and Wyatt. As I turned around slowly, I remembered the main reason why I wanted to get back home. Not for Wyatt and not for school. Not for my clothes or my future car, but my parents.

My parents.

My crazy, neglectful, insane, oblivious parents.

My mom stood there on the sidewalk a few yards away from me with expensive mascara running down her sunken face. Her cheeks were flushed. And her eyes were stunned.

"Is it really you, Lyris?" She was already running towards me. I had never seen her run before.

"M-mom," I muttered as I opened my arms to let her embrace me. "Mom," I croaked as she squeezed me tight. I could smell her familiar perfume mixed with red wine. "Mom," I whispered as I nuzzled into her shoulder. More arms wrapped around the two of us as sirens continued to blare and voices continued to shout.

"Lyris." My dad's soft voice came next. "You're back. You're alive. You're back."

I pinched my eyes shut and enjoyed their hugs more than anything I would or could have ever gotten from Wyatt or Brindt.

I was home.

"Mom," I whispered. "Dad, I'm so sorry..."

"Don't be..." my mom said as she squeezed me so tightly that I almost passed out, "...I'm just glad you're home."

"Yeah," I muttered through tears. The house collapsed to the ground right in front of us as my parents hugged me tighter. The firemen did their best, but before long the Shaw place was nothing more than a pile of ash and rubble.

I still smiled. "I'm home."

Months passed.

It was hard going back to school at first, knowing what I knew. For some reason gossiping about my father's latest raise, my mother's latest nose job, or the decision for my first car didn't really seem to interest me. I felt vapid and shallow and alone.

I stayed in touch with Grace for a few months after we both got home, but our communication had died down significantly after a surprisingly short while. It was like the whole thing had never happened. No giants. No other world. No Shaw place. No portal.

Despite our remarkably detailed and consistent accounts of the giant's world, since the house had been burned down to the ground there was no proof of what had happened to any of us. People talked about Wyatt, but he never came back – and if he had found a way home he certainly hadn't come back to see me.

It didn't really matter.

Come the next summer I had completely moved on, or so I told myself. A year had passed and that fall I would start college. Of course I was going to the college my parents worked at. My education would be free and it was a good school, after all. I didn't really mind. My future was always pretty planned out and I was okay with it. I'd go for my English degree and probably end up with some corporate job where my education could be put to good use in writing beautiful e-mails that no one would ever read.

Still, there were days when I looked at the ruins of the Shaw place and wondered how Wyatt was doing.

How Brindt was doing. He would have been sixteen and I wondered if he was driving. I wondered how much trouble he got into and I wondered if he thought about me as much as I thought about him. I missed him so much and it didn't help that the guys I went to school with all seemed so boring. They only wanted to talk about the same things I tried to avoid.

288

The coolest sports car.

What prestigious college was the best party school.

Their latest (insert something here).

I missed Brindt's innocence and I missed his kindness. I missed the way he looked at me and tried to process everything I said despite our differences in language. Sometimes when I was alone in my room, I'd thumb the collar that I kept hidden in my desk and frown. No guy here looked at me like Brindt had. No guy sought to protect me the way he had.

I only wanted to see him one more time.

To ask how he was doing.

To see what he'd been up to.

To find how much trouble he gotten into.

I smiled and knew I had another question I wanted to ask.

Was he putting his amazing talent to good use?

I never let go of the outfit I had come home with despite my mother's insistence. I finally got her to bend on buying me a new leather jacket – so long as I got rid of the old one. But I couldn't. Despite the message behind that coat, I loved it because it gave me a connection to Brindt. I kept my jacket, my scarf and my sweater and I wore them proudly – probably more often than my parents wanted me to.

I didn't care.

The sweater smelled like starmelon – one of Brindt's favorite foods and I'd be damned if I lost that part of him.

I smiled as I looked at the burnt down Shaw place on a

particularly warm June morning and thought of him as the scent of the fruit wafted into my nose even after all those months. I never thought about it then, but his fingers always smelled like citrus.

"I hope you're okay," I whispered as I stared at the tattered home.

I wondered how long it would be before someone bought the lot and built a tacky new home to replace it. I glanced over my shoulder at my home and turned back a second time. My parents were both teaching summer courses so they could comfortably afford my older brother and older sister's weddings next year so I was alone a lot of the time. It took a few months before my parents trusted me enough to walk around by myself... especially because I never spoke to anyone but the police about what happened.

I had been abducted.

I was back.

That was all they needed to know.

When stories hit the news about another world and a portal and giants, the media laughed and made jokes that we were all on drugs.

I never spoke to the media about anything.

It was over. After all, I hadn't been a puppet in a world of giants so I certainly wasn't going to be a puppet back home.

As I crossed over the property line from my parents to the Shaw's, I noticed the difference immediately. Where my parents had paid someone to keep our grass lush and green, the Shaw place was dying. The dried up grass crunched under my sneakers as I ventured into the backyard. I still had so many unanswered questions.

What was the portal and how many more were there?

How had Wyatt become a Targeter in the first place?

How many people had suffered/were suffering in that world because of what Wyatt and other Targeters had done?

So many questions.

I had too much time on my hands.

As I ventured onward, a flash of white came into view amongst the gray rubble. I narrowed my eyes as I approached, surprised to find something had not been damaged by the fire.

Everywhere else was gray and ash.

Everywhere else was lifeless.

Grey and lifeless.

Just like how I'd felt since I'd gotten back home.

I wondered. *Was it so wrong to want to go back? To want to change things? To want to make a difference?*

I sounded like a crazy person because I wanted to go back to that horrible world. Had I already taken for granted how happy I was to be united with my parents again? Why was I even thinking for a moment that going back was a good idea?

"You really need to get a job," I muttered with a smile. Since I returned back home, I had whipped my body into better shape, remembering how easily Wyatt was able to move in that giant world. How easily he swung from tables and climbed up chairs without trouble. I was probably just as strong as he was, but there was no way to test it.

I ventured a little closer to the sliver of white paint hidden amongst the rubble and used the tip of my sneaker to push some of the gray away. I started working mechanically, shoveling the piles of old ash aside as I cleared off the white rectangle. Finally it was completely uncovered and I stood up to make sure it was what I thought it was.

The door.

The exact same door from the haunted room, and yet, despite the fire it was somehow perfect. As though the fire hadn't touched it. Flawless. My breath hitched as I knelt over the familiar white door and touched the knob. Memories of Brindt flooded over like waves and all the questions that had remained unanswered taunted me because there was a chance they could all be answered with the flick of my wrist. Just a turn and I could find out what had happened to Brindt. What had happened to Wyatt. It was all right there in front me hidden behind this door. Somehow the fire hadn't touched it.

My fingers brushed against the cool metal for a few moments as I waited for something to distract my attention from this mad, dangerous impulse.

I wanted the distraction.

I gripped the knob harder.

C.E. Wilson is currently living in Pittsburgh, Pennsylvania with her husband, beautiful daughter, two dogs and two cats. They are all the loves of her life. She loves horror movies and shoujo manga. When it rains she feels at peace and loves a sweet cup of coffee with way too much sugar and cream. She loves the fall because of football and all things pumpkin. Her favorite subject to write about is size difference, but she enjoys to try her hand at all things fantastical.

Other titles by C.E. Wilson

The Punishment Series

Oath of Servitude

Permanent Shadows

Standalone Works

The Promise

Coming soon

The Boy with Words (Late 2015)

This is Me. (Early 2016)

Untitled Beauty (Early 2016)

Cruel and Unusual (Summer 2016)

Connect with C.E. Wilson online:

Twitter: https://twitter.com/cewilson1

Facebook: http://www.facebook.com/people/Ce-Wilson/100003313330557

Deviantart: http://cewilson5.deviantart.com/

24483559R00187

Made in the USA
Middletown, DE
26 September 2015